THE **DARK** EDGE OF NIGHT

THE DARK EDGE OF NIGHT

A HENRI LEFORT MYSTERY

Mark Pryor

MINOTAUR
BOOKS
NEW YORK

First published in the United States by Minotaur Books, an imprint of St. Martin's Publishing Group

THE DARK EDGE OF NIGHT. Copyright © 2023 by Mark Pryor. All rights reserved. Printed in the United States of America. For information, address St. Martin's Publishing Group, 120 Broadway, New York, NY 10271.

www.minotaurbooks.com

Designed by Omar Chapa

Library of Congress Cataloging-in-Publication Data

Names: Pryor, Mark, 1967- author.
Title: The dark edge of night / Mark Pryor.
Description: First edition. I New York : Minotaur Books, 2023. I Series: A
    Henri Lefort Mystery
Identifiers: LCCN 2022059551 I ISBN 9781250825049 (hardcover) I ISBN
    9781250825056 (ebook)
Subjects: LCSH: World War, 1939–1945—France—Paris—Fiction. I
    France—History—German occupation, 1940–1945—Fiction. I LCGFT:
    Thrillers (Fiction). I Historical fiction. I Detective and mystery fiction. I
    Novels.
Classification: LCC PS3616.R976 D37 2023 I DDC 813/.6—dc23/eng/20221213
LC record available at https://lccn.loc.gov/2022059551

Our books may be purchased in bulk for promotional, educational, or business use. Please contact your local bookseller or the Macmillan Corporate and Premium Sales Department at 1-800-221-7945, extension 5442, or by email at MacmillanSpecialMarkets@macmillan.com.

First Edition: 2023

10 9 8 7 6 5 4 3 2 1

This book is dedicated to my amazing child Blake.
Thank you for being you.
I love you.

THE DARK EDGE OF NIGHT

CHAPTER ONE

Paris, France
Monday, December 2, 1940

I slipped into the lobby of the Gaumont-Palace cinema and went to the ticket booth, glad to leave the chilly December wind to the few people trudging along rue Caulaincourt. The sky was heavy and gray, and the radio had warned of snow to come, the first of the year. I didn't used to mind a good dose of the white stuff, but since the Germans had confiscated most of the motorcars that hadn't fled the city months ago, we detectives had to flat-foot around the city like the uniforms did. So much for that perk of promotion.

"One, please," I said to the old man behind the counter. "And a seat in the back corner. Back left corner."

"Of course, sir, and would you like me to shine your shoes

and perhaps bring you a glass of Bordeaux while you watch the movie?"

I stared for a moment. "I'll shine my shoes with your backside if you don't show a little more respect to an officer of the law."

"A policeman?" The man pouted and handed me a ticket. "How was I supposed to know?"

"How about you save your sarcasm for the bastards who've taken over our city?" I looked at the ticket. "It doesn't have a seat number."

"We don't do that anymore." He waved an arm toward the double doors into the theater. "*They* like to sit wherever they want, even move around during the film. There's no point to numbers."

"I'm shocked," I said, completely unshocked. To begin with, back in June and July, the Boche had been polite, respectful, and tried to get along with us Parisians. As the days and weeks went by, though, the veneer of decency had cracked and too many of them acted like the schoolyard bullies they were. "How much do I owe you?"

"Don't worry about it." He waved his hand again. "But I'm curious, where is that accent from?"

"South. Pyrénées. And thanks." I moved away quickly to avoid any further interrogation, as I always did. My history was a little more complicated than most people's, and the less I talked about it the better. Especially with strangers.

I found a seat in the back left corner, but was less than happy to see the place more than half full for the afternoon showing. No wonder there was no one on the street, they were all here. A collective groan went up as the lights dimmed and a cheerful German propaganda film whirred onto the big screen. This one was a preview for something called *The Eternal Jew*, directed by someone called Fritz Hippler. The translation was so bad I could only gather it had something to do with Jews being sex crazed and money hungry, stereotypes the invaders had been force-feeding since they arrived.

Just for kicks I let out a low "boo," and then a louder one after I was shushed. A large man at the front stood, turned around, and yelled, "Silence!"

I thought about telling him where to go, just to give the audience some genuine entertainment in place of the mandatory mindless slop the Krauts served up before every good film. But it was my day off and I'd come here to be left alone, be distracted from the world and its problems, not cause more.

The movie began and I settled into my seat to enjoy it, but my attention soon fixated on the end seat two rows ahead of me. A small boy, judging from his height and haircut, was tapping something on the wooden armrest.

This is why you don't go to the cinema, I thought, teeth gritted. My downstairs neighbor and sometime psychotherapist, Mimi, had named my condition "misophonia." Basically, I have an aversion to sounds that is so strong it provokes a physical reaction in me—racing pulse, fast breathing . . . "rage" is a fine word for it. Not annoyance, not irritation, but pure red-hot anger. Mimi, who was better known as Princess Marie Bonaparte, great-grand-niece of the short man himself, said it probably had something to do with what I went through in the previous war. I couldn't see the connection myself, but whatever the root cause my sister had long resigned herself to eating apples, celery, and carrots in a different room. Not that finding fresh crunchy vegetables was possible these days, so I had this new war to thank for that.

After a full minute of that kid tapping—*And, my god, why doesn't it drive his father mad?*—I called out in a low voice, "Hey, kid, stop that tapping." Several heads turned, including those belonging to the boy and his papa, who seemed to stare at me in the dark, but at least the noise stopped.

For less than a minute.

I gritted my teeth when it started up again, hoping against hope the action and pretty people on the screen would distract the little rat. They didn't.

"Kid, stop tapping," I growled.

He did for a moment, but the problem with misophonia is that when a noise starts and stops, your blood pressure keeps tipping higher and higher, not just from the noise but the expectation of the noise. Pressurized anxiety, wasn't that what Mimi called it?

He started up again, this time interspersing the tapping with his foot knocking against the base of the seat in front of him, making a veritable orchestra of antagonization.

Why is no one else strangling this kid? I truly couldn't believe this didn't anger other people, and that worked me into even more of a frenzy. Finally, I snapped.

"Kid, shut the fuck up!" I shouted.

The father instantly stood up and whirled around. "What did you say to my son?"

"I'm saying it to you, too. Shut him the fuck up. And sit down, you make a shitty movie screen."

"You can't speak to me like that!"

He stepped past his son and headed for me, pausing when the big man from the front of the cinema, and his equally big friend, stood and told him to stop. He paused and we both watched them stride toward us.

Merde. They're Boche. One chump I could handle, but one chump plus two hefty Germans in uniform made things a little too spicy.

"It's a movie theater, not a playground," I said, preparing my defense in case I got to present one.

"Yes, it's a movie theater, and you are being disruptive," one of the uniforms said, looming over me.

"This has nothing to do with you," I snapped, now extra raw that they were wading into this on the wrong side.

"We paid for our tickets, just like everyone else."

"You didn't just take them from the old man at the front?" I said.

This was not the smartest approach. They conferred quickly and a moment later I was being hauled out of the room by my armpits. I thought about putting up some resistance but I didn't know of a single case where a Frenchman had fought a German in uniform and won. Temporarily, perhaps, but not for long.

The old ticket-seller, to his credit, tried to get them to drop me in the lobby but their danders were up and they breezed past his protests. I wondered if I was getting dumped in the street or pummeled there. I could tell them I was a policeman, but these days you didn't know what that might mean to them. "I beat up a French cop" might get them more admiration than if they just beat up your average Parisian moviegoer, so I kept my mouth shut.

Outside, they pinned me to a large poster of Danielle Darrieux, which under other circumstances I would have taken the time to admire, but only now did I see why they'd been able to carry me like a baguette—they weren't large men, they were downright huge. The huger of the two leaned in, his gigantic square head barely an inch from mine.

His French was understandable but almost as bad as his breath. "You need to learn some manners, Frenchie."

"This from the men who help themselves to other people's countries." The old man popped his head out of one of the doors, so I asked him: "Hey, did these apes really pay for their tickets?"

"Please, leave him alone. He's a policeman, we don't have many left."

Great, there goes my undercover status.

"You don't fight like a cop," the big face, which was still too close to mine, said. "You don't fight at all."

A female voice piped up behind the giant, and for a second I couldn't see who it was.

"That's because you're both German, enormous, and he's not an idiot." The two soldiers swiveled to see who was talking. "Well, I take that last part back. He's a complete idiot, otherwise he wouldn't be in this situation."

"Who are you?" the man holding me asked. His tone, as always happened when this particular savior showed up, had softened considerably.

"I am his colleague, Nicola Prehn, and I was sent here by your superior to bring him to the Préfecture. Immediately." The ape still didn't let go, so Nicola took a step forward and gave him her most serious glare. "And in one piece."

The man finally released me and I quickly moved to Nicola's side. "Who's my superior?" he asked, his broad brow furrowed.

Nicola looked him up and down, taking in his uniform and thereby his rank. "You're a private, yes?"

"*Ja. Oui.*" He nodded.

"That's what I thought." Nicola performed a slow turn, but

looked back over her shoulder as she started walking away with me in tow. "Then all of them."

•   •   •

We walked in silence for a moment.

"I had that under control," I said mildly.

"Yes, you certainly seemed to. Apologies for butting in."

"Apology accepted." We were walking more quickly than usual. "You weren't really sent to fetch me, were you?"

"I was, as a matter of fact."

"It's my day off."

"Don't be ridiculous, no one gets those anymore."

"A man can dream." I sighed. "What's going on?"

"The chief wants to see you."

"Well, of course but . . . Why send you?"

"Full of questions, aren't we?" she said. "I volunteered because I wanted to talk to you."

"You know I go to the cinema to be not talked to, don't you?"

"I do. And since you're not at the cinema, we can talk."

"But I would've been if—"

"If you hadn't gotten yourself thrown out." She stopped and turned to me. "Which is precisely what I want to talk about." She set off again, at a slower pace this time.

"How can you have come here to talk about me getting ejected from the movie when it hadn't happened yet?"

"Henri, you're being intentionally obtuse."

"I don't think one *can* be unintentionally obtuse," I said quietly. I knew why she was there, what she wanted to say, but she laid it out just in case I didn't.

"You've been a complete bear to live with this past couple of months. You're rude, angry, and I can't decide if it's because you're working too much, or if you're working too much to avoid being around me."

"And here I am, on my one day off—"

"Henri!" she snapped. "You know perfectly well what I'm talking about."

"If you'd not noticed, we're in the middle of a war. Or the beginning of one, who the hell knows?"

"Yes, I'd noticed. We are, but we all are. You're the one acting differently."

She was right. Just as the winter days had been getting shorter and the nights longer, my mood had been darkening, too. If you've lived through a war, you know what it is to suffer hardship and hunger, fear and frustration. But if you've fought in a war and lived, then you know the real terrors it can unleash. When the Germans moved into Paris I was sickened and sad, but for a time it looked like life would maybe settle down to some bearable way of living. But in the past few months I'd started to see that that wasn't going to happen. Every aspect of life was getting worse, from the attrition at work leaving us shorthanded to the daily assault on decency and humanity that our Teutonic occupiers were inflicting on us: random roadblocks and searches, raids on suspected agitators (no real proof required), and more lately the rounding up of people the Germans thought undesirable. And they thought *a lot* of people were undesirable. To see the stricken faces of the parents and the confused faces of their children as they were pressed into the backs of trucks was enough to make the most optimistic soul bitter. And it'd been some time since I'd been an optimistic soul.

Nicola didn't see as much of this as I did. Not just because she was a secretary at the Préfecture and therefore out and about less, but because some of the biggest problems other people suffered had been alleviated for us by Mimi. From her position of power, prestige, and wealth, she was able to get food and supplies that others couldn't. And, now that she was Nicola's best friend, she shared them with us.

"It's just the war getting me down," I said. "And the work."

"Then when you're home you should be better, and you're not." I saw her glance over at me. "Mimi says you resent her a little."

"Does she, now? Why would I do that?"

"I don't know, why don't you talk to her about it?"

I groaned. "Because, at the end of a long day, I don't want to talk about my feelings with Princess Marie Bonaparte and have her pick them apart and point out how unreasonable I am."

"You're happy to drink her wine and eat her food. Seems like you should be willing to talk to her, too."

"So now a condition of her sharing is my compliance?"

She laughed. "It was before."

Also true. In July, when all this was new, I'd saved Mimi's life during a robbery at her home. She'd taken a shine to me, or my foibles at least, and when she moved into the apartment below ours she said she wanted to practice her witchcraft on me. She called it psychoanalysis, of course, and told me all about her friend Sigmund Freud and how he'd taught her everything she knows. In our evening sessions, she poured me fine wine and then the next day a basket of food would arrive on our doorstep.

That food and wine had been free, but they cost me plenty. I trusted Mimi and told her my story, about who I really was and about some of the things I'd done to survive the war. How I'd saved myself. I still trusted her, but I was less happy now that she knew these things; widening that circle to include her made me vulnerable and gave her power. A regal background was all very well for getting you fresh asparagus and the occasional ox tongue but, as I'd been seeing lately, it wouldn't keep the Germans from kicking in your door and asking pointed questions if they had a mind to. These goose-stepping Boche were as happy to spill blue blood as red and, from what I was hearing recently, being a woman was no protection at all. That meant if they wanted her to talk, and spill my secrets, she inevitably would.

And if there was one more headache I didn't need, it was the Boche finding out about my past, about who I really was and what I'd done to make it through the last war.

CHAPTER TWO

We walked in silence much of the way, but as we got close to the Police Préfecture I noticed Nicola kept clasping and unclasping her hands together. And she only fidgeted like that when she wanted to tell me something, but was afraid to.

"We'll be there in five minutes," I said.

"I know. So what?"

"So spit it out."

She smiled. "I'm that easy to read, am I?"

"Only occasionally. This isn't more about Mimi, is it?"

"No, it's about me."

"Just a moment." I put a hand on her shoulder and we both stopped in our tracks. She was confused until she saw where I was looking—across the road three German soldiers were confronting an old couple in front of a bakery. The man's white apron suggested he was the proprietor, and I guessed the box he held in front of him contained his wares. And the Germans looked very interested in them.

"Let's just keep walking," Nicola said. "I'm sure it's fine."

"I'm not, they look aggressive."

I stayed put, and Nicola did, too. One of the soldiers had flipped up the lid of the box and pulled out a pastry, which he waved in the old man's face.

"Crime of the fucking century," I said, my blood pressure rising. "A croissant, for god's sake."

Which would have been perfectly normal and fine a few months ago. But the bastards had banned croissants, actually banned croissants in Paris, in what I and most people saw as the most petty, insidious, and hurtful anti-French measure yet.

All three soldiers were pulling the pastries out and stood there with handfuls of the damn things, waving them and yelling at the cowering couple. They knew they'd done wrong, I'd seen the *I've been caught* look a lot in my career, but it was equally obvious they had no clue what the Germans were saying. Or were about to do.

Nicola and I gasped as the smallest of the three jammed a croissant in his mouth and used the same hand to draw his pistol. He stuck it in the baker's face, and Nicola grabbed my arm as we watched the wife burst into tears.

"Surely he wouldn't . . . ," Nicola said in a whisper.

"For a croissant. Please no." I raised my voice and shouted over to them. "That's not the penalty."

Three heads snapped around to glare at me and one of them said something I didn't understand.

"I'm police," I shouted back. "That is not the penalty. Please, don't shoot him."

The small soldier still had his gun in the baker's face and when he said something to his colleagues they drew their pistols, too.

"Henri, please, let's go. They're going to do whatever it is they want to do. We're not involved."

One of the Germans slowly, intentionally slowly, began raising his gun toward us and Nicola tugged at my arm. She was right, I knew that, and I didn't want to get us shot over a pastry, so I let her drag me as those bullies watched us slink off, powerless to do anything for that couple except distract their tormentors for a few seconds.

We were quiet for a minute, and I was doing what I found myself doing too often lately: trying to forget what I'd just seen. It was getting harder and harder to see these moments, and there seemed to be more and more of them. Each time I saw an injustice like this a red-hot filament burned my insides with the frustration of not being able to do anything about it.

"So you were about to tell me something," I said, to shift us a little toward normal.

"Right, yes." She took a deep breath. "Fine, I'll just say it. I've been talking to someone. Someone I quite like."

That's all? "No harm in that. Anyone I know?"

"Sort of."

We walked on a little farther but eventually I prodded at the silence. "Someone I don't like, I assume from your reticence."

"Actually, no, I think you quite liked him."

"*Liked?* Dear god, tell me he's not dead. I know we have some tough rules about who we can and can't see, but a dead man seems a little desperate, even for one of us."

That got me a smile, but I was expecting a chuckle at least.

"Right, the rules," she said quietly.

These tough rules weren't set in stone, but they were in place for good reasons. One good reason, anyway: Nicola and I were prepared to do pretty much anything to keep my past a secret, and that meant seeing people on a superficial level, and only certain types of people, or not at all. In more than ten years neither of us had developed long-term relationships. Nicola's short marriage to a now-dead drunk made the lack of companionship easier for her in a way—if she didn't have a boyfriend, she couldn't marry another loser. And I had too much at stake to risk falling in love with someone who may or may not be good with my past. So Mimi was the only person to penetrate the closed circuit that was Nicola and me, and even that allowance weighed heavily on me.

Nicola elbowed me in the ribs. "And don't be stupid, Henri. He's not dead."

"Blind, perhaps, if he finds your visage less than repulsive."

"You're a child, Henri. And an unoriginal one, at that."

"Well then, out with it. Who is the poor young man?"

"Daniel Moulin." She glanced at me as I struggled to put a face to the vaguely familiar name. "You met him once, a few months ago."

"And I liked him?"

"Yes, you did."

"That's pretty unusual, but I can't quite place the—" Then it hit me, and I stopped in my tracks. She stopped, too, and turned to face me.

"Henri, just wait, I know what you're going to say."

"Of course you do. Because I'm right." My mind went back to the case of the dead German in the Louvre, which I'd solved back in July. He was some high-ranking Boche who'd been put in charge of redistributing the museum's works of art. His demeanor, and who he'd been redistributing to, had landed him a sharp object in a fatal place. Daniel Moulin had been put in charge of guarding the body, and we'd met him when inspecting said body for clues. Moulin had been given that job because he was a police officer. And when it came to relationships, police officers and employees were at the very top of the "no relationships" list.

"You remember how when we met him, he was reading a book?" Nicola said.

"Oh, a policeman who can read, that's what we're aspiring to now?"

"One who *does* read is quite different from one who just *can*," she said firmly. "You're the one who was so impressed that it was Russian literature and not a newspaper or something pornographic."

"And yet he's still a policeman."

"Yes, I know." She hung her head for a moment, but when she looked up again I saw a resoluteness in her eyes. "I'm not young, Henri, and if I am I won't be for much longer. And I'm not sure I want to spend the rest of my life darning your socks and drinking red wine with you."

"Nonsense, of course you're still young. Younger than me."

"I'm a woman. It's different for men, and you know it." She shook her head slowly. "You can chase women half your age and no one cares. Hell, other men will cheer you on. But when a woman starts racking up the years, she's done for. Except maybe for some ancient widower too grotesque for the younger gold diggers. And I don't want to be a gold digger, young or old."

"We've talked about this."

"Yes, once and about a decade ago. And for more than a decade I've abided by whatever we call this—a rule or an unspoken agreement."

"Because we can't afford for anyone to find out. Because *I* can't afford that, at least."

"Neither can I, Henri. Don't be like that. It's my secret, too."

"And who better to uncover it than a policeman? That's quite literally their job, Nicola. We both know that if you have a serious relationship with a *flic* then there's a high likelihood that somehow, either intentionally or carelessly, you'll spill the beans. Or they'll see something or hear something that wouldn't register with a regular person."

"And then again, maybe they wouldn't. The only reason they'd know would be if you or I told them, and we've managed not to for a very long time."

"I don't think starting a serious relationship with a grand lie is a sound idea," I said.

"So I remain single for the rest of my life? A spinster because we . . . no, because *you* won't trust someone enough to tell the truth."

Thing was, she had a point. Condemning her to a life alone was not what I wanted, but I didn't see a way around it. She could hardly marry someone and then come out with the truth. Or maybe she could. Without a crystal ball, there was just no way to know how it'd all shake out.

I softened my voice. "You could wait until I retire, then it wouldn't matter."

"Great, I'm sure I'll find lots of eligible bachelors when I'm sixty."

"I could retire a few years early."

"Oh, so when I'm fifty, great, so much better." She cocked her head. "How about right now?"

"That's funny. Apart from everything else, we've lost enough detectives in the past five months. They can't handle losing another right now."

"I'm serious, Henri. What if you found another line of work, a different career?"

"These days?" I laughed out loud. "Like what? The only people hiring are the army recruiters, and no thank you very much."

"There must be something you could do."

"There's a war on, Nicola. Do you seriously expect me to find a new line of work right now? It's hard enough to find a potato that's not rotten."

"We can get all the potatoes we want from Mimi, you know that."

"Yes, and I'm just wondering how beholden to her we are, and for how long."

"She doesn't see it that way, and neither do I," she said firmly. "She's a friend who's able to help us out. That's all."

"And I trust things will remain that way."

"Trust is a big problem for you, isn't it?"

"I trust you."

"You *only* trust me. Which is precisely the problem." She turned and started to walk. "Come on, we're taking too long."

"We didn't finish talking about this Moulin fellow." I hurried after her.

"Later." She gave me a devilish grin. "I want to get Mimi's opinion about it all."

"I wonder whose side she'll take," I grumbled.

"Yes, I agree, she *is* very wise."

•   •   •

To date, I'd survived two disasters—the war of 1914 and the invasion of my city—and in my experience people respond to such *disastres magnifiques* in one of two ways: they either become more selfless, or more selfish. In the present microcosm that was my world, that meant my colleagues were either more helpful or more likely to stab me in the back. And when I think of the latter, a certain Georges Guyat comes to mind. We all call him "GiGi," partly for his initials and partly because of his unnaturally long face.

Nicola and I walked into the Préfecture together and had the displeasure of running into him on his way out. GiGi had never liked me, and liked me even less after his partner got shot while the three of us were at a crime scene together. Mimi's house as it happens. I'd managed to kill the bastard before he could shoot anyone else, and somehow GiGi's horse brain had translated that into me shooting too slowly to save his partner, and yet also shooting too quickly and making him look bad. I'd heard this through other sources, though, because we'd barely spoken in the months since, which is why I was surprised when he stopped to chat this time.

"A new case, Lefort," he said. His nostrils twitched a couple of times, and I wasn't sure if I smelled or it was part of his horsiness.

"No idea, just know the chief wants to see me."

"I was telling, not asking. There's someone important gone missing and the boss wants you to find him."

"We're murder squad, not missing persons."

"True. But the junior detective gets the shit cases." It's true, I was junior, and GiGi loved to remind me of that. "And I suspect he wants you to find this *mec* before he goes from missing to murdered."

"Who is he?"

"No idea. Someone important, though, so why don't you run upstairs and find out?" I turned to go, but his voice stopped me. "Oh, and Lefort."

"What is it now?"

"I don't know what you've heard, but I have no hard feelings over the Marie Bonaparte scene. If anyone says so, they're lying."

"Glad to hear it."

He turned and walked away, wrapping his scarf around his long neck as he stepped out of the main doors. Nicola moved to my side.

"Do you believe him?" she asked.

"About what?"

"That he has no hard feelings?"

"You're joking. Those are the only kind he has."

Nicola snorted with laughter and led the way up to our floor, where my boss, Louis Proulx, was waiting in the doughnut—the large, open, and round room stuffed with junior detectives and secretaries—with a cigarette in one hand and a cup of coffee in the other.

"Either of those for me?" I asked.

"No, but I do have a special treat for you. In my office, please."

He was acting unusually grim, and since he was the veer-toward-selfless kind, I didn't like his tone.

"Chief, last time we had this kind of talk there were two Nazis in your office waiting to hang an assignment around my neck."

"Not this time," he said, walking toward the closed door of his office

"Glad to hear it." I followed.

He paused with his hand on the doorknob and gave me a tight smile, and when he spoke he kept his voice low. "This time there's just one of the bastards."

Before I could object, or run away, he swung the door open and waved me ahead of him. Sitting behind Proulx's desk, and with his feet up on it, was a man in a dark wool suit. He was clearly tall, and looked very thin from this angle. He didn't stand, just looked me up and down. To his side, leaning against one of the chief's bookcases, was a man also dressed formally, this one in a three-piece tweed suit.

I turned to Proulx. "Am I seeing double, or did you just lie to me?"

Or do I play "guess the Nazi"? I thought, but didn't say.

"Henri," Chief Proulx said, and gestured to the man in his chair. "This is Stefan Becker. He is with the German security services."

Ah. My Nazi.

"So, you're the great Henri Lefort." He spoke French, and quite well. His sarcasm was especially clear.

I nodded in acknowledgment and turned to the standing man. "And you are?"

"Dr. Andreas von Rauch." He stepped forward and offered his

hand. I thought perhaps I saw an apology, or regret, in his eyes as we shook. "And we have a mutual acquaintance."

"That seems unlikely," I said.

Von Rauch didn't seem to mind, or perhaps notice, my insolence. "Well, true, you probably only met her the one time. But I recognize your name from the headlines because of Princess Marie Bonaparte."

That got my interest. "You know her?"

"We've met on several occasions, yes. Our families have known each other for almost a century." He smiled. "And so I now formally thank you for saving her life."

"You're welcome, but only partially since that's apparently the reason I'm here." I threw a dirty look at Chief Proulx. "Again."

"You are good at your job," Becker said, and von Rauch stepped back to his place by the bookcase. "I imagine we will call on you in the future. Assuming you continue to succeed."

That last phrase dripped with menace but I tried to look indifferent to his meaning. I looked Becker over.

"Security services?" I asked, keeping my tone light. "Given the expensive suit and lack of jackboots, I'm guessing Gestapo." I reached for my cigarette case and hoped Becker couldn't see my hands shaking. Mostly from fear, but also from the intense hatred I had for this band of murderous bullies.

"There, you see, you *are* a good detective." This time I got a sneer to go with my sarcasm.

"Most kind, thank you." I turned to Chief Proulx again. "Well, assuming I was invited here to collect a few compliments, I think my work is done."

"Not so fast." Becker snapped out the words as he swung his

legs off Proulx's desk. "Whatever you're working on, you have a more important case now."

"More important than murder?" I let my skepticism show. "Seems unlikely."

"More important than the murder of any *Frenchman.*"

"I don't differentiate." *Unless it's a Boche, then my standards slip a little.*

"You will today." Becker picked up a manila folder from the desk. "This man has gone missing. His case is your priority, and you will find him."

"Who is he?"

"Everything you need to know is in here. I expect a telephone report in a day or two, to know where things stand." He glared at me. "You will make this investigation quick."

"I can tell you a little more." Von Rauch spoke up, and I liked the way he ignored the scowl Becker gave him. "The man's a colleague of mine. We're doctors at the Blériot Hospital."

"Do you know him well?"

"Not at all. He only arrived here from Germany last week. I saw him maybe two days, I was away from the hospital on business."

I nodded, noting not just the information but the man's cultured accent. He wasn't just fluent, and it was more than him having a good French accent. He sounded like a wealthy Parisian.

"Can you tell me whether—" I began, before Becker cut me off.

"On your own time, Detective."

"Come see me at the hospital," von Rauch said with an apologetic smile. "I'm there all day tomorrow, I can tell you what little I know about him."

"Thank you." I looked at Becker. "Speaking of time, do I get a full week this go-around?" The last time the Nazis did this to me, I had five days to solve the murder before they slipped a noose around my neck.

"Just find him." Becker stared at me, as if daring me to waste hours of the time arguing with him. I didn't. I leaned over and snatched the folder from the desk. I gave von Rauch a nod and my boss a glare, then walked out. I went straight to my office and shut the door, plopped down in my squeaky wooden chair and stared out of the window that overlooked the River Seine. The snow hadn't started yet but the sky was dark with its coming, and the river roiled and swirled like molten lead, its mood today: hostile and dangerous.

With a deep sigh I opened the folder and turned my attention to its contents. My missing person was a Dr. Viktor Brandt, who was six feet tall, was of average build, and looked like no one you'd ever remember. A photo of him showed light brown, maybe sandy hair, wire-rimmed glasses, and an expensive suit, or maybe just a new one. These Germans and their suits.

The folder contained a one-page summary of his recent movements, which consisted of arriving in Paris the previous week, as von Rauch had said, checking in at the Ritz Hotel, and going to work every day at the Blériot Hospital close to the Gare du Nord in the Tenth Arrondissement. His job description was included, but meant little to me: neurological research specialist. The single page didn't list any of his last whereabouts, nor any friends or colleagues he may have visited. The file gave me flashbacks to the last case I handled for the Boche, only this one had less information. Next time I saw one of those bastards at the Préfecture I'd turn around and run away because they'd probably ask me to solve an unnamed crime before it happened, or it'd be my head.

Or, maybe I should take Nicola's suggestion and retire. Maybe I could make it retroactive to about ten minutes ago. Somehow, I didn't think the Nazi and his wool suit would allow that. And even if he did, some other poor detective would find his neck on the line and I hadn't become quite that selfish or coldhearted. Not yet, anyway.

I looked up as someone knocked on my door. "Come in."

I expected to see Nicola offering help and condolences, but it was the chief. He closed the door behind him and sat down.

"Henri—" he began, but I cut him off.

"Come to apologize for dumping me in the shit again?"

"Actually, yes. I tried to get them to use someone else, but you're a victim of your own success."

"Great, then I'll remember to fail more in the future."

"Fine, just not on this case, Henri, else there may not be a future."

"I've always admired your encouraging management style, Chief, thank you."

"Look, it's worse than you think," Proulx said, not looking me in the eye.

"I don't think that's possible."

"Oh, it is. Thing is, we got a call less than an hour ago about a body pulled from the Seine. GiGi just left to look into it, it'll be his case."

"You're surely not going to ask me to work it with him," I said, firing up my outrage.

"No, no. We don't have the resources for two people to work cases, you know that."

"Then what?"

"We just got a second call."

My heart sank. "Another murder."

"Yes. And you're the only one who can take it."

"No, Chief, I'm the only one who *can't* take it."

"I'm sorry, Henri." He rose. "Look, go check out the crime scene and interview anyone who's nearby. Then put that case on the back burner, and tomorrow focus on finding the missing German." He opened the door and looked over his shoulder. "Hell, maybe you'll get lucky and this new corpse will be him."

CHAPTER THREE

I grabbed Nicola, ignoring Proulx's feeble protests that he needed her there, and set off for the Left Bank and my new murder scene. I needed her to tag along because, to me, she was more than just a secretary in the murder division, she was twice as useful as any of the other detectives in the unit. She was bright, observant, and with her looks and smarts could extract information faster and more accurately than a pair of heated tongs applied to the genitals. And, since she wasn't a detective, people paid her no mind at crime scenes, all too often letting their guard drop and their tongues wag. Quite the asset, in other words. And while the others in the office had thrown us suspicious looks in years gone by, they no longer assumed we were lovers, just as they had no clue what our history together, and our current relationship, truly was. People had other things to worry about these days.

Outside, it was colder than it'd been just an hour ago, and the heavy sky and soon-to-be setting sun made the city look dour and grim. I pulled my coat tight around me and together we set off. En route, she asked why Proulx had wanted to see me. "I know it wasn't this new murder because I just took the call. And who were those men in his office?"

"'Men' is a bit generous. Do you remember last time a Nazi invited me in there for a chat?"

"Oh, Henri. They've given you another murder case to work on?" She paled, remembering how close I'd come to blowing the deadline the last time around.

"Yes, only it's a missing person." I frowned. "Not even the benefit of having a dead German this time."

"Who is he? What do you know?"

"Some doctor, he worked at the Blériot Hospital doing research."

"Into what?"

"No idea. That's my focus for tomorrow. Today we do the basics on whatever we find, and then this case will have to wait."

"Can I help you with the missing person, too?"

I smiled wryly. "You better."

"What are you going to do first?"

"I think visit his workplace and his room at the Ritz."

"The Ritz?" She raised a questioning eyebrow. "Nice quarters for a doctor."

"Yes," I agreed. "I had the very same thought."

We reached boulevard Saint-Germain, and paused outside the Café de Flore as the smell of fresh coffee melted the cold air and tempted me inside for a shot of the stuff to warm my stomach. The toll of a church bell reminded me that I could spare the change but not the time, so I lit a cigarette and settled for warming my lungs instead. Beside me, my sister, Nicola, threw me a disappointed look.

"Maybe on the way back," I said, and started walking.

"I'm just hungry is all." I got the same sideways look, but this time with a hint of recrimination.

"Ah, yes. I'm sorry, I didn't know it was the last of the bread this morning."

"And the last of the butter, and the last of the jam."

"Mimi has food, surely."

"I knocked on her door on my way to work. No answer, she must have gone out early."

"Where to?"

"No idea."

"You've not eaten all day?" She shook her head to say no. "*Merde*, we'll find something for you." I blew out a stream of smoke, knowing we probably would but not soon enough for her hungry stomach. Two meals a day was our norm now, and she didn't have enough meat on her bones to miss both of them.

We heard the *clip-clop*s before we saw them, weary beasts struggling through the semidarkness toward us. We stood and watched the procession, a dozen or so raggedy-looking horses plodding down the middle of boulevard Saint-Germain, tethered together and led by a scruffy man wearing a cap that looked four sizes too big. It was hard to judge who looked more miserable, them or him.

"What's that about?" Nicola asked.

"You don't want to know."

"Yes, Henri, I think I do."

"Those poor bastards are taking their final walk." I glanced over and took another pull on my cigarette. "You may have noticed more horses in the streets lately."

"I have, yes. Usually pulling carts."

"Right, but some not. In a normal year, these sorry creatures would be loaded into the back of a truck and driven to their final destination. Nowadays, they have to walk to their own demise."

"The abattoir?" She cringed as the lead horse passed us, its nostrils flaring with puffs of air visible in the cold.

"Shh, they'll hear."

Nicola punched my arm. "You're awful, Henri Lefort. Those poor creatures, they have no idea."

"If you have to endure the indignity of a long march before you face the firing squad, it's better you don't know where you're headed." I dropped my smoke on the pavement and crushed it under my heel. "Like these fellows."

"I suppose so," Nicola said quietly. Then she nudged me and gave me that wicked smile. "Still, maybe there'll be some meat in the shops tomorrow."

"You're awful, Nicola Prehn. Just awful." A gust of cold air made us pull our coats tight and I made sure my hat was firmly planted on my head. "Come on, it may be a murder scene, but at least it'll be warm."

We were headed to boulevard Raspail, roughly a mile from the apartment Nicola and I shared in the Sixth Arrondissement on rue Jacob, close to the River Seine. I was a little apprehensive about where we were going because, like too many neighborhoods, it had seen many of its fine buildings taken over by the Germans. The thing was, you could never quite know what they were being used for—we'd heard about, and even come across, everything from living quarters and admin offices to torture sites. As a result, each of those neighborhoods took on a slightly sinister air and, if you didn't live there, you hurried through it, just in case.

We trudged along silently in the growing darkness and, as always lately, I noticed the absence of those quiet but helpful bastions of normality: streetlights. Surprisingly I noted also the lack of cars to light the street at this normally busy hour. Even the stores with something to sell had closed already—they didn't have enough stock to keep them open an entire day—and I missed the aromas that just six months ago would have escorted us on our way: the freshly baked bread, soul-stirring aromas of ground coffee, and alluring wafts of garlic and grilled meat. Nowadays you couldn't even buy a croissant—the Germans had banned them and all other pastries as of the first of August. I shook my head at the loss, and the absurdity.

"What's wrong?" Nicola had noticed.

"Nothing. Reminiscing."

When we reached our destination, an older, uniformed police officer stood smoking at the doorway to the stone, five-story building typical of the area—two spacious apartments per floor, places I couldn't have afforded on a police salary. I liked the building but the *flic* was irritating me with his attitude.

"Put that cigarette out, man, and stop lounging."

"Why? The guy's dead already."

I stopped in front of him. "What's your name?"

"Bissett. Albert Bissett. And you can spare me the lecture, I've been walking these streets since you were in shorts."

"That so?" I reached up and plucked the cigarette from his lips. "And yet here I am, your superior officer." He didn't like that, the tightening of his mouth and the narrowing of his eyes told me so. "Also, you should stop smoking, Albert Bissett. Mademoiselle Prehn here says these things will kill you."

His eyes slid over and appraised Nicola, and for once it seemed a fellow cop wasn't sizing her up for his bedroom. I liked that. And when he addressed her, his tone was respectful. "A lot more out here will get me first, mademoiselle. Especially these days." He turned back to me and straightened a little. "You must be Henri Lefort."

"*Oui*. How did you know?"

"I heard about a murder detective who takes his secretary to crime scenes. You have a good reputation." He glanced at Nicola again. "You both do."

"I don't take her, Bissett. She follows along." I moved past him into the doorway.

Behind I heard Nicola speak sotto voce to the *flic*. "He'd be lost without me." I could hear the smile in her voice, and Bissett chuckled.

The door to my victim's apartment was open, and was on the right side of a tiled reception area used for storing bicycles, boxes, and the ground-floor apartments' rubbish bins. It was clean, tidy, and didn't smell.

"Hey, Bissett," I called back. The *flic* stepped into the building. "The Boche come by yet?"

"About ten minutes ago. Nothing of interest for them."

About two months ago, the Germans had decreed that we not work a murder until they'd been by to check it out. There was no explanation for this new rule, so I figured they just liked seeing dead Parisians. Even better for them if it was a dead Jew, homosexual, or person with any shade of skin that wasn't shiny pink. At the murder scenes I'd attended, some arrogant prick in a starched uniform had shown up, cracked a couple of hilarious German jokes, jotted down a few details, and left us to it.

"Thanks. And do you know how many people have been through the place?"

To my surprise, Bissett pulled a notebook from his jacket and flipped through it.

"The housekeeper who found him. Two uniforms who got there before me, I have their names if you want them, and then me." He jerked a thumb over his shoulder. "And those mange-touts ten minutes ago, of course." That was one of my favorite nicknames for our unwelcome invaders. It was the name of a kind of pea where one could also eat the flat, tender pod, but literally translated it meant "eat everything," which was how we felt about the bastards—we starve, they eat their fill. "But they barely went in and I know the *flics* who did, they wouldn't have touched anything. They know better."

"Thanks." I nodded, and contemplated the idea of always having someone like Bissett at a crime scene, logging who came in and what they did. I filed that away to suggest to my superiors later as Nicola followed me into the apartment, and Bissett hovered close behind.

"Just so you know, sir, I'm off duty in about three minutes. Someone will be along to replace me, though."

"Make sure they have your notes, if you don't mind."

"*Bien sûr.*" Of course.

The place smelled musty, which surprised me given the neighborhood and cleanliness of the reception area. Its front door led into a short hallway, with a hat rack to my right and the living area away to my left. I glanced directly into the kitchen as I made my way down the hall, but nothing seemed out of place, then stopped at an open door that connected to the living room, where beyond it I knew lay a bathroom and two bedrooms.

From the doorway it certainly looked like a burglary gone wrong—the large living room was a mess. Drawers had been opened and emptied, furniture overturned, lamps and knick-knacks strewn among reams of papers. And in the middle of the sitting room, facedown amid the chaos, was our victim, dressed in a nice, new blue suit. In days gone by I would have waited for the police doctor to show up and tell me all he could, but in recent months I'd seen enough bodies and waited around for non-appearing police doctors long enough not to bother anymore.

"Wait here," I said to Nicola. That was her cue to get out her own notepad and write down any observations I might make, or questions I might ask. I stepped carefully through the wreckage of the room to the body, my nose twitching from the dust. "Bachelor, is my guess. Doesn't clean much." I knelt. "Clean incision in the back of the neck, maybe a stab into the brain." I looked behind me. "Bissett, we have any information about this *mec* at all? Name, whether he lives here, anything?"

"*Non, monsieur.* You're the first investigator here. The two young *flics*, I would've had them knock on doors but they were at the end of a double shift." Policing, like every other profession, had suffered losses in the last few months. Not just from the war directly, but from the exodus of people from Paris in May and June, as the Germans arrived. A huge number of them had come back by December, but the police force had been hesitant to rehire people so quick to abandon the city. "The poor bastards were completely exhausted, and"—he nodded toward the corpse beside me—"I figured this gentleman would not object to waiting for the murder squad to arrive."

"Well, true, I don't hear him complaining." I looked around. "So, we're thinking a bad guy or two was rifling through the place, our bachelor friend comes home and interrupts. Maybe the burglar hears him coming in, lies in wait, and stabs him in the back of the neck."

"You see a weapon?" Nicola asked.

"There." Bissett pointed to the handle of a hammer that poked up at us from the floor.

"That didn't kill him, the injury is too precise." I looked closely at the floor around me. "So no, I don't see the murder weapon. But this place is a mess so it could be here, or maybe he took it with him." I put my fingertips on his wrist, not to feel a pulse I knew wasn't there, but to see if there was any semblance of warmth in the body. There was none. "Right, now for the fun part," I said. "I need to flip him over, look through his pockets and see who we have here."

With a grunt and a groan I rolled the body gently onto its side, and then let it keep rolling onto its back.

"Oh, my goodness!" Nicola said from the doorway.

"*Merde*," Bissett said. "What the hell happened to him?"

I didn't answer, I couldn't. All I could do was stare at what once was the face of a man, stare down at a visage beaten flat, bloody, and utterly unrecognizable.

CHAPTER FOUR

I sat back on my heels and grimaced. "Well, that explains the hammer." I glanced toward the implement and saw what I hadn't noticed before, the bloody flat end of it. *Did he bring it with him?* I wondered.

"Angry burglar?" Nicola mused from the doorway.

"Maybe not a burglar after all," I said.

"Why not?" Bissett chirped up. "Seems damned obvious to me, just look at the place."

The sound of footsteps drew our attention, and a uniformed *flic* appeared behind Bissett, who turned and said, "Excellent, now I can go home and eat my one meal of the day."

I felt Nicola's eyes on me but when I glanced at her it wasn't recrimination I saw, but worry. She turned her head and looked back at the new officer, and I did the same.

"Good evening, sir," he said. The same shadow of anxiety was in his eyes, but it disappeared when he looked over at Nicola.

I gritted my teeth. "Good evening. Moulin, isn't it?"

"Yes, sir. Sorry we have to keep meeting over dead bodies."

"That's right, you guarded the last one for me."

"And he didn't escape, sir, not once."

He said it deadpan, and I had to suppress a smile. "Right, I remember that." I turned to the older *flic*. "Thank you, Bissett, you should get home. Just brief Moulin before you do." I spoke directly to Nicola. "You arrange this little coincidence?"

"I'm not that good," she said. "But I would have if I could have."

Moulin got the briefest of briefings from Bissett and stood in the doorway.

"What are you reading these days, Moulin?" I asked.

"A book of short stories by Edgar Allan Poe."

"The American, yes." I grimaced. "Not sure we should support the bastards since they won't support us."

"I think they will, sir. They'll have to."

"Maybe you're right. They were late for the last war, maybe they're just late for this one."

Moulin smiled nervously. "I think so, sir."

"In the meantime, do me a favor. Knock on some doors and find out who lives here." The young *flic* nodded and left the apartment while opening his notepad. Nicola watched him leave, then turned to me.

"Thank you," she said.

"For what?"

"For not bullying him."

"I hate bullies."

"You know what I mean. You were almost nice to him."

"We're at work. I'm always almost nice to people at work."

Nicola laughed. "Right then. So, why is this not a burglary?"

"Look around." I gestured with a sweeping arm. "Burglars open drawers and cabinets, which admittedly we have here. What they don't do is overturn chairs and lamps, which we also have. What are they going to find under a lamp?"

"You think this is a faked burglary."

"Quite possibly. Or a real one that someone wanted to make look suspicious."

"Why would anyone do that?"

"No idea. They probably wouldn't." I gestured at the corpse. "And look at his face. Mimi would say that this was a personal attack."

Mimi's other interest, when not psychoanalyzing me or someone else, was crime. She loved hearing about my cases and, before Sigmund Freud died, she'd been working with him on a theory that you can glean valuable insight from a crime scene, in that each one tells you something about the perpetrator. At first I was dubious, she had some intriguing and odd theories, but this one meshed with my experience as a detective.

"'Personal'?" Nicola asked.

"Yes. A person's face is who they are, it's how the world sees and knows them. By disfiguring someone's face, the killer is destroying *that* particular person. In random robberies or street murders, that doesn't happen. Here, our killer intentionally destroyed this poor fellow's last remaining connection to the people who know and love him."

"Which happens to be very few people," Moulin said, from behind Nicola.

"Meaning?"

"I found two neighbors talking to each other. Apparently, this gentleman was, how did they put it?" He consulted his notebook. "Ah, yes, here it is: *un salaud et un fils de pute*."

"A bastard *and* the son of a whore?" I said. "Not the building's most popular resident."

"I'm guessing not," Moulin agreed. "Also, they were surprised he was at home."

"Why is that?"

"He moved in with his brother about a year ago, rarely came back and when he did he looked like shit. Sick with cancer or something."

"Another direct quote?" I asked.

Moulin grinned. "You know it. Anyway, I didn't invite them down to identify him, for obvious reasons, but they say the owner of this place is called Edouard Grabbin."

"Well, Monsieur Grabbin, let's see what you have on you." I opened his jacket, noting the expensive wool, and stuck my right hand into each of the inside pockets. The first was empty, but the second contained keys, a train ticket to the nearby city of Rennes, and an identity card. I inspected it, and when I saw the name I said, "Edouard Grabbin, indeed."

I stood and gave poor Monsieur Grabbin the once-over. His suit, while expensive, was slightly too large for him, which made sense if he'd gone to stay with his brother out of illness and lost weight. I planned to visit that brother next, make sure Edouard wasn't still there and someone else had been murdered in his suit and apartment. And maybe the brother could explain who would detest this man enough to kill him so precisely and then bash his face in? *Why not let cancer do the dirty work?* I wondered.

"You have plans for tonight, Moulin?" I asked.

"Just a normal night shift, sir, nothing special planned." He gave me a rueful smile. "But I'm thinking I do now. What do you need?"

"Good man. Can you comb through this mess and look for two things? First, a murder weapon. Second, evidence supporting the burglary theory, or"—I held up a cautionary finger—"evidence disproving it."

"Wallets, jewelry, that kind of thing." Moulin nodded. "Understood. You headed back to the Préfecture?"

"*Pas encore*," I said. *Not yet.* "First, I have some bad news to deliver to this gentleman's brother."

"You know where he lives?" Moulin asked.

"*Non.*" I stooped and picked up a stack of envelopes and other papers that had been spread over the floor. "But there are letters here, and a few other papers, with the name Jean Grabbin." I waved an envelope. "And Jean's address. Seems like the place to start."

"Very good, sir."

"Come by my office first thing in the morning, let me know what you find."

"Yes, sir. Good night. Good night, Nicola."

"*Bonsoir*, Daniel. It was a nice surprise to see you here."

"All right, you two," I said, trying to be gruff. "There's work to be done."

Nicola and I stepped outside, buttoning up our coats as we did so. I glanced up at the shapeless gray clouds and felt the gentle tickle of the winter's first snowfall. This was a thought I had at almost every crime scene, no matter the weather—the poor *mec* lying dead inside would never again feel the snow, the wind, or the sun on his face. No matter the discomfort I might endure walking back to the Préfecture or, in this case, to the home of a relative, it was a sensation my victim would never feel again. Thoughts like that made my sore feet and tired back bearable at the low ebb of an investigation, and made me not mind the first heavy snowflakes that slipped down the back of my neck as Nicola and I set off for the long walk across the center of the city to the Seventh Arrondissement.

• • •

As we crossed rue de Babylone the air turned colder still, and the stone buildings around us seemed to lighten with the coming of the snow. For a brief while it came down hard, the flakes hissing gently as they flew down past us onto the sidewalk, giving me a sense of invisibility, comfort even, as we made our way west to carry out the first and most necessary task after a murder.

We call them "death knocks," and there's never been a good one. Some are worse than others, of course, and some people dread doing them more than others, but every single one of them is hateful. And, in the moments before I deliver the news, I always have the same thought: the death has already happened, the loved one is already gone, but it's not the death itself that shatters someone's world, it's the knowing about it. That moment while I'm talking when something changes in their eyes, the moment of realization that nothing will ever be the same again. In some ways, I wonder if it's worse than the flicker of lights out when a man dies. At least what follows that is peace.

A thin dusting of snow had started to settle on the bushes and railings as we turned into rue de Varenne and, more importantly, my toes were beginning to numb. I leaned on the doorbell of Jean Grabbin's building and an elderly woman opened one of the tall doors.

"Can I help you?" She blocked the entrance and, quite frankly, did not seem particularly interested in helping us at all.

"We're here to see Monsieur Jean Grabbin," I said.

"It's *Dr.* Grabbin," she said. "And you are, Monsieur . . . ?"

"I am *Detective* Henri Lefort, Paris police." I waited for her to challenge me, insist on some identification, but apparently my tone worked wonders. She stepped out of the doorway and gestured across a cobbled courtyard to a pair of double wooden doors.

"Knock loudly," she said. "His hearing is not good."

"Merci." I gave her a nod and walked past her, with Nicola in tow. When we got to the doors I rapped loudly and we waited.

"Nice place," Nicola said, looking around.

"I hear he's a doctor."

"Funny."

The doors opened and a short, elegantly dressed man stood there. He wore a cable-knit sweater and corduroy trousers that were only slightly redder than his face. His receding gray hair was swept back over his head, and he ran a hand through it when he saw Nicola beside me.

"Can I help you?" Wariness lingered in his eyes, as if he were expecting bad news.

"Are you Dr. Jean Grabbin?" I asked.

"Yes."

"We're police. May we come in for a moment?"

He hesitated for a second, then looked upward. "It's snowing. First time this year, isn't it?"

"I believe so."

"*Oui, bien sûr*, come in." He led us through a tiled reception area into a kitchen, where a kettle was boiling on a new-looking electric stove. Given his obvious wealth, I was surprised that the room was cold, and I could see why he wore the knit sweater and heavy trousers. He gestured to a kitchen table. "Please, sit down."

All three of us sat, and I cleared my throat. "Doctor, are you the brother of Edouard Grabbin, who lives on boulevard Raspail?"

"Yes, I am." The wariness in his eyes was still there. That wasn't surprising, though; police rarely arrive unannounced with good news.

"Then I am sorry to have to inform you that your brother is dead."

He stopped breathing for a moment, his eyes flicking between me and Nicola. Finally, he said, "Dead? My brother? Are you . . . certain?"

"Yes. I'm quite certain."

He swallowed and looked down. "How did . . . it happen?"

"I'm afraid he was murdered. It looks like someone broke into his apartment and he came upon them, and was attacked."

"Attacked?"

"*Oui, monsieur.*"

"They shot him, or . . . ?"

"He was stabbed, once. It looks like he died instantly." *No need to mention the disfigurement just yet.*

"I see. I see." He was nodding slowly, taking it in. He looked up. "When did this happen? And do you know who did it?"

"The housekeeper found him late this afternoon, so we're thinking last night. There's a lot more sneaking around in the dark these days, the blackout is wonderful for criminals. And I don't know who did it, not yet, as I came straight from there. Do you know of anyone who might want to hurt him?"

"I thought you said it was a burglary gone wrong."

"That's what it looks like." *Or maybe that's what it was made to look like.* "But I have to ask, just in case."

Dr. Grabbin shrugged. "He was a grumpy, irritable person. He didn't have any friends but, as far as I know, he didn't have any enemies, either." He looked at me. "Do you need me to . . . identify him or anything like that?"

"Normally, yes. I have to tell you, though, that he appears to have been assaulted postmortem, and so the normal identification procedures may not be possible."

"Good god." Grabbin recoiled. "Someone . . . disfigured him?"

"That's another way to put it. Did he own a dark green tweed suit that was slightly too big for him?"

"Yes. It used to fit him, but he'd been ill."

"Then I think that, along with him being found in his apartment, and the identity card in his pocket, will be enough. Then again, if your brother strolls through the door in the next couple of days, let me know."

My attempt at lightening the mood bypassed Grabbin, and probably for the best. "Poor Edouard," he said, shaking his head slowly.

"A neighbor of his said he'd moved in with you a while back," I said.

"About a year ago, yes. Because of the cancer."

"Why did he go back to his apartment? And when?"

"Yesterday morning. He went back from time to time to check on the place, collect his mail." He shrugged again. "Sometimes he stays one night, if he's tired. He didn't like being out in the dark, the way things are these days, you never know."

"Very true. Do you mind if I look in his bedroom?"

"His bedroom?"

"Just in case."

"That won't be possible." Grabbin stood suddenly. "I'm afraid I have an appointment, you see. If there's nothing else for now, I will show you out."

Nicola and I exchanged glances. "Nothing else right now, but I'm sure we'll see you again," I said.

Grabbin walked us across the courtyard to the main entrance, and opened it for us himself. Either the old battle-ax was unavailable or, it struck me, Grabbin wanted to make sure we left the property.

On rue de Varenne I looked up and blinked as a snowflake landed in my right eye. I ignored the sour look from Nicola as I popped open my silver cigarette case and lit up. Together, she and Mimi had been trying to get me to quit.

"What did you make of him?" I asked her.

"Hard to say. But you really don't think this was a disturbed burglary, do you?"

"I can't say for sure." I blew out a stream of smoke. "Someone certainly wants us to think it was."

"But you're keeping an open mind."

"Of course, always. I'm especially open to finding out why he didn't want us looking in his brother's room."

"That was odd," Nicola agreed. "And suspicious."

"Odd certainly. Probably nothing because guilty people are usually more subtle than that." I held up a correcting finger. "The intelligent ones, I mean."

"And he is a doctor."

"Indeed. But still, it was definitely odd." A pair of German soldiers was making their way toward us, and I shivered. "Come on, I'm cold and there are too many questionable characters in this neighborhood."

CHAPTER FIVE

After Nicola and I had eaten a meal of vegetable soup, there was a knock at our door. We'd left the dishes in the sink and were reading, so I got up to see who it was. I opened the door to see a smiling, well-dressed woman holding a bottle of wine.

"Nicola," I called back into the sitting room. "There's royalty at the door, bearing gifts."

"Then you better let it in," Nicola said. "At least take the gift."

"It's not one or the other," Princess Marie Bonaparte said, pushing past me. "You have to accept both. And I'm not an 'it.'"

I closed the door and followed her into the kitchen, handing her a corkscrew. A minute later we were settled into comfortable chairs in the living room, savoring a flavorful Burgundy

"I hope you don't mind the late visit," Mimi said, then looked at me. "I ran into Nicola earlier, she said you had a new case."

"Two new cases," I corrected her. "One murder, one missing person. Well, I say 'person,' but he's a Nazi doctor, so who knows? He may once have been a human being."

"Reasonable accusation." Mimi smiled. "Anything interesting about the murder?"

"Yes. Victim is in his sixties, stabbed once in the neck in his apartment, which is a wreck, and had his face bashed in with a hammer."

"Unusual." Mimi took a sip and sat back in thought. "Interesting to have a single stab wound, then a more brutal act of violence. Makes me think it was personal."

"My thinking also." I gave Nicola a *Told you so* wink. "It's possible it was made to look like a burglary that went wrong, but I can't tell if anything was taken, and it looked *too* burgled."

"Meaning?"

"Things like lamps and chairs were overturned. Burglars don't look under lamps for treasure to steal. It was all too much."

"Any suspects?" Mimi asked.

"I'd go for his brother," Nicola chipped in. "He didn't seem overly shocked, and wouldn't let us see the dead man's bedroom."

"Oh, why not?"

"No idea," Nicola said. "He shooed us out, saying he had an appointment to go to."

"And I checked," I said. "He's been retired for two years so, if he really did have an appointment, it wasn't with a patient."

"Will you go see him again?" Mimi asked.

"Yes, but not tomorrow. I need to start looking into this missing Boche; they have me on a short leash to find him."

"How long has he been gone?"

"Three days." I grimaced. "Not a good sign. Anyway, what about you? Keeping busy?"

"Yes, but not through my practice. I see a client every day or two in my apartment, if I'm lucky, and none as interesting as my first and favorite." She gave me a big smile. I'd been her first, and we'd talked about more than just my aversion to sounds. Apart from Nicola, she was the only person in the world in whom I'd confided my heavy past and yet, despite my fears, she'd never violated the trust I showed in her. I felt a little guilty about what I'd said to Nicola earlier, because in truth Mimi had been nothing but a good friend to us. Not just providing food and wine, which we deeply appreciated, but being there for anything else we needed. Mostly talking. And that in itself was fun because she was a woman of immense intelligence and energy, always curious and always wanting to help others.

Maybe I should *work on my trust issues with her.*

"So if not your practice, what's keeping you busy?"

"I've been volunteering at two different children's homes. Today was my third day at this new place, and quite the day it was," she said.

"How so?" I asked.

"Well, that's why I'm here, I wonder if you can help."

"Something bad happened?"

"I'm not sure. Two of the children were taken away from the home."

"Taken away?" Nicola asked.

"Yes." Mimi frowned. "Two women and a man appeared, showed the director some papers, and took the children."

"What kind of home is it, exactly?" I asked.

"It's essentially an orphanage, but they have medical staff and try more modern methods of treatment and discipline than most. That's why they wanted me there, to conduct psychoanalysis, even though I'm not used to working with children."

"Oh, I don't know," Nicola said. "You were great with Henri."

We laughed, but Mimi still looked worried, so I tried to reassure her. "You said they had paperwork, so it sounds official. Maybe an adoption?"

"No, no. The director said they were being sent to a treatment center. A better one."

"What treatment do they need?" Nicola asked.

"Both were boys, aged sixteen. One had a misformed spine, the other was blind." Mimi shrugged. "I don't think you can treat, let alone cure, either of those conditions."

"The people who took them, they were French?" I asked.

"Yes. I'd assumed they were Germans but the director said they were definitely French." She sipped her wine. "Maybe it's all fine but it just seemed very sudden, and the director, well, she didn't know what to do except cooperate."

"Where is this new treatment center?" I asked. "Here in Paris? If so, I could pay a visit and make sure all's in order."

"That's what I was thinking," Mimi said. "But I just remembered, it's not in Paris. It west of here. In the city of Rennes. Where I also heard the Germans are building a weapons factory or something like that."

Nicola's head snapped up at that and we locked eyes for a moment, no doubt our thoughts mirroring each other's as well. But coincidences do happen, and Rennes is a fairly large city—probably in the top ten in France. And nearby, of course, so a common destination for people escaping Paris for a day or so. In sum, there was no real reason to think there'd be a link between the dead Edouard Grabbin and the seemingly official removal of these children. No reason at all.

Then again, I thought, *this little coincidence might just merit a little bit of my time and interest. Once I've found that missing Boche, of course.*

"I can ask a few questions," I said. "Not about the factory, I don't care about that. Glad for it to be away from here; those things explode from time to time."

"Thank you," Mimi said. "It's probably nothing sinister but these days that's always the first assumption, isn't it?"

"It most certainly is," I agreed. "Maybe I can even bring you positive news. That'd make a nice change."

CHAPTER SIX

Tuesday, December 3, 1940

The following morning I was awoken by the sound of shouting in the street below my bedroom window. It was five o'clock, too late for it to be drunks and too early for anything else, except one of those damn German raids. They'd begun targeting Jews recently, but so far this part of Paris had mostly escaped the raids. The winding streets of the Sixth Arrondissement, where we lived, were more popular with students and working people than the large, wide boulevards that the richer homes and businesses inhabited on the Right Bank. The homes and businesses of wealthy Jewish bankers and moneymen so despised by our occupiers.

I peered down into the street and my worst fears were realized. A unit of German soldiers had stormed a nearby building and were loading a family, a man and his wife and two children, into the back of a truck. They were still in their pajamas.

"They woke you, too?" Nicola said from my doorway. I hadn't heard her open it.

"Yes." I shook my head because there was nothing more to say about it.

"Coffee is brewing," she said. "I won't be able to sleep now."

"Same. Long day ahead, may as well get started with it."

"Need company?" she asked. "I have a lot to catch up on, but your cases are a priority."

"Saving my neck is a priority, you mean." I smiled at her. "But no, get caught up and I'll check in with you later. If I need help, I'll ask for it. For now, just that coffee."

"Black and sweet, coming up. And give me your list, please, if you know it."

I nodded and started writing down a list of people and places I planned to visit that day. A lot of detectives had started to make a record of where they were going, a list of destinations handed to a secretary or family member. The reason for that was twofold: first, if the detective went missing or got into any kind of trouble with the new authorities there was a trail to follow, a way to find him. Second, with communications in poor shape throughout the city, especially with the scarcity of working telephones, if a detective was needed while he was out conducting interviews, then a bicycle courier could be sent to the places on his list to catch up with him. I handed Nicola my list and went in search of my hat, coat, and a fresh pack of cigarettes.

It was still dark when I let myself out of the building. My heart sank as I remembered the family taken just an hour before, but I pushed the image of them from my mind. I had to. We all had to. I wanted to believe I'd help people like that if and when I could, but I knew I couldn't let my mind linger on thoughts of where they were being taken, or what was going to happen to them.

The sky above me was dappled with stars, one of the very few benefits of the blackout of Paris, and the only source of light in the narrow, empty street that bounced the sound of my footsteps back to me. It was even colder than yesterday, too, and I noticed the hoarfrost that sparkled like diamond dust on the iron railings as I passed by.

My first visit was to the Ritz Hotel, where my missing Dr. Brandt had been staying. It wasn't the sort of place I frequented, of course, but my occasional visits while working a case were always eye-opening. Not just for the wealth and opulence, but for the ways in which a place like the Ritz, even in a war, managed to stay a cut above the rest of us poor working slobs—around the time the Germans were preparing to take over the city there were fears of bombing raids, and the Ritz had turned its cellars into shelters for the lucky few, complete with fur rugs and Hermès sleeping bags.

I took the walk slowly, using a flashlight on occasion because the blackout had never been lifted—the French were no longer scared of the Germans bombing Paris, the Germans were now scared the British would. Now we just needed the Brits to reclaim the city and keep us in the dark in case the Yanks wanted to join in late with a few bombs. I made jokes about the Americans always being late, like they were in the 1914 war, but having lived there until I was fifteen I did see their refusal to step in and stop Hitler as something of a personal grievance. I'd fought with that army, I knew its might and power, and I believed with all my heart that alongside the English it could destroy that horrible little man and his horrible little Nazis.

The Pont du Carrousel was empty when I started across, and despite the chill wind that whipped at me from the river below, I paused when I got to the middle. I looked to my right, toward Notre Dame, but she was a black figure in a black cloak. Normally, the riverside would sparkle with light, to my left and right, but now in the freezing morning the city felt deserted, as if the million or more people who'd left in June and July had stayed away, and the rest of the city had joined them. I sighed, straightened up, and kept going.

The Ritz was an odd place these days. Frenchmen with money and drooping mustaches still frequented the place, almost as if to make a point. The problem was, though, they were forced to see the multitude of Germans and German sympathizers trooping in and out of the hotel. I got there soon after six, and the downstairs lobby was beginning to wake up. As was I when I smelled the fresh coffee and pastries. I'd assumed the pastry ban extended citywide, but reminded myself about those Hermès sleeping bags; the rich and powerful didn't suffer the privations forced on the rest of us. If they wanted *pain au chocolat* or an almond croissant with their coffee, by god they were going to get one.

The receptionist was a tall woman with a nose that was slightly too large to not stare at. Which, of course, she noticed.

"Can I help you?" It wasn't the friendliest tone, but then I didn't deserve that.

I showed her my police identification. "I need to see the room that is being used by Dr. Viktor Brandt."

"You need to see Dr. Brandt?"

"No, just his room."

She hesitated. "Have you asked him? I mean, do you have his permission?"

"Ah, no." I leaned across the counter and lowered my voice. "He's missing. It's my job to find him."

"Oh. And you think he might be in his room?"

I can usually tell when someone is being sarcastic or whether they're just stupid, but in this case I really couldn't. Maybe it was the way her nose blocked a proper view of her eyes and generally dominated her countenance, but I was at a loss.

"That would be nice," I said. "It'd certainly make my job easier."

"Then you are welcome to knock on his door." She frowned. "Although it is quite early."

"Would you be good enough to tell me his room number? And perhaps a key, in case he's not there."

"A key?" She hesitated. "If he's not there, then you won't find him there. So you don't need a key."

"Mademoiselle." I took a deep breath and tried to remain calm. "I am not playing hide-and-seek with the doctor. I am a policeman and he has gone missing. If he is not in his room, it may contain clues as to why not, and as to where he might be."

She looked dubious but nonetheless handed me the key, which had the room number on it. "Please bring it back when you are finished," she said.

"I most certainly will." I took the elevator to the fourth floor and padded along the carpeted corridor to Dr. Brandt's room. I even raised my fist to knock, before shaking my head at myself and slipping the key into the lock and turning it. I pushed open the door and stepped into what felt like a completely different world.

The room had obviously been made up since Dr. Brandt had last shut the door, and it was a bright, clean haven of the lightest ivory. In front of me the giant bed was covered with an impossibly smooth bedspread, the pillows plumped and waiting for their guest. The walls were painted white, too, and the light-cream drapes had been swept aside from the two sets of windows to my right to let the morning light in. At the far end of the room, a fireplace and two ivory chairs nestled together, and I just stood there staring, wondering how one room could be so beautiful, so perfect, and how anyone could afford such a place. I even thought about taking off my shoes so as not to risk dirtying the pristine cream carpet.

I first took a general look over the room, trying to ignore the splendor and look for anything out of place, but the maids had obviously righted any glaring wrongs suffered in the room. To my right, between the sets of windows, sat a large chest of drawers (that looked like they were made of *actual* ivory). I started there.

In my years as a detective, I've seen and even touched a lot of things that made my skin crawl but even so, sifting through the neatly stacked and perfectly pressed clean underwear of a Nazi doctor ranked near the top of my most disgusting moments. This man ironed his own underwear and socks, he must have, even the Ritz wouldn't have provided that service. Surely.

I went through each drawer methodically, checking the undersides in case something had been taped to the bottoms, but I finished in five minutes and was none the wiser. I crossed to the wardrobe and opened it, finding three suits and a heavy winter coat. *Does he have two of these, or did he go out without it?* I wondered. The way the Germans had been buying up French food, art, and clothing, I'd not be surprised if he had three or four coats. I began to go through the suit pockets but came up with nothing but lint and frustration. It was only when I looked inside one of the four shoes in the wardrobe that I struck gold.

"What do we have here?" I used my fingertips to pull out a black-and-white business card. "Well, look at that. For Club Monocle." There was a graphic of a monocle to match the name, and while that name rang a bell I couldn't dredge up anything specific from the depths of my coffee-deprived brain. But the one benefit of being awoken at five was that I now had time to not only visit Dr. Brandt's place of work, but maybe add in a visit to this club.

I searched the rest of Brandt's belongings, and the room itself, but didn't find anything that might suggest where he'd gone. I closed the door behind me, still wondering how a mere medical doctor, even a Gestapo one, either afforded or warranted such an expensive room. That kind of privilege, in my experience, came with either a bodyguard or, at the least, some kind of aide-de-camp. As far as I knew, Brandt had neither, and that suggested one of two possibilities to me: either he was a senior member of the Gestapo but was operating relatively unsupervised on some secret endeavor, or he was of a lower rank and had somehow finagled the privileges of a more senior man.

Whichever the correct answer, I couldn't shake the feeling that something fishy was going on, over and apart from just the disappearance of Dr. Brandt.

In the hallway, I saw a maid pushing her cart of toiletries and cleaning supplies. I stopped her and showed her my police identification.

"Excuse me, mademoiselle. Do you clean Monsieur Brandt's room?"

"*Oui, monsieur.*"

"When did you last have to make it up?"

"I don't really know . . ." She thought for a moment. "Come to think of it, I've not had to make his bed or replace any soaps for . . ." Again the frown. "Maybe three or four days?"

"So, to be specific, Friday night was the last time he slept in his room?"

"*Non.*" She shook her head. "I cleaned on Friday morning, so Thursday was the last time he slept in it. Or, as far as I can tell, used it at all."

"*Merci*, mademoiselle, you have been very helpful."

I walked downstairs and through the hotel lobby toward the exit, my stomach rumbling as the rich smell of coffee reached out to me again. I couldn't afford to eat at the Ritz, assuming I was even allowed to, so decided to go in search of food. So after I returned the key to my front desk friend, I found some bread at a supermarket on rue de la Paix. It wasn't fresh, but I didn't mind that as much as I minded almost getting myself shot before I could eat it.

CHAPTER SEVEN

I'd paused on the way out of the store, watching a large unit of the goose-steppers clomp toward me in the dark. I looked at the faces of the men as they passed, grim and determined, and wondered if they liked being all serious while in Paris. I mean, it seemed utterly incongruent to me: marching as a military squad, with great purpose, in a city where there was literally no one to fight. And, of course, in a city whose greatest charms called for strolling not marching, and led one precisely away from fighting (unless it was over a pretty girl or a glass of absinthe).

What happened next was by no means a frequent occurrence, but it was an occasional act of defiance that made the Boche as mad as hornets.

The soldiers drew level with the supermarket, watched by maybe a dozen Parisians on either side of the street, and suddenly it began to snow again. This time, though, with *papillons*—hundreds of paper toilet–thin pieces of paper, which drifted down from the dark sky above, curling and dipping in the cold breeze. They settled on the shoulders of the marching soldiers and piled up in front of their perfectly shined boots. I saw several of those grim faces glance upward in irritation.

I'd heard of these air assaults but never seen one in person, and it was a delight. I knew they were let loose from rooftops or thrown into the air from speeding bicycles, designed to drift down onto the heads of our occupiers, irritating them like falling pollen, each scrap of paper with a slur or some other anti-German message. These flurries were a boon to those of us who witnessed—or even heard about—them, and they agitated the Boche because they were a reminder that despite the smiles and nods and lack of overt resistance, we hated them. A reminder, too, that there were mimeograph machines hidden away out there, printing words and images they did not want to exist, let alone see. And the beauty of these acts of defiance was not just the embarrassment of the Germans, but the invisibility (and therefore un-catchability) of the perpetrator. A perfect pairing, in my view.

I grabbed a falling *papillon*, and read the words: *Go home, sausage-eaters!* The message was accompanied by a cartoon drawing of a German soldier with crossed eyes, crooked teeth, and a sausage sticking out of each ear. I showed it to the old man standing nearest to me, and we both grinned. We looked up at the squadron as it came to a sudden halt, the silence as threatening as the stomp of boots had just been.

An officer was striding toward me and my new friend, and I let the *papillon* flutter to the ground while turning my facial expression to neutral.

The officer stopped in front of us, his face crimson with anger. "Did you do this?" he demanded in bad French.

"How could I?" I said mildly, then gestured to the sky. "They came from up there, and I'm down here."

"Don't be insolent!" he yelled. Before I could open my mouth and be insolent again, he drew his hand back and slapped me across the face. I staggered back, pain searing my right cheek, anger exploding inside me. I stepped forward, but the old man tugged on my arm, holding me back.

"He didn't do it, monsieur," the old man said. "He couldn't; he was here with me."

But the officer wasn't convinced, stepping up to face me again. After a brief stare down he sneered. "Well, let's see if he has more of these hilarious messages on him, shall we?" He leaned in even closer. "You do find them funny, do you not?"

I chewed my lip, declining to answer. Telling the truth was only going to get me another slap, at the very least, and I sure as hell wasn't going to lie. I spread my arms wide so he could search me, realizing too late what he'd find—the moment his hand brushed over the pistol under my arm he pulled his own and began shouting.

"On your knees, get down on your knees, now!" He waved two men over and they roughly searched me, removing my gun and my wallet. "Why do you have a gun?" the officer was yelling.

"I'm a policeman," I insisted. "I'm a detective and on duty, investigating a case."

"Hauptmann Gurtz," one of the two helpers was saying. To my relief, he'd found my credentials and held them up for the officer to see.

Gurtz studied them for a moment, and it seemed to me he was

buying himself some time to figure out his next move. Eventually, he turned to me.

"Detective, you said?"

"Yes." I had to consciously swallow the *sir* that would normally have followed.

"In that case, I have a job for you."

"Thanks, but I already have one. And from someone a little more senior than you." I shouldn't have, but I couldn't resist. If there's one thing that makes these sausage-eaters stop in their tracks it's a call to authority.

Usually.

"Is that so?" He looked around dramatically. "I don't see anyone here but me. So . . ." He glanced at his watch. "I will give you an hour to find the criminal who threw those papers on us."

"What? How the hell am I . . . ?"

"He must be in this building, correct? I mean, they fell from the roof so he's either up there still, or has made his way down. My men will make sure no one leaves until you find him, how about that?"

"Very helpful."

"Solve this little mystery, and only the perpetrator gets what's coming. Fail to solve it, and I'll pick a couple of people from the crowd and blame them." He leaned in close and his eyes narrowed. "Maybe you'll be one of them."

"I'll do my best."

"Excellent, off you go." He shooed me away like I was a small child, and I gritted my teeth as I walked back into the supermarket. I stopped by the cashier.

"Stairs?" I asked.

She pointed to the back of the shop. "Through the double doors, staircase on your left."

I nodded and trudged through the store and the doors, finding the stairs on my left as she'd said.

And if I find the kid, it's always a kid, who did this? What then? But I knew the answer. If he was real young he might just get beaten to a pulp for his offense. Any older than ten and he'd either be shot right there and then, or shipped off on one of those transport trains to an even worse fate, one of the work camps I'd been hearing about. I shook my head and walked slowly upstairs to the roof, sure whoever had dispersed those *papillons* was gone, but hoping I could waste enough time that my friendly Hauptmann Gurtz would get cold, or bored, and find someone else to harass.

The clouds seemed especially low from up here, gunmetal gray and lurking like an evil being keeping watch over me. My heart lifted, though, when I confirmed that the rooftop was deserted and, even, better, I found who had sent the *papillons* fluttering down on us. Well, technically it was a *what* and not a *who*. It was a mousetrap and it sat on the ledge of the building, overlooking the street. I'd never seen one, but we had a collection at the Préfecture—a tin can full of water, and with a tiny hole in the bottom, is placed on the snapper arm, along with a light cardboard box filled with the *papillons*. The can of water holds the bar down until enough water drains out that it suddenly doesn't, and the bar snaps up and sends the *papillons* flying into the air. The beauty of the device is, of course, that by the time it goes off the perpetrator is well away from the scene—no doubt lingering on the street to admire his handiwork, then melting away when the finger-pointing begins. *Merveilleux!*

I picked up the trap and headed back downstairs.

"Where's the culprit?" Hauptmann Gurtz demanded.

"Right here." I handed him the device.

"What the hell is this?" Hauptmann Gurtz demanded.

"It's a time-delay device. Whoever set it was away from here before it went off."

"Then you have a problem, policeman. Don't you?"

"With respect, Hauptmann, you said if I solved this mystery you'd let these people go on about their business. I solved it."

I could see his mind working, thinking back and conjuring up the exact words he'd used. When he realized I'd quoted him correctly, he smiled, knowing he was in a bind. He could either lose face by lying, or lose face by being outwitted by a kid and a French detective. To my surprise, he picked the latter. He dropped the mousetrap on the floor, then flattened it with the heel of his boot. A small victory for him, and one he was welcome to, given the situation. Without another word, he turned and marched to the front of his unit and in seconds had them lined up like tin soldiers, ready to march on. We all watched in silence as they headed down the street, the ominous sounds of their boots echoing off the stone walls, gradually fading away like an outgoing tide. An outgoing tide that had almost swept me away for good.

Seeing the violence in that Nazi's eyes, his casual, easy approach to hurting people, suddenly made me wonder something. Everyone knew the Germans were buying up or otherwise acquiring everything they could, regardless of the effect on us Parisians. What if Edouard Grabbin was merely another one of their victims? What if he'd owned something that one of those bastards wanted for themselves? It didn't even need to be something valuable, clearly if these callous invaders decided something now belonged to them, why would they hesitate to take it? So maybe Grabbin's murder was a simple burglary gone wrong, but one carried out by a greedy German soldier.

I groaned inwardly at the possibility, as it would be an added complication I didn't need. Accountability for a Frenchman's death didn't seem like it'd be high on the Boche's list of moral attributes, and if this was the right answer my overlords would likely be less than happy about it. And I had no doubt they'd be just as happy to shoot the French messenger as the German culprit.

A few of us exchanged glances before we moved off in different directions, stepping safely back into the new normal of our lives, this time untouched by violence, but only just.

CHAPTER EIGHT

The Blériot Hospital smelled liked every hospital I'd ever been in. I wrinkled my nose the second I stepped inside, and wondered why cleanliness had to smell so unpleasant. At the reception desk I was greeted by a stern-looking *boniche*, one of the older nurses the Germans foisted on the hospitals they took over. We called them *boniches*, or maids, for the ridiculous white bonnets they wore and the contrast between the silly hat and the sour face made me smile. This *boniche*, however, rewarded my friendliness with a cold stare, and my police identification did nothing to warm her up.

"You will need to speak to the chief of administration."

"I'm here to see Dr. Andreas von Rauch. He's expecting me."

"No."

This was unexpected. "What do you mean, 'no'?" I asked, still smiling. "No, I'm not here to see Dr. von Rauch or no, he's not expecting me. Because, frankly, either way—"

"The chief of administration first. All requests and visits go through him." She pointed to a row of chairs nearby. "Sit."

I did so, and fiddled with my hat as she spoke rapidly in German into a telephone. She said nothing when she hung up, so I waited a moment before speaking.

"Is someone coming to meet me? This matter is of the utmost importance."

"If not, I would have said so." She spoke firmly and without looking up.

It was of interest to me, her attitude. My experience in the five months since Paris had been taken over by the Germans was that most of the bastards tried to ingratiate themselves with the local populace. More often than not, those attempts at friendliness were greeted with passive resistance—perhaps a cold stare, or a pretense of not hearing, but for the most part, quite a few Germans continued to try to win us over. As the weeks and months rolled by, though, I became increasingly aware that this politeness and attempted warmth from the Boche was more my experience than that of others. I came to realize it was because I was a policeman and not a regular civilian (much less a street beggar), and it was also because my skin was the right color for politeness. More than those things, it was because my blood and name didn't set off any of those fine-tuned German alarms that I might be a Jew or a gypsy. I'd not earned any of these merit badges, which is what my name and skin were, and I was a little annoyed at myself for taking so long to realize that not every Parisian was treated with such respect.

After a five-minute wait, a door opened to my left and a small, somewhat rotund man with thinning hair and round spectacles hurried toward me.

"Detective Leport, I am sorry to keep you waiting. My name is Leon Werner."

"Henri Lefort," I corrected him and stood. We shook hands. "And I wasn't waiting long."

"Good. Please, follow me." His French was slow but clear, and I trailed him into his small office, taking one of the two wooden chairs across the desk from him. I noticed photos on a low bookcase to his right of, presumably, his wife and two young children. "How can I help the Paris police?" he asked once we were settled.

"I've been assigned to find Dr. Viktor Brandt."

"Ah, yes." His eyes slid away from me, and I got the feeling he didn't care much for the doctor. "What do you need from me?"

"Do you know him?"

"Not well. I am in charge of personnel here at the hospital, so my work is administrative, not clinical."

"Then you hired Dr. Brandt?"

"Non, monsieur." The slightest of smiles played on his lips. "He is part of a special team that was . . . placed here."

"The team that includes Dr. von Rauch."

"Yes. But I don't know much about them. Research, is all I have been told."

"Research into what?"

"Again, I do not know."

"Then who placed that team here?" I pulled out my notebook. "And who else is on it?"

"Who's to say? If I had to guess I'd say either Gestapo or SS." He pursed his lips and I knew he was choosing his words carefully. "Whichever of those two, my function is to provide the support requested and not ask too many questions. Or any at all."

"Understood. And the team consists of . . . ?"

"Dr. Brandt and two others. Von Rauch, as you know, and Dr. Denis Berger."

"Thank you. I would like to speak to them, now if at all possible."

"Perhaps. That would be up to them."

"Well, von Rauch has already invited me to speak to him here, so I think that one is decided."

"I am not aware of that."

I wasn't sure whether it was the language barrier, or if he was intentionally stonewalling or withholding information, and perhaps it was just because I needed a cigarette, but I was beginning to run low on patience with this man.

"Is there a reason you should be aware, monsieur? Are you their keeper?"

"Not at all, I just meant—"

"Good, because I'm fairly sure they'd be delighted to speak to the detective searching for their lost colleague, don't you think?"

He looked at me for a moment, then picked up his telephone receiver. The rest of the city was resorting to carrier pigeons and telepathy for communications these days, but this *mec* had his own private telephone. He mumbled in German, waited, then mumbled some more, then said: "Dr. von Rauch will be down in a moment."

•   •   •

"First of all," von Rauch said with a deprecating smile, "a thousand apologies for my colleague's demeanor at the Préfecture. Truth be told, it makes me wince to call him a colleague."

"We could go with *conard*," I suggested.

"Yes, I suppose from your perspective that would not necessarily be inappropriate."

Werner had left us alone to talk, and I wondered briefly if that was at the suggestion of von Rauch. He was most definitely a man of authority, and that would be true regardless of military rank. Aristocrats like him, like Mimi, seemed to be born with a commanding air. Or maybe they had it piped into them at the succession of private schools and institutions they were subjected to as children. But, like Mimi, von Rauch seemed to be aware of his effect on others and not overly arrogant about it.

"I don't understand types like him," I said. "Seems like a pure sadist and psychopath. I should certainly hope a man of medicine would distance himself from such a brute."

"Indeed. But medicine can be a brutal business in itself," von Rauch said mildly. "Decisions about life and death, sometimes pure guesses as to which treatment. And always the risk is with someone else's life."

"But you're always looking to preserve that life, at least. Those pointy-toed fascists don't seem to care one jot about anyone, they just want results."

"If I may." Von Rauch cleared his throat. "I think, Detective, you may want to be careful in front of whom you throw about certain words and accusations."

"Oh, you mean words like 'fascist'?" It gave me a perverse pleasure to see his face darken a little. "Because 'fascist' is a good word in my book, and one that is very applicable. Fascist. Are you one of those, Herr von Rauch?"

The first rule of being a good detective is knowing how to make your subject feel comfortable in your presence, feel able and even willing to open up to you and tell you the truth. Clearly, I needed a refresher course because von Rauch was closing up bit by bit before my eyes.

"I am a German patriot," he said stiffly. "And I would remind you that you are a conquered nation."

"For now," I muttered.

"Indeed." His attitude seemed to soften. "And while this may be of cold comfort to you, Detective, I am delighted to be in Paris, and am strongly encouraging the powers that be to continue to help the city live as normally as possible."

"'Normally'?" I really had no idea what he meant. People were eating scraps, waiting in lines for hours, freezing, starving, miserable. In other words, nowhere close to normal.

"Yes. Opening cinemas, theaters, bringing back the opera." He sighed with delight. "Ah, the opera, how I've missed it."

"Yes, me too," I lied. I knew slightly more about opera than I enjoyed it, thanks to Nicola's love of the arts.

"Ah, yes? Which are your favorites?"

"Anything French," I said, not particularly interested in being interrogated about any one specific opera. "I imagine you're partial to marathons like *Die Meistersinger von Nürnberg.*"

"A masterful work, no doubt. But it's always struck me as too long to absorb in one sitting."

"No concerns about the Jewish stereotypes or unrealistic depiction of the German people?"

"Stereotypes exist for a reason," von Rauch said earnestly. "And how is the depiction unrealistic? We are a fine and noble people. And a conquering people, as you well know." To his credit he managed to say that with the smallest of smiles that blunted the sharp and immediate truth of his words.

"True enough" was all I managed to say.

"No, in fact I, too, prefer the French operas. As a military doctor I have all the bombast I need, so I'm happy to leave Wagner to the German purists in favor of, say *Lakmé*."

"Ah, the flower duet is perhaps my favorite moment in any opera." I meant that, too. Performed in act one, and with the right soprano and mezzo-soprano, after that duet I was happy to leave the theater early, knowing that the opera's highlight had come and gone.

"Ah, yes, I agree." He seemed to grow wistful. "The lushness, the sensuality, even the humor of the French operas are unparalleled. And Bizet's *Carmen*, what boldness, what brashness!"

What breasts, was my memory of the only performance I'd seen. The gypsy Carmen had been dressed by, well . . . Whoever it was appreciated not just the quiver of her voice, that was for sure. I dragged my thoughts back into the present, somewhat pleased that von Rauch and I had forged an artistic bond.

"So, we should talk about why I'm here. Tell me, what kind of doctor are you?" I asked.

"I am a neurologist."

"I see. Same as Dr. Brandt, yes?" Von Rauch nodded. "And your other colleague, Denis Berger. . . . What's his specialty?"

"He's a neuropathologist."

"And how does that differ from your neurology pursuits?"

"Detective Lefort, please do not misunderstand me, nor take offense about what I'm about to say. But I do need you to consider that I am a very busy man. What does my specialty have to do with the absence of my colleague?"

"Just trying to get a full picture of the man and what he's doing here." The edges of von Rauch's mouth flickered down, but

I carried on. "What is it you are working on here? Anything in particular?"

"Not really." He shrugged. "There is so much to learn from the brain, our focus is neither specific nor static."

"What is he like?" He gave me a dubious look, so I explained my thinking. "I'm just wondering if there's a way he could have upset someone—a patient, an assistant, someone like that."

"He . . . didn't really see patients."

"A doctor with no patients?"

He shifted in his seat, impatient. "It's complicated, what we do. But no, as far as I know he's not upset anyone."

"Any professional jealousies?"

"Are you asking if Dr. Berger or I are responsible for his disappearance?"

"Are you?"

"No."

"And Dr. Berger?"

"Ask him yourself, but the idea is ridiculous."

"Probably." I thought for a moment. "Are you friends outside work, the three of you?"

He let out a short laugh, and instantly I could see he regretted it. "Excuse me. But no, we are not."

"Why not?" I leaned forward. "And don't tell me 'no reason,' because that laugh meant something."

Von Rauch held my eye for a moment, then said: "Dr. Brandt is a private man, I don't know that he has many friends at all, and since he just got here, why would he? As for Dr. Berger, he is . . ." He cast about for the right words. "Of a different personality type than I am."

"Meaning?"

"Again, what does this have to do with—?"

"Dr. von Rauch," I interrupted. "Your colleague is missing. He has been for days, which means maybe he's unlikely to be found, not in any sort of decent condition, anyway. That means I need to know who his friends are, and if he has any enemies. I need to know about his life, his movements, his work, and his home. All of it."

Von Rauch sighed. "Dr. Brandt, to my knowledge, has no friends and no enemies here. I know little about him, especially his life outside of work."

"What about Dr. Berger?"

"He is neither friends nor enemies with Dr. Brandt. He certainly wouldn't have done him any harm."

"That's an odd thing to say."

Von Rauch's eyes shifted to the door, then back to me, the aristocrat about to share a secret with the staff and not wanting to be overheard. "I just mean that he is dedicated to our work. To the research. He would never do anything to undermine what . . . our superiors want us to do."

"To accept your reassurance, it would help to know what it is your superiors are wanting you to do."

He looked at me, unmoving, for a moment. "I apologize. But you will have to take my word for it that our work is confidential, and the nature of it has nothing to do with Dr. Brandt's disappearance." I started to protest but he held up a quieting hand. "I say that as a gentleman, as a military man."

"And if those aren't enough for me?"

"Then I say it as a senior officer of the army that has conquered your people." He grimaced. "Which I would much prefer not to do."

"But you see, that wouldn't be enough, either."

"What on earth do you mean?" He sounded truly baffled, as if one of his subjects had failed to grasp the lowliness of his place in the world.

"I'll be glad to explain. You see, I didn't volunteer for this little exercise in frustration. I was ordered by one of your mighty fellow conquerors to locate Dr. Brandt. They didn't ask the Gestapo or the SS, or some other member of the victorious German forces. They asked me."

"Ordered you, I believe," he said stiffly.

"You believe correctly. So, one of two things must therefore be true. Either you people want Dr. Brandt found and so should therefore cooperate at every turn. Or, as is seeming more and more likely, you don't actually want him found."

"Well, that's preposter—"

"But let me make myself clear, Dr. von Rauch. Very clear." I leaned forward so there was no mistaking my words. "I will do my job, and if this man can be found, I will find him. With or without your help."

"Very commendable, Detective." I couldn't tell in the moment if he was being serious or sarcastic. The French aren't big on it and the English, at least, make their sarcasm evident to you. My interactions with Germans had mostly been at one end of a rifle or another, so I was left to guess.

"So, which is it to be?" I pressed.

"With my help, of course." Which reassured me greatly, until he stood up. "And I have given you all I can."

With that, he turned and walked out.

CHAPTER NINE

I got up slowly and wandered back into the reception area, narrowly avoiding being run over by a large man, both tall and wide, who was stuffing a hat on his head and storming toward the main doors. I still needed to talk to Denis Berger but von Rauch had made his escape before I could ask for the French doctor.

"Dr. Berger?" the receptionist said, after making me wait for her attention for a full minute, and even then acting like she had no interest in being of assistance. "You just missed him."

"That was him with the hat? Large fellow?"

She nodded and I turned and went after Berger, not bothering to thank her for her lassitude.

Outside, the sun had lifted over the city and her rays felt good on my face as I happily stepped away from the astringent smell of disinfectant and bleach. I looked both ways and spotted

Denis Berger about a hundred yards ahead to my left, still making haste. I hurried after him and quickly gained, but when I got within hailing distance something inside me said to keep quiet and just follow.

Berger kept up the pace for a while, wending his way back into the center of the city and deep into the Eighth Arrondissement. Not necessarily a place I would expect an esteemed physician to go for a late breakfast, so my curiosity grew by the second.

And then it hit me. I grinned as I imagined the good doctor showing up at one of the places I knew well from my days walking the beat: known as One-Two-Two, that was its street number on rue de Provence. From what I remembered, it had twenty-two rooms for clients, each with its own theme. If it was still as busy as it used to be, its working girls could service up to three hundred clients a day.

Sure enough, as we got close I ducked into a doorway and watched as Berger looked over both shoulders and slipped into the building. I hurried across the road and, giving him a few minutes head start, went in, too.

"Marcel, it's been too long," I said. "How are things?"

Marcel Jamet stood up and came around the table that served as his desk.

"Monsieur Lefort, what a surprise." He was a small man, but energetic and also smiling, dressed in his usual red velvet waistcoat, his mustache impeccably trimmed as ever. A lot of *flics* on the beat hated dealing with brothels, for moral reasons or because the clientele you had to help them eject was either the dregs of society or powerful enough to ruin your career if you weren't tactful. One-Two-Two attracted the latter and on several occasions Marcel Jamet and his wife, Fernande, had been grateful for my resourcefulness and discretion as much as my truncheon.

"You look well," I said. "Business still booming?"

"Ah, there's a war on, yes, but you know the other side of the coin from fighting, yes?"

"Loving?"

"*Exactement.* You are here on business, or perhaps a day off and looking for something a little special? We have a couple of new girls who are exceptional, especially if you like things a little kinky."

"Sorry to disappoint them, and you, but I'm here on business." I looked around. "Are you even open for business? I thought you were closed in the daytime."

"Officially we are open from four in the afternoon for exactly twelve hours, you are correct." He frowned a little. "However, the Boche aren't good at following our rules and so when one of them calls ahead we have found it in our interest to make exceptions."

"That sounds about right," I said with a shake of the head. "I trust they pay well for the added privilege."

"They do not. They pay my fee and nothing more. Not even a little extra for the poor girl who is only wanting to sleep after a busy night." He jerked a thumb toward the staircase. "Take that one, the *mec* who just came in. Gives us very little notice and turns up sweating and panting like a dog. And he's French, for god's sake!"

"Then why let him in, if he's not German?"

"Because the traitorous goat is working with them. I can't refuse." A smile spread over his face. "I do take some pleasure in knowing what he is paying for."

"What do you mean?"

"Well, professional discretion forbids me from going into detail but, as you know, each of our rooms has a specialty, as do some of our girls."

"And he's not picked one of the gentler flowers on offer?"

"More like a cactus." His brow furrowed. "Is he the reason you're here?"

"Very astute. Yes, he is." I lowered my voice. "And, to be perfectly frank, a casual chat while he is in flagrante delicto could be quite beneficial."

"What did he do?"

"Nothing that I know of. I've just been told he may not be as cooperative as I would like."

"Well, then, you should probably find him before the gag is put in."

"My plan exactly. Which room would I . . . ?"

"Ah, yes, about that. Without some form of warrant, I couldn't possibly direct you to his room. I have a reputation for discretion to uphold."

With that, he stepped to one side, revealing the board that had twenty-two hooks, one for the key to each room. Only one was missing, room 18.

"Of course, I wouldn't dream of besmirching your reputation for discretion," I said. "Now, if you'll excuse me I wish to pop upstairs. The doors are still left unlocked?"

"For the girls' safety, yes they are."

"*Merci*, Marcel." I shook his hand and then started up the staircase, turning left at the top and finding my way to room 18. I didn't bother knocking, just opened the door and slipped quietly inside. At first, I couldn't see much, but my eyes quickly adjusted to the low light. When they did, I saw my interview subject perfectly placed for questioning—his wrists and ankles were strapped to a large wooden cross in the shape of an X. He was a hairy man, about the hairiest I'd ever seen, and he looked like a rug strapped up and ready to be beaten clean. Which, in a way, I guess he was.

The wooden cross he was attached to was bolted to the wall to my left, which was why it took a second for him to notice me. Well, he may also have been distracted by the lithe, raven-haired beauty standing beside him, stark naked but for a leather thong, a pair of thigh-high boots, and a thin horsewhip. In the back right corner, a tall candelabra held four fat candles, only one of which was alight, but it filled the dim room with the strong aroma of sandalwood.

When the doctor did finally spot me, I enjoyed the look of surprise on his face, and watched as it turned to confusion.

"Who are you? I didn't pay for anything that includes—"

"Silence!" the woman snapped. She turned to me, hands on hips, and looked me up and down. "Well?"

My own sexual tastes run to the mundane, I confess, but even my knees went slightly wobbly at the sight and tone of her. I imagined her to be very good at her work.

I cleared my throat and steadied my legs. "I need a brief word with your friend."

"You can have him when I'm done with him."

I showed her my police credentials. "I rather like where he is right now."

"There's nothing illegal going on," she said. Her eyes narrowed. "Wait, don't I know you?"

"I don't think so. Not professionally, certainly."

"Yeah, you used to be a uniformed *flic*, yes?"

"I'm a detective now, but yes."

"I remember. I'm Cassie."

I looked more closely at her in the dim light and recognized her at last, half Chinese she'd once told me and, as so often happens when different ethnicities procreate, she was stunning.

"Yes, of course. Cassie. You've developed a specialty, I see."

"One I've always aspired to," she said with an evil grin, and she glanced at her captive and flicked the crop across his rapidly wilting, yet still impressive, manhood. He flinched and she laughed. "That's Mistress Lau to you, worm." She laughed again and looked back at me. "What did he do?"

"Nothing as far as I know. I'd just like some answers and was told he wasn't very talkative."

"Is that so? Well, go ahead and question him. Maybe I can help."

The poor fellow seemed confused, as if he still thought this might be part of the session he'd paid for.

"You're not a *real* policeman, are you?" he asked.

"Very real. I'm looking for your friend Dr. Brandt."

He rattled his restraints, but neither I nor Cassie moved to release him. "I don't know anything about where he is. Now go away."

"When did you last see him?"

"I don't know. Two days ago, I suppose."

"At the hospital?"

"Yes, we work together, you already know that." He tugged his wrists again and earned himself another swipe from Cassie.

"Stay still!" she commanded, and his eyes dropped to the floor like he was a scolded puppy dog.

"Tell me what you are working on," I said. "You're a neurologist, too, are you not?"

"Close enough. Pathology is my expertise." He was answering, but I could tell he was unhappy in the extreme. "Look, can't we talk after, I paid good money—"

"I'm more than happy to slap you around for free," I said. "Answer my questions and I'll be out of your way. How long are you hanging around here?"

Cassie snickered but Berger's face reddened. "One hour," he said.

"What are you working on at the hospital?" I asked again.

"Nothing special. Brain research."

"Looking for anything in particular?"

"Mapping the parts of the brain as best we can." He seemed to shrug, but then again he might just have been chafing against his bonds. The next few seconds of silence were interrupted by his rhythmically tapping his wrists on the wooden cross. Which instantly irritated me.

"Stand still when I'm talking to you, man!" I snapped.

"Yes, sir!" he said instinctively, then seemed embarrassed about it. "I mean, er . . ."

Cassie chuckled and turned her head so he couldn't see her laughing. I could.

"You're all doing the same thing?" I asked.

"Yes, basically."

"You're a Frenchman. Why are you working with the Germans?"

That struck a chord with him, and also with Cassie. She moved in front of him and when she spoke her voice was a growl. "You're paying me with German money? I don't mind taking it from them myself, but not from a Frenchman."

With that, she took one step back and delivered a hefty kick to his groin, and the poor doctor folded into himself with a howl of pain, or as best he could pinioned as he was. I didn't like the man, but it was all I could do not to collapse to the floor in sympathy.

"Answer him!" she shouted, then kicked him in the groin again. Looking past my own squeamishness, I rather wanted to take a turn. It looked fun.

"Because it's a job," he gasped. "They pay me and pay me well. I have to earn a living, like everyone else. Like you."

"Not everyone has to collaborate," I said.

Cassie turned to me and I thought I saw shame in her eyes when she spoke. "You know, some have to. If you're looking for a missing German, aren't you working for them right now?"

"On pain of death, not for silver." Still, she had a point, collaboration was both a matter of degree and, sometimes, a matter of necessity. It was a complicated issue, more so than many people dared to admit. After all, here she was kicking a doctor in the balls for paying her with his German salary, when the same evening she'd happily take money from some profligate and horny Boche. If there was a principle to be observed, a line not to be crossed, it was blurry at best, and probably in constant motion. If pressed, I couldn't say why I was angry at Berger for working for the Germans, while being fine with Cassie making her money from them. But I was.

"Well, thanks for being no help," I said to Berger. "And don't worry, your secret is safe with me. But next time I talk to you, I expect more cooperation else I'll be the one putting the boot into you." I gave Cassie a little bow and let myself out of the room, pausing after I closed the door long enough to hear the swish of her whip and his high-pitched squeal in response. It gave me more satisfaction than any of his answers had.

I started down the hallway but stopped when I heard a voice

behind me, by the door to the back staircase. Something about the voice was familiar and I turned to see who it was. My line of sight was taken up by a pale, blue-eyed woman I'd dealt with before, a sassy minx known in the streets as Margot le Chatte—descriptive if not original. She wore a light blue kimono that almost covered her bottom, but not quite, and while that sight distracted me the man behind her slipped through the door to the stairway. I just caught the briefest glimpse of his profile and then the back of his head before he disappeared from view, and I stood there waiting to see if my brain had correctly processed what I'd seen. Who I'd seen.

I'd not known him long, and didn't know him well, but I'd seen him often and recently enough that I'd have bet a fair few of my weekly francs that the man slipping out of a tart's bedroom was none other than my sister's new beau, Daniel Moulin. I blinked a few times in case I came to my senses but the image of the man remained, and so I stood there for a moment longer and stared at the half-naked woman who now looked back at me and saw my mouth hanging open, but not for the reason she imagined.

CHAPTER TEN

The sound of a door closing below me brought me back to the present, and I hurried down the main stairs to the reception area. I looked around for Marcel Jamet but didn't see him, or anyone else. I stepped past the main desk and opened the office door, to find Marcel sitting in a chair with his head very close to the crotch of someone sitting on his desk, someone I presumed to be one of his employees.

"Health check," he said curtly, pulling away and glaring at me. The young lady closed her legs quickly, but didn't bother pushing her dress back down.

"You're a doctor now?" I asked.

"How can I help you, Detective?" His friendly manner had gone, apparently this was one businessman who didn't like being interrupted while checking his inventory.

"I just saw a man leaving. I need to know who it was."

"I don't know. I've been in here."

"Then can you please find out? I can tell you which room he was in."

"No," Marcel said. "We have a duty to protect the privacy of our clientele."

"You just let me walk in on one of them while—"

"I said 'clientele,' not collaborators."

"So you're confirming that the man I saw was a Frenchman."

"I didn't say that." Marcel bit his lip, annoyed that he'd given me even that clue.

"And yet you don't open for your French customers until four in the afternoon, so . . ." So it made sense to me, it was another policeman that the good Monsieur Jamet was accommodating. *It must have been Moulin!*

"Is there anything else?" Marcel asked curtly.

"No, thank you. I'll see myself out." I did so at some speed, hoping I could see the bastard in the street and give him what for. In principle, I didn't have too much of a problem with men who used establishments like those of Jamet. I'd never done so myself, but I'd be a liar if I said I'd not thought about it. With the pact Nicola and I had to not get overly involved with members of the opposite sex there were times, many times, where the easy and no-strings release of long built-up frustration was tempting in the extreme. I couldn't even say what stopped me from frequenting a place like this, I just . . . hadn't. And these days especially, people were looking for comfort, for distractions, and the warm embrace of a paid-for bosom was unquestionably a worthy escape from the stark realities that Paris under the Germans thrust at us daily. So yes, I was willing to allow the men of Paris to fornicate at their own expense, to line the pockets of Marcel Jamet and his ladies. But not if they were seeing my Nicola. That would not do at all, and as unpleasant as it would no doubt prove to be, I resolved to tell her in no uncertain terms what I'd seen, and give her the reason she needed to end her association with young Moulin. She'd hate me for telling her, but only for a little while.

Or so I hoped.

When I stepped outside, the man was nowhere in sight, and I didn't have time to waste trying to track him down right now. I had a job to do, so I put thoughts of that conversation to the back of my mind and tried to focus on what came next. I was tempted to take one of the pedicabs that had come into being in the past few months. Paris was a walkable city, but not if you were old or very young, or were one of the many left crippled by the last war. We're an imaginative bunch, we Parisians, so it was no surprise when alternative methods of transport filled the gap when all the cars were requisitioned or simply ran out of petrol.

I opted to walk, though, as I do my best thinking when my shoes are slapping the pavement. And I felt like what I needed to do right now was think, and maybe over a cup of coffee. I angled up to stay alongside the Seine, hoping that a few Germans might have gotten overly drunk the night before and fallen in. Seeing their bodies drifting by would have been as uplifting as the weak but warm rays of sun that were melting away the frost and whatever snowflakes had managed to cling to their frozen forms until now. My hopeful glances at the river, however, were rewarded with nothing more than the sight of driftwood bobbing along in the gray waters. I squinted as the sun rolled free of the clouds, brightening my way and warming the air by ten degrees.

A café appeared on my left, and I crossed the street to take one of the last open tables on the pavement. A man sat next to me, a camera and a notepad in front of him, but as soon as he saw me walking in his direction he scooped them up and put them into a canvas shoulder bag.

The waiter appeared and I ordered coffee.

"Why so busy out here?" I asked.

"A flood inside, burst pipe, everyone had to move outside." He gestured to the patch of blue sky above him. "But the sun is joining us, at least."

The waiter lingered while I searched my pockets for change so I could pay in advance. This was one of the new habits we'd gotten used to—it began before the Germans took over the city, when we were expecting air raids. The cafés and restaurants had started insisting customers pay as soon as they ordered because too often meals, and therefore bills, had been abandoned when air raid sirens went off. For some reason we'd all kept doing it, probably because, even though the air raid fear had dissipated, we were all so aware that some other hideous fate could befall us at any moment.

"*Vous êtes journaliste?*" I asked the man beside me after the waiter had brought me coffee. "It's fine, some of my closest friends are journalists."

"*Vraiment?*" He looked surprised, and more than a little re-lieved.

"*Non*, not at all. But you don't have to hide anything from me."

"Good," the photographer responded. "*Je suis des États-Unis.*"

"American?" I smiled and switched to English. "I keep hoping you guys make it over here, but with guns not notepads."

"The pen is mightier than the sword, didn't you know?"

THE DARK EDGE OF NIGHT

"Not in my experience," I said grimly.

He smiled. "You speak English better than I speak French. Mind if I join you?"

"Please do. I've not spoken English in a while, forgive me if I can't find the occasional word." It was true, and it felt strange to be speaking it again now.

"Eric Sevareid, CBS News." He extended a hand and we shook.

"Henri Lefort, Paris police."

"Policeman, eh?" He looked impressed, or maybe just surprised, then a knowing look crossed his face. "Wait, aren't you the cop who saved Princess Marie Bonaparte a few months ago?"

"That's me." My name and face had been splattered across a few newspapers in the days after I shot the man who had broken into her home. Some outlets went for the good-news-amid-all-the-bloodshed angle, and some used it as propaganda to show how well the French police were working alongside their invaders. Neither was particularly true.

"What are you working on now?" he asked.

What indeed? I wondered. I should be looking for the man who killed Edouard Grabbin, who was definitely murdered. I should probably also be looking into missing children who, although less certainly at risk, would be a much bigger deal if something bad was indeed happening to them. Instead, I was chasing after a Nazi doctor who was probably drunk in some other's man apartment having the time of his life.

"I suppose you could say I'm juggling a few cases right now," I said.

"Ah, I see. Nothing as dramatic as a princess almost being killed?"

"It's funny, how people remember an event so differently."

"What do you mean?"

"One of my colleagues died that night. Killed by the man I shot. But he was just a policeman and she was a princess." I shrugged. "I suppose that's how the world turns."

"Newspapers, definitely. I remember now, the policeman being killed."

"I bet you don't remember his name, though."

"That's true," Sevareid conceded. "I don't. But that's something of a professional hazard for me."

"What do you mean?"

"I cover a story and move on to the next one. And there's always another one. Do you remember all the names of the victims you come across?"

"All the dead ones, yes."

"That's good." Sevareid took a sip of coffee. "I've been covering the war. Too many killed to remember even a fraction of them."

"I'm aware of the irony," I said.

"Irony?"

"Of trying to solve one murder in the middle of a war."

He nodded. "That's Paris for you, though."

"I don't follow."

"You're all trying to live your normal lives. You buy food and clothing, you go to work." He gestured toward me. "You solve crimes. Meanwhile, outside of Paris, the world burns. People starve and fight and die by the thousands. You're an island of relative normalcy, so it makes sense in that normal world for a single life to matter."

"We're not an island," I corrected him. "We're the beating

heart of Europe. But the rest of our body is poisoned, and soon it will die and take us down with it." I gave him a sad smile. "Unless you can convince your politicians to send a few good men our way. With guns, not pens."

"I think it will happen," Sevareid said. "Especially if Roosevelt is reelected next week."

"You think he will be?"

"I do. His isolationist rhetoric is just that, by the way. Wendell Willkie is far more likely to keep America out of the war than Roosevelt."

"Then let's hope for the best." I finished off my coffee. "You think you'll stay here much longer?"

"Why do you ask that?"

"The way you reacted when you saw me coming toward you. You don't feel safe."

"That's true. And I probably won't stay too long. Unless the case you're working on is interesting enough to keep me here . . ."

I couldn't tell if he was joking or meant it, but I answered anyway. "Not the murder case. Looks like a burglary gone wrong."

"Like with the princess."

"This victim was a retired doctor. Nothing as sexy as a princess, believe me."

"Ah, shame."

"The other case I'm working on . . ." I hesitated to tell him, though. The Boche didn't like anything that put them in a bad light and losing one of their top research doctors was nothing to boast about. On the other hand, this *mec* was a journalist and I was looking for someone so he could be an asset. Just not yet. "Do you have a card, or a number? Some way to reach you?"

"Not going to tell me right now?"

"Correct. Mostly because right now there's no story."

"You'd be amazed how often people say that." He slid a business card across the adjoining table. "And they're usually wrong. But sure, call me anytime. Even if it's just for a drink one night."

"I may do that." I was thinking about Mimi and the missing children. I'd not had a chance to delve into that, but she would be expecting an update. And since I'd suggested I could bring her good news, the two missing boys needed to slide up my to-do list a few notches. Their disappearance could even be a story for Sevareid, but I didn't have the mental strength to worry about it, not now, not until I knew there was something definite to worry about. "So what are you working on?"

"I heard rumors of a new munitions factory being built. I don't suppose we'd dare run a story about it, but you never know."

"I heard about that, but is it really newsworthy? And you're right, the Germans would not like that at all. Not one bit, so if you're worried for your safety now, just wait until you publish that story."

"I know, I know. And you're right, in a war it's not all that newsworthy. There's just something about this one . . ." His voice trailed off, and he shook his head.

"What do you mean, 'something about this one'?"

"All I can find are rumors about it, not definitive information."

"That's hardly surprising. Those places are always kept secret as long as possible."

"I know," he said again. "They're high-value targets for the Brits to bomb, so yes, I agree it makes sense to keep things hush-hush. But with my sources, I just find it odd I can't get a definite location or anything else solid."

"What's the general area?" I knew where Mimi thought it was, but since Rennes kept popping up I wanted to hear about it independently.

"The city of Rennes, is what I'm hearing. That's as specific as I can get right now. I should get back to the office," he said, and stood.

"If I find out anything about that factory, I'll let you know," I said.

"Thank you, I would appreciate that very much."

"Of course. Nice to meet you, Mr. Sevareid. Until next time."

He shook my hand. "Sooner rather than later, I hope."

I sipped from my little coffee cup and watched him walk away, my view then switching to a tall woman who smiled as she, somewhat awkwardly, sidled into the small space Sevareid had just vacated and plopped down. I noticed she was wearing trousers, extremely rare for women in Paris, and she sighed with relief as she stretched out her left leg. She seemed at first glance an unconventional woman, she had the aura that was neither ladylike nor uncouth and while she was not pretty or beautiful in any sense I'd normally use those words, she was most certainly striking, with dark hair and dark eyes and a wide mouth. On the one hand, a typical Parisian woman, albeit in trousers, but on the other hand . . . somehow glamorous. I couldn't really put my finger on the attraction I felt for this complete stranger.

Confidence, I thought. *That's what it is, she doesn't much care what others think about her.*

I thought about making conversation, which was most unlike me, but before I could think of anything witty or incisive to say another woman swerved off the sidewalk and into the chair across from her.

"Darling Virginia, I'm sorry I'm late," the new arrival said in English.

"Not at all, I just got here myself."

I started, visibly, and stared at the women. *Not Parisian at all; they are Americans.*

The striking woman had noticed my reaction and turned her head to look at me. I felt like a schoolboy being chastened by a particularly ravishing headmistress.

"I'm sorry," I said in English. "I was just surprised to hear you speak. Not many Americans left in Paris these days."

She appraised me for a moment then smiled. She held out a hand. "Virginia Hall, pleased to meet you. This is my friend, Marie Johnson. Also American."

I shook hands with them both. "Henri Lefort."

Her eyes darkened as I leaned forward and she saw what was under my coat.

"You have a gun, monsieur."

"Tool of the trade," I assured her. "I'm a detective with the Paris police."

She raised an eyebrow and smiled. "How dashing."

"Occasionally, but mostly rather mundane, I'm afraid."

"And you do speak English very well indeed. Better than most Parisians I run into."

"Thank you, I'm . . . I read and practice a lot."

"Good for you," she said with that broad smile again, and turned back to her friend Marie.

I let their chatter drift over me as I thought about the case, but my heart stopped cold when I felt something against my right foot. I knew without looking it was Virginia Hall's left foot, resting on top of mine. I scarcely dared to breathe—no woman had been this forward with me in . . . a very long time indeed.

Then again, we'd all heard about how forward American women had become.

She shifted in her seat as the waiter brought them coffee, but her foot stayed on mine. I wasn't sure what to do next.

Show some sort of recognition, some signal? I can't speak up and say anything, of course.

Slowly, inch by inch, I slid my foot out from under hers, over the toes of her shoe, and into the crook of her ankle. I stayed like that for a full minute, my entire body frozen and yet buzzing with anticipation at the same time. I felt her shin push against my foot and I rattled my cup on its saucer as I reached for something to do. She turned her head again and smiled, what I definitely took to be a knowing look in her eye.

Even for an American this seemed brazen, but the truth was there were plenty of women who had a thing for policemen. Sometimes it was the uniform, sometimes the power, sometimes maybe the gun.

She took a sip of her own coffee as Marie Johnson stood and excused herself for a moment, heading inside the brasserie in the direction of the *salle-de-bain.*

With another sigh, Virginia Hall put down her cup and leaned slowly forward, her hands reaching down to where our feet were entwined. My throat closed up and I thought desperately of something to say but my mind was a blank, my eyes widening as her hands got closer and closer to her leg, and mine.

She looked up at me with a twinkle in her eye and without saying a word grabbed her shin and pulled it toward her. She obviously saw the confusion on my face, and enjoyed it, because she then took a fork from the table and quickly jabbed it into her left shin. My mouth fell open and beside me she laughed.

"The leg is wooden and the foot is aluminum, Henri, so don't worry, I can't feel a thing."

Can't feel a thing . . . that means . . .

"You look like you've seen a ghost," she said. "Did something happen?"

"No, no, not at all," I stammered, trying to regain my composure.

"Shot myself in the foot while hunting snipe in Turkey," she said matter-of-factly, sitting back again. "Got tangled up in a fence like the damned fool I am. Anyway, I hope my little party trick with the fork didn't upset you."

"No, I just wasn't expecting . . . that."

"Full of surprises, aren't I?"

"You are indeed, Madame Hall."

"Oh, please, we're in a war and I'm American, so let's keep it informal with Virginia, shall we?"

"Yes, of course." It was with boundless relief, and yet a twinge of disappointment, when I saw a lad from the Préfecture screech to a halt on his rickety bicycle in front of the café. He wore the white-and-blue armband of a police messenger boy, and couldn't have been more than twelve years old.

"Detective Lefort?" he called out.

"That's me."

"I know, sir. You're famous. Especially among us bicycle lads."

"Oh, is that so?"

"Yes, sir. You're about the only one who tips us."

"Message first." I signaled with my hand for him to hand over the envelope. He hopped off his bike and did so, lingering like a bad smell.

"Thanks. Now bugger off."

"But, sir . . . ," he began.

"Nice try, you little twerp, but the only tip you'll get from me is the tip of my boot up your arse if you're still standing there in three seconds."

The fact was, these minions had been trying on this new racket for the past couple of weeks. They told every detective he was the favorite because of his tipping, trying to trick us all into *actually* tipping. No one much minded, because it was funny— they were gamely trying to con a bunch of people whose job it was to expose cons. I watched as the boy sloped off to his bicycle and climbed on. He threw me a doleful look and I returned it with a cheery wave, and he peddled away, muttering to himself.

I opened the envelope and recognized Nicola's handwriting.

Body found south of Montparnasse station. Officers waiting for you at NW end of rue Ampère. Your missing doctor?

I took a deep breath, unsure if I wanted this dead man to be the doctor. *Will that get me off the hook, or will I get skewered for not finding him in time? Only one way to find out.*

I tucked the note away and turned to my new acquaintance. "Forgive me, but I'm afraid I have to get back to work."

"I understand."

"But I am curious. What's an American lady doing in Paris these days?"

"Would you believe I'm a tourist?"

"No," I said with a smile.

"I am trying to obtain a position with the *New York Post*. I'm a writer."

Two American journalists in one day. Within the space of an hour. Coincidence? "Do you know Eric Sevareid?"

"I've heard of him, but haven't met him. Why?"

"No matter. This must be a popular café for writers, is all." I jammed my hat on my head, offered her my hand, and turned my mind, and my feet, toward the northwest end of rue Ampère. As I strolled away, I resisted the almost overwhelming urge to look back.

CHAPTER ELEVEN

"Suicide?" a uniformed officer behind me suggested, and on the available evidence, it was a reasonable assumption. I turned to look at him and was surprised at who was standing there.

"Officer Moulin."

"Yes, sir."

I narrowed my eyes and looked into his for some recognition that I'd seen him at the brothel. He looked back at me, innocent as a baby.

Was I wrong? Was it not him? It certainly looked like him . . .

"Where were you this morning?" I asked.

"Working extra patrol hours, filling in for someone."

"Where?"

"Up in Montmartre. Quite the trek."

Nowhere near the brothel. If true.

"I see. And what are you doing here?"

"After that shift ended, I went by your office like you asked, but they said you were out looking for the missing German. And when the call came in about this fellow, Nicola said she'd sent a note your way. I figured I'd meet you here and let you know what I found last night." He patted a leather satchel that was slung over one shoulder.

"You could have left that in my office, you know."

"I wasn't sure when you'd be back, sir. And Nicola didn't seem to know."

"Oh, didn't she?" I grumbled. "Never mind that, let's take a look here, see who and what we have." I knelt beside the body, which was badly mangled. One arm had been severed and lay nearby between the rails still. The skin had been torn from his face, and his nose, too, so as with Edouard Grabbin a visual identification wouldn't be possible. I didn't like, not one bit, that two corpses in a row were disfigured, although it wasn't surprising in this case. Even so, I filed away the coincidence, if that's what it was, for future reference. "Anyone been through his pockets?"

"No, sir. We were waiting for you."

"Good." I took a moment to eye the dead man's clothing, the cut of his suit, and tried to ignore the cold, gray hand poking out of the still-attached sleeve, now spattered with blood that was mixed with oil and dust from the train. Grimacing, because even a fresh corpse has its smell, I went through his pockets and pulled a wallet from inside his jacket. I opened it and looked through the contents. "Well, will you look at this." I held up the identification card with the name "Viktor Brandt" on it. I stood. "He's also the same height by the looks of things, and his suit is the same quality as the ones from his hotel room."

"Well, looks like you found him, sir."

"For better or worse," I muttered. "What's this then?" My eyes widened with surprise as I pulled a train ticket from the wallet. A ticket stamped for the city of Rennes, no less. I didn't know what was in that city for the good doctor, but I did recognize a coincidence when I saw one. I showed it to Moulin, who raised an eyebrow but also apparently had no explanation for me.

"Did anyone search the area?" I asked him. "Just in case there's something else to be found."

"Yes, sir, I helped with that. We didn't see anything suspicious or out of place."

"If this was suicide, he lay down on the rails and didn't move as the train got close. If it wasn't suicide he would have felt the rails vibrating, heard the train coming, maybe seen it, though I don't suppose they're allowed lights these days."

"They're not, sir, no," Moulin said. "But I agree, suicide is more likely than accident even so. And it happened overnight so the train driver wouldn't have seen him. Not in time anyway." He cleared his throat. "And he may not have seen him even if it'd been daylight."

I glanced up. "What does that mean?"

"I spoke to the driver just now. He has all the symptoms of a man whose closest relationship is with a bottle."

"That's less than helpful of him. So, Moulin. Why would a high-ranking German doctor commit suicide by lying on a railway track?"

"I don't know. Maybe it wasn't suicide after all. Maybe he was in his cups, too, tripped, and fell onto the track. Hit his head on the rail and then the train came along."

"Maybe. Then the next question: What is a high-ranking German doctor doing out here, drunk, at night?"

"He's lodging near here?" Moulin offered.

"He's staying at the Ritz Hotel. Which is not exactly close and, I am confident, has a nicer bar than you'd find out here."

"Not everyone likes nice bars, sir."

"Very true." *Smart fellow. Or is he letting me know he likes brothels?*

"Did you find anything helpful there?"

"Not really. Oh, do you know what Club Monocle is?"

Moulin gave me a strange look, and said, "No idea, why?"

"He had a card from there, makes me think he's been there for some reason." I waved a hand dismissively. "I'll check it out tomorrow."

"Wait, though. Club Monocle, a black-and-white card with a picture of a monocle on it?"

"You know the card but not the place?" I asked, surprised.

"I saw one at Edouard Grabbin's place. I didn't think anything of it, but he had one, too."

"Are you sure?"

"Yes, absolutely."

"How very interesting. All the more reason for me to visit the place."

"Definitely. And while you do that, maybe I'll see if I can find a drinking hole or two around here and ask if Brandt was in there getting himself drunk enough to die out here."

"*Bien*, take a couple more uniforms with you, it'll be quicker."

I looked around and saw a small crowd of people staring at us, and the body. "Let's not announce who he is just yet, eh? Keep it between us for now."

"Yes, sir."

"I'm not sure there's much more we can do here, then." I moved away from the body. As much as I didn't mind finding dead Nazis strewn about the place, I wanted a patch of fresh air to turn my mind to the other case I needed to solve. I gestured for Moulin to follow me. "So then, what did you come up with at the other crime scene? Tell me you found the murder weapon and it has the killer's name inscribed on it."

"No such luck." He shook his head. "No weapon at all, sorry."

"Next time, maybe. Anything good?"

"Nothing definitive, sadly. About the Rennes coincidence, I didn't see anything in the house that would indicate family there, but then again I didn't see anything in the place that indicated family anywhere, except his brother Jean. Other than the junk thrown about in the living room, the place seemed cleaned out."

"He'd been living with his brother, just went back occasionally to check on the place. What else did you find?"

"This in his back pocket."

"A passport. Seems like an odd thing to be carrying about."

"Not really, sir. All those random German checkpoints, if you're not carrying some sort of identification you can find yourself in handcuffs."

"Right, of course." I riffled through the passport. "Do you think the Boche accept expired identification?"

"Oh, I didn't notice that." I think he flushed a little, embarrassed at the oversight.

"Well, next time you'll look more closely, won't you?" I said it mildly, not wanting to be too harsh with the young man. I opened it and showed him that it expired on September 31, 1940. "Not that anyone's traveling anymore. Not voluntarily, anyway."

Moulin had brought a few other things, examples of the man's handwriting in case that became important, which I doubted. Also, a few photographs of Edouard himself, a journal that he'd not written in for eight months, and a broken pocket watch.

"Not a lot of use, I'm afraid," Moulin said.

"Could you tell if anything had been taken?" It was a stupid question, I knew, and Moulin, to his credit, tried not to look at me and show he knew it was, too. "Never mind, no way you could know."

"You still thinking burglary interrupted or burglary staged?"

"It's one of those two. I'm thinking I want to talk to his brother again before I reach any final conclusions."

"Yes, sir. I also asked all the neighbors if they'd seen or heard anything Sunday night. No luck there, either."

"Not the most successful night."

"For Monsieur Grabbin, most certainly," Moulin said.

Despite myself, I liked the young fellow, and he was smarter and more thorough than many *flics* his age. But he was still a *flic*.

"About you and Nicola. How close are you?"

He looked at me for a moment. "I don't know how to answer that, exactly."

"You think it's none of my business?"

"Unless you want to take her out yourself, sir, honestly I do think it's none of your business."

I smiled at that. "No, no. Nothing like that. I am no romantic competition, rest assured."

"Glad to hear that, sir."

"She and I have known each other for almost twenty years. Did you know that?"

"No, sir."

"A little old for you, don't you think?"

"That doesn't bother me at all."

"What are you, twenty-five?"

"Almost thirty, sir."

"She and I share a belief when it comes to seeing people. As a rule, we don't get into relationships with people who work for the police, either officers or administrative staff."

"Why is that?"

As if I can tell you. "Long story."

"Are you telling me to break it off?" he asked.

"What if I am?"

"Well, sir, since you don't really have the authority to do that, it would make working with you awkward and I'd ask for a transfer."

"It won't work out, I can assure you of that."

"With all due respect, sir, you've not given me one good reason why it wouldn't, or why I should break things off now. I understand she's your friend and you're protective of her. Especially these days. But I have a sister, so I know what it means to feel protective. But I am very fond of Nicola and have real feelings for her. And I think she does for me."

"She's told you that?"

"No, not in so many words. But I can at least speak to the truth of my feelings."

"You can indeed."

"So, are you ordering me not to see her?"

"As you said, I don't have the authority to do that."

"I'm glad you agree, sir." He gave a wry smile. "But you can make my life difficult if you want to."

"True enough. Seems to me, we've lost enough policemen this year, Moulin, so I don't plan to chase a good one away. But I need you to answer one question honestly."

"I can probably do that."

"Did I see you at the One-Two-Two this morning?"

"You were at a brothel this morning, sir?" His surprise seemed genuine enough.

"On police business, of course."

"Of course, sir."

I couldn't tell if he was being sarcastic, but I did know he'd not answered my question. "Well, was that you I saw coming out of a tart's bedroom?"

He straightened and looked me in the eye. "I give you my word, sir, I have never engaged the services of a prostitute, and I never will."

"Never say never," I muttered. "But all right, I'll take you at your word."

"Thank you, sir."

"Very well." I nodded. "Oh, and do me one more courtesy."

"What's that, sir?"

"When we're talking about you and Nicola, or if I happen to see you out of uniform, don't call me 'sir.'"

CHAPTER TWELVE

"Nice work getting carrots." I slipped my coat off and hung it up, my hat going atop it next. A crate of vegetables sat just inside the doorway and my mouth watered at the thought of those carrots soft-boiled and served up with a drizzle of real butter and a sprinkle of parsley. "Or should I thank Mimi?"

"You should."

I walked into the living room to see Nicola pouring two glasses of wine. "One of us is going to get in trouble sooner or later."

"She's not doing anything illegal," Nicola said.

"As far as you know. And these days things suddenly become illegal just because the Boche don't like them."

Nicola handed me a glass of red and I settled into my armchair.

"This isn't about vegetables, is it?" she said, looking down at me with a frown on her face.

"Don't hover over me." I took a sip. "God, I wish the wine she gave us wasn't so good."

"We're spoiled, I know." She went over to the couch, and sat with her legs stretched out on it. "So what's bothering my grumpy detective?"

"I always feel a little out of sorts after seeing a man squashed like a bug by a train. Especially when it's the man I've been tasked to find and bring home."

"And *especially* when the person who tasked you is a mange-tout."

"Precisely. On the plus side, I ran into your new friend again."

"Daniel?"

"I prefer to think of him as Officer Moulin."

"I'm sure you do."

"I saw him this afternoon, but I'm fairly sure I saw him this morning, too."

"Oh, where?" she asked.

"At a brothel." I watched closely for her reaction, which was to almost choke on her wine.

"What? You can't be serious."

"Oh, but I am."

"He was there on business, then. Interviewing someone?"

"He wasn't in uniform, so not that."

"And you're sure it was him?" She exuded dubiousness.

"I was sure at the time. And he was there when it should have been closed, which means the person I saw was either a Boche or a policeman."

"You must be mistaken. Did you ask him about it?"

"He said he was on patrol in Montmartre this morning. We keep a log of assignments now, which he probably doesn't even know about. I'll check the list in the morning."

This seemed to irritate her. "You'll do no such thing."

"Why not? Don't you want to know if your boyfriend is picking up diseases at a whorehouse?"

"First of all, he's not my boyfriend. And second of all, he doesn't frequent those places."

"Then there's no harm in me checking."

"He doesn't, Henri," Nicola said firmly.

"How would you know?"

"I just do."

I laughed, a little too loudly. "You can't possibly know that. Half the men who use those places would swear up and down they'd never set foot in one."

"Have you?"

"This morning, I told you."

"Apart from that, Henri."

"No, never."

"Should I believe you?"

"This isn't about me. It's about you seeing a ne'er-do-well."

"I'll ask him myself. He won't lie to me."

"No, of course not, a man has never lied to his wife or girlfriend about using whores. Come on, Nicola, you're the very first person he'd lie to." I shook my head. "No, no. Let me check the patrol assignments in the morning."

"You're wrong about him, Henri. He's a good person."

"Even if he is, how do you think this relationship is going to go?"

"Well now, why don't I try it and see?"

"Or I can just tell you." I sipped my wine again, keeping my tone firm but not overly harsh. I didn't think so, anyway. "You two will go out and have fun. Not too much fun, because the Germans won't allow that. So that means you'll be looking to have your fun indoors."

"Henri, for heaven's sake."

"So your first problem is that you can't bring him here. I mean, you could but I'd have to be elsewhere and you'd also have to make sure there were no photos of me for him to see, no other signs that I live here. Organizationally difficult, I'm sure you'll agree."

"And I'm not likely to get any assistance from you making it less so, am I?"

"None at all," I said with my most evil smile. "That leaves his place and, assuming he doesn't have a secret sibling, your tryst will happen there. Which brings about your second problem."

Nicola didn't take the bait on the subject of secrets and siblings; instead she sighed dramatically. "Does it now."

"Indeed it does. Because soon as that happens, and we both know what 'that' is, you two will be attached at the hip. More importantly, you will be emotionally invested, which means you will have a much harder time doing all the things normal people do, like keeping secrets."

"I'm not going to tell him anything, Henri. When have I ever?"

"You haven't, because you haven't been in a long-term situation with anyone."

"And that's because you are like this. Do we really live the rest of our lives single and alone?" She wagged a finger at me. "And don't you dare say that I'm not alone because I have you."

"And Mimi."

"I'm serious, Henri. And maybe people knowing we're siblings wouldn't be as bad as you think."

"The problem is, if it *is* as bad as I think, my career is over. And you'll be out of a job, too."

"Not necessarily," she said.

"We've been through this before." I was getting exasperated, and didn't mind showing it. "Countless times. If, after twenty years, it's suddenly revealed that we're brother and sister, people will start asking questions. And maybe it will be people like GiGi, who would just love to see me booted from the force. Imagine what he'd say about our lack of transparency. We already had one close shave with someone finding out about me. And that was one dumb reporter. Imagine a few curious detectives trying to figure out why good old Henri Lefort had hidden this secret for so long. People are going to ask why, you know that."

"We can come up with something."

"When you do, let me know. I can't think of a single thing that would satisfactorily answer why we kept this hidden so long, that doesn't also put us out on the street. And right now, for heaven's sake, in the middle of a war. Life's hard enough without both of us being unemployed, we simply can't take that risk."

"There's always a reason with you," she said, her voice quiet. "It's always the wrong time. When the right time does finally roll around I'll be too old to climb the steps to this place, let alone find a husband."

"Well, maybe the Boche will be so upset at the death of their comrade they'll remove your one obstacle."

"Stop it, Henri, you know I don't want that."

"Neither do I." I drained my glass. "I would, however, like some of those vegetables before they wilt. You chop, I'll cook."

Nicola sighed again, then stood. "Mimi put some butter in the cooler for us, too."

"And I know we have some parsley lying around." I rubbed my hands with delight. "Let's get to it."

"Do me a favor. Run downstairs and get me some garlic."

"Garlic?" I threw her a look. "From Mimi, you mean."

"Of course."

"She was able to deliver this fine basket of vegetables, but the garlic wouldn't fit in it?"

"Don't be difficult, Henri, just go, *s'il te plaît.*"

I sighed as loudly as I could manage and headed down one flight of stairs to Mimi's door, which I knocked loudly enough to let her know that I was there, and that I was mildly irritated. She, however, opened it with a large smile on her face.

"Henri, what a lovely surprise."

"Yes, I'm sure it is."

"Do come in." She turned and walked inside, giving me no option but to follow. I was beginning to wonder if I had a thing for bossy women. That notion just made me grumpier. "What can I do for you?"

"Garlic, please," I muttered.

"You want some garlic? There was none in the box?"

"Apparently not."

"Well then, take a seat while I locate some." Again with the orders, and again with me following them. I slumped into the armchair that had held me for most nights back in July, when I'd told her my story, who I really was and what I'd done. The chair was somehow less comfortable than back then. I glanced to my right, and my suspicions were confirmed: a glass of red wine sat beside me, letting me know that the garlic ruse had, indeed, been to get me to talk to Mimi. I felt suddenly exhausted, deflated. Just when I wanted to relax after a hard day, here I was being tricked into a no doubt heavy conversation about . . . *feelings*, or some such thing.

Then again, I knew it was a trick and went along with it anyway, didn't I?

I reached for the wine and took a delicious mouthful before my brain could psychoanalyze itself any further. After all, I had Mimi for that. A moment later she reappeared, nodded at the fact I was seated and holding her wineglass, and then sat down opposite me.

"I hear you are working two cases at once," she said.

"I am, and it's exhausting." I thought about mentioning her connection to Andreas von Rauch, but I didn't. Frankly, I had no desire to hear about what a fine, upstanding gentleman he was. After the distressing scene outside the bakery, I didn't want to hear about any nice, admirable German, especially if it was the truth.

"Then I won't keep you past that glass of wine. I did want to ask about a couple of things, though."

"Be my guest."

"First, did you get a chance to inquire about those two boys who were taken from my school?"

"Not at all. Haven't had a second to even ask about it."

"Do you think you will tomorrow?"

"Unlikely. I'm sure it's nothing, and it's most definitely nothing when compared to what I will be looking into."

She arched a disapproving eyebrow. "You're telling me that looking into the cases of dead people is more urgent than looking into the case of missing live children?"

"They're not a case. They're probably not even missing. From the way you described it before, their removal sounded fairly official."

"Well, these days 'official' can mean something that just a few months ago would have been criminal."

I held up one hand in surrender. "If I remember, I'll ask. I promise."

"Thank you."

"Was that all?"

She smiled. "I think you know the answer to that."

I groaned. "Is this where I get a lecture about . . . something?"

"No, it's where we have an adult conversation about your trust issues."

"And who says I have those?"

"I do. And I know Nicola would agree with me."

"She's talked to you about her policeman friend."

"We talk about a lot of things. But yes, he was one of them." She fixed me with a stern look. "She has a right to be happy, Henri."

"And I have a right to keep my own secrets."

"You're assuming that her having a boyfriend, or god forbid a husband, would automatically mean your secret would get out."

"Would you like to explain to me how it wouldn't? Either she tells him who I am, or she lies to her husband for the entirety of their marriage. There's no in-between, here."

"And your solution is that she never, for as long as she lives, has a satisfying long-term relationship." I didn't have a good answer for that one, and she knew it. "That's incredibly selfish, Henri, and you know it is."

"I don't get to have one, either," I protested, but it sounded weak even to me.

"I agree, you're selling yourself short, too." She leaned forward, earnest. "Don't you want to fall in love?"

"Get married and have a family?" I laughed. "Honestly, no. I might once have wanted that but with what's going on out there, no."

"What about sex?"

I knew she was forward on the subject, but I couldn't help but blush a little. Not as much as when she told me about her research related to the placement of the clitoris and the female orgasm, but then again that was the mother of all blushes.

"I can have sex when I want."

"Do you visit brothels for it?" She pointed a finger at me. "And let me be clear, I think that you should."

"That reminds me." I snapped my fingers with excitement, thrilled to be able to change the subject. "I don't suppose you would encourage a respectable young man to secretly visit a brothel if he was pursuing a respectable young woman?"

"Well, no, of course not."

"That's what I thought. But guess who I saw in a brothel this very morning?"

"You were at a brothel this morning?"

I sighed. "That's beside the point. I was there for work, interviewing someone."

"At a brothel?"

"Yes," I said firmly. "At a brothel. And guess who I saw there?"

"I have absolutely no idea, Henri. Absolutely none."

"Nicola's new beau, that's who." I sat back and grinned with the satisfaction I usually reserved for unmasking a killer.

Mimi, however, was unimpressed. "Your point?"

"Wait just one moment," I began. "You *just* told me you'd be horrified if a young man courting a respectable woman used a tart."

"I said nothing of the sort. You asked if I would *encourage* someone in that situation to use a brothel. I said no. You're the only one who's horrified, Henri."

"Apparently I am." I heard the sulkiness in my own voice, and tried fixing it with a gulp of Mimi's fine wine.

"Ah, interesting." A smile spread across her face. "Very interesting."

I waited for a moment, but she just sat there smiling.

"Fine, I'll ask. What's so interesting?"

"Well, clearly you've told Nicola about this. I'm sure you took enormous pleasure in telling her, in fact."

"I did tell her, yes, but took no pleasure in it," I lied.

"Mm-hmm. Of course. And yet if you're the only one outraged at this, it seems to me she doesn't mind."

"It's not that she doesn't mind, exactly."

"No?"

"No. She doesn't believe me."

"Why not? Surely she doesn't think you'd make this up, Henri, you wouldn't do such a thing and she wouldn't believe that of you."

"She thinks I was mistaken."

"Well, are you sure it's him? Did you get a clear look at him?"

"I'd call it fleeting, rather than lingering," I admitted.

"Not a clear look, so then maybe you are mistaken."

"I don't think so. Although I asked Moulin about it directly, and he denied it was him. I told her that and she chooses to believe him, and not me."

"'Fleeting,' you said?"

"Well, I mean . . ." I shrugged. "It was him, I'm almost positive."

"'Almost positive'?" Her eyes were wide with disbelief. "Henri, for goodness' sake, you cannot cast aspersions about a man, especially a policeman, when you aren't absolutely sure. You know that."

"But I am sure. Almost certain."

"Not good enough." She shook her head, like a disappointed school teacher. "Not nearly good enough. And, if you ask me, this comes back to your trust problems. A manifestation of them."

"I have no idea what you're talking about."

"You're finding reasons to exclude people from your life, seizing on something either insignificant or maybe not even real, and justifying your continued and unhealthy life of isolation."

"That's nonsense. Did you read that in a book somewhere and feel the need to practice how it sounds in the real world?" I stood, tired of being psychoanalyzed. "I'll tell you how it sounds. Ridiculous, that's how."

And ignoring another of her stern gazes, I gave her a little bow and showed myself to the door. I trudged slowly up the stairs to my apartment, with a bulb of garlic in my hand and the weight of the day and her words sitting heavy on my shoulders. The truth was, I didn't want to condemn Nicola to a lifetime of solitude, a lifetime of just *me*. I didn't even want that for myself. But I didn't see a way out of it, and I still believed the last person we needed to trust with our truths was a policeman. An image of Daniel

Moulin popped into my head, which in turn made me think about how he kept popping up in my life. First at the murder scene, then at the brothel, and once more where we found the body of Dr. Brandt. Intentionally trying to ingratiate himself? the cynical part of me wondered. I shook my head to clear the image and let myself back into the apartment.

Nicola was in the kitchen chopping garlic, which I pointed to before snatching up my already refilled wineglass.

"And you wonder why I have trust issues," I said with a glare.

CHAPTER THIRTEEN

Wednesday, December 4, 1940

The next morning, I got up early and was at the Préfecture by seven o'clock. I had a long day ahead of me, and I wanted to start it by checking out young Moulin's whereabouts the previous morning. It took me two brigadiers and one *gardien de la paix*, but I finally got my hands on the assignment sheet.

"So tell me," I said to the custodian of the overtime log, a weary brigadier with a drooping mustache that seemed to fit his current mood. "Who has access to this?"

"Just about anyone who works here. The commandants who fill it out and the *flics* who are assigned overtime. It's not exactly a secret document."

"I thought it was. Command staff only."

"A secret? In this place?" He snorted. "Some chance."

"Disappointing, but I get your point." I leaned against the wall and turned to yesterday's entries, but didn't see one for Daniel Moulin. I looked up and down the list again, and then checked the previous pages to be thorough, but his name wasn't there. The lying toad.

I went up to my office and was surprised to see Nicola at her desk.

"*Bonjour.* You didn't happen to bring me coffee, did you?" I said, my voice low so no one else would hear.

"The flask is in your office." She smiled, and I felt a pang of remorse at the position I'd put her in, and my fierce opposition to her seeing Moulin. I'd planned to tell her about his lie that I'd just uncovered, maybe even gloat a little, but all of a sudden I didn't want to.

"Thank you," I said, and started for my office.

"Wait," Nicola said. "Autopsy report on Edouard Grabbin, and a note from his office. Apparently, the autopsy was done yesterday morning, his brother retrieved the body in the afternoon, and he's set to be buried tomorrow."

"That's a little hasty." I took the report and the note from her, intending to read it immediately so I would know if I should call a halt to the suspiciously fast burial. I settled in behind my desk with the door closed and hot coffee in front of me.

According to the report, Edouard Grabbin had been killed by a single stab wound into the base of his brain. The facial abuse had taken place after he was dead, the doctor opined, and even if not it was probably not serious enough to have been a cause of death. In all other respects, the dead man was quite healthy. Which was to confirm, just for the record, that this was most definitely murder.

But who, and why? I wondered. *Did the killer sneak up behind him, stab him in the brain, then smash his face in?*

As I well knew, in this line of work anything was possible. But this was an odd series of events, speaking neither of a burglary gone wrong, nor of an angry outburst by someone who hated him. It was a very strange mix of both things. It crossed my mind that the facial attack had been done to disfigure the poor man, hide his identity, but he'd been found dead in his own apartment and identified by objects on him.

I had the strongest desire to talk to Jean Grabbin, the dead man's brother. Was he mixed up in this? But, again, why? One thing was for sure, Jean was very eager to keep us from seeing his brother's room, and also keen to stick him in the ground. I resolved to attend the funeral myself and get an answer to that latter peculiarity, at the very least.

A brisk knock on my door startled me.

"Come in."

The door opened and Nicola poked her head in. "How's the coffee?"

"Too hot, probably. I haven't tried it yet."

"You're welcome, Detective. There's someone to see you at reception downstairs."

"Who?" I said to a closing door. I took a sip of coffee, and proved myself wrong. The perfect temperature, and strong and sweet just how I liked it. I took it with me on the walk down to reception, since I now lived in a world where everyday pleasures, like a good cup of coffee, were becoming hard-to-find luxuries. I planned to savor it while I still could.

At reception, a harried *flic* pointed me to the back of the room, where stood a tall, handsome woman in a long wool coat and sporting a brown tam hat with a bow on the crown.

"It's happened again," Princess Marie Bonaparte said in her most imperious tone.

"What's happened again?"

"A child. Taken away."

"Ah. I see."

"Do you?" she pressed. "This isn't normal. They can't just come and take children like that."

"Who are *they*, remind me?"

"How on earth am I supposed to know?" She waved an arm. "Them. The authorities. Maybe your lot. People with papers and grim faces that don't seem very child friendly."

"Why don't you refuse, if you think they're up to no good?"

"Because they also carry guns," she said, a little sulkily.

"Why do they need guns to do that?"

"Precisely!" She poked me in the chest. Not always very ladylike, our Mimi. "Why indeed? Something you need be looking into, I should think."

"Mimi, I've told you. I will, but right now I'm up to my ears in—"

"Oh, take your time, Detective, I'm sure those poor children will understand as they're being dragged away from their beds to goodness knows where."

"Why do I have to do it?" I protested. "This place is full of cops. It's not even my department."

"Oh, for heaven's sake, Henri. Not your department? Who cares which *department* it should be. These kids are disappearing left, right, and center, and we're playing the department game?"

"Mimi, calm down—"

"Do. Not." Her eyes blazed. "Do *not* tell me to calm down, not now and not ever."

I held my hands up in surrender. "I'm sorry, I am just trying to get a handle on what is happening and what you expect me to do about it."

I turned as I felt a hand on my shoulder.

"Everything all right, sir?" Daniel Moulin asked.

"Yes and no. Mostly no." I gestured toward Mimi. "Allow me to present Princess Marie Bonaparte, known to her closest enemies as Mimi. Mimi, this is Daniel Moulin."

There was a pause, which might have been because he wasn't sure about the princess thing, but it might have been something else, too. Did they know each other? My immediate thought was that Nicola had introduced them behind my back, which if true would make me bristle. But that odd little pause was brief, and they shook hands and said hello like they'd never seen each other before, even though surely Mimi recognized his name.

"And which department are you in, Monsieur Moulin?" Mimi asked, dripping with niceness that she knew was poison to me.

"It's all changing, all the time. I have been helping Detective Lefort here with his murder case, as much as possible anyway."

"And there's something I need you to do for me, Moulin," I said. "Right now if you can."

"I'm at your disposal, sir."

"Excellent. Take a statement from her highness, and then start looking into it."

"Into what, sir?" I enjoyed the confusion and disappointment on his face.

"Disappearing children," I said. "Of the utmost urgency. Report back to me at the end of the day and let me know what you've found."

"But—" Moulin's face flushed with either anger or frustration. Either one was good with me.

"Excellent, thank you." I turned to Mimi. "He's very good. Now, if you'll excuse me, I have a murder to investigate."

And with that, I turned on my heel and hurried back upstairs, and fast enough to ensure that I escaped further verbal molestation. I'd wanted to confront Moulin about his lie, but right now I wanted more to get Mimi out of my hair. She was like a dog with a bone, and I didn't want those teeth settling into me, not while I had Nazis breathing down my neck. Having Moulin look into her concerns was a stroke of genius, killing two birds with one stone. I'd maybe get Mimi some answers, while keeping Moulin busy and knowing what he was up to all day.

Such a stroke of genius I couldn't stop myself from telling Nicola about it, and I didn't bother removing the smug grin from my face as I did.

"Oh, that's splendid," she said, rather unexpectedly.

"Splendid? He's mad as a hornet, how is that splendid in your book?"

"I've told Mimi about him, of course. But not really told him about her, so this will be a nice chance for them to get to know each other."

Damn it. I didn't think of that.

"*Merde,*" I said, and stomped back to my office, where I slammed the door behind me, dropped into my creaking chair, and sipped my coffee, finding it still warm and, in that moment, my only measure of comfort.

•   •   •

I'd been putting off visiting Club Monocle but felt like it was time. I grabbed my hat and coat and trotted downstairs to begin the hour-long walk to Montmartre. But as I exited the building a black Mercedes swooped toward me, its impressive metal bumper stopping inches from my knees. A driver hopped out and opened the rear door and my heart managed to sink and speed up at the same time.

"Detective Lefort. I need an update on the case." He did not look happy. "I've telephoned twice and both times you've been out."

"Herr Becker, two whole times?" I kept my sarcasm light because, well, I'm not completely suicidal. "My apologies, I'm busy working on the case."

"I do not appreciate having to drive down here to look for you myself."

"Feel free not to."

That was a step too far, apparently, and I found that out from the stinging slap that scorched my left cheek. I blinked away the tears that sprang into my eyes but resisted putting a hand to my face. Resisted, too, pulling out my pistol and sticking it up his Nazi arse. When I managed to focus on him again, his face glowed with rage and he jabbed an angry finger at me as he snarled.

"You would do well to remember that although you are good at your job, you are also entirely expendable. You do *my* bidding. You are the lackey, not me. Do you understand?"

"I most certainly do." I hoped that the disgust in my eyes conveyed the hate I had for this man, a hate my words didn't dare express.

"Why have you not told me about the body you found yester-day?"

"Because we don't know who it is." True enough, if you take the word "know" very literally. "Look, there are a lot of bodies lying around Paris these days, I'm not going to bother you every time a new one shows up. If it turns out to be him, you will be the first to know. I promise." I meant it, too, because I could still feel the outline of every single finger on my face. This man was a practiced and expert face-slapper, and I was certain he was fairly experienced in other methods of discomfiting people he didn't like.

"What else have you found?"

"Nothing from his hotel room, for one thing. Why did he have a room in such a nice place, by the way?"

"That is not your concern."

"Right, understood. Well, I'm about to go to a nightclub I believe he visited recently."

"Nightclub?"

"Yes." I declined to expound on that; he didn't need to know the details. Not yet anyway. "Depending on what I find out there, that will inform my next move."

He seemed suddenly bored, looking at his watch and frowning.

"I don't have time for this." He poked me in the chest and leaned in close. "And I do not have time for failure."

"Got it." I nodded eagerly.

"If I have to come down here again, there will be consequences." He tapped me lightly on my still-stinging cheek. "And if you fail, those consequences will be permanent."

With that, he turned and went back to his car, climbing into the back seat without giving me another look. I watched the Mercedes drive away, a trail of exhaust spinning behind it in the cold air, and breathed out a long sigh of relief.

With a new sense of dread and worry, I set off for Montmartre. It was cold again, but the skies were clearing and every now and again the sun warmed my face, and the farther I got from the Préfecture, the scene of my morning disasters, the happier I felt.

That ended, however, when I stepped on a sharp pebble and felt a searing pain in my foot, radiating all the way up my leg. I hopped about for a moment, then perched on a low stone wall to pull off my shoe and inspect the damage. My foot would be fine, just a red mark where the stone had pressed into a nerve, but the shoe itself was more of a hat for my foot than a useful item of clothing. The sole had worn as thin as paper and, being me, I'd waited until the paper was torn to worry about it. No wonder the recent snow had felt extra cold on my feet.

I looked around and saw an empty cigarette packet on the ground close to me. I retrieved it and flattened the thing out with my hands, then stuffed it into my shoe. As long as it didn't rain, it'd be a serviceable fix until I could find a cobbler to do a real job. Although even that might not do it—too many people were stomping around the city with wooden soles on their shoes, thanks to a shortage of leather.

Maybe Mimi can help me out, I thought, and immediately felt guilty for using her while dismissing her worries about missing kids. *Just three of them,* I reminded myself. But still.

Club Monocle sat among the bars and seedy storefronts in the Pigalle section of Montmartre, where sex and alcohol were the main commodities for sale. The club looked very closed, hardly a surprise at that time of day. I was a little surprised the uptight sausage-smellers hadn't shut the place down altogether—Nicola had informed me that it was a club for women seeking the company of other women. Maybe Montmartre was too far out of the city center for the Germans to see, and therefore get upset about, women enjoying each other over a drink or three. Or perhaps this area was so full of artists, painters, and other irregulars they felt it a lost cause. Either way, I'd not seen a Boche uniform for the last thirty minutes, to my great relief and delight.

Being there, seeing only my fellow citizens, I once again felt a stab of regret, or maybe frustration, that I was letting down a fellow Parisian by the name of Grabbin. Everyone in this business knows that the more time ticks by in a murder investigation, the harder it is to solve. And here I was galivanting around nightclubs in Montmartre, which was no doubt successfully putting time *and* distance between me and Grabbin's killer.

When I reached the club, I put him out of my mind and banged on the front door loudly enough to attract the attention of some neighbors. Finally, a disheveled person opened the front door to me and introduced herself as Lulu, the owner. She had short hair and from any distance more than a few feet could easily be mistaken for a man.

"You're police," she said matter-of-factly before I could introduce myself.

"Well, yes, actually I am."

"I wondered when you'd get to it."

"Get to what?"

"Persecuting us. Been expecting it since the Germans moved in."

"It'll probably happen," I said. "But not today."

This took her by surprise. "Oh. Then I'll let you in."

Club Monocle was like any other bar, smelling of cigarettes, alcohol, and human need. This place had a slightly perfumy lilt to it, though, which made it more pleasant. We sat at a small table and I offered her a smoke, and lit hers and mine before speaking.

"I'm looking into a murder. Maybe two."

"Around here?" Lulu asked.

"No. But both of my corpses had tickets to your club, here."

"Both were women, then."

"Actually, no. Both were men."

She took that in, then gave me a wry smile. "You may not know this, Detective, but we don't get a lot of those around here."

"I'm well aware. But I was hoping you could shed some light on why not just one, but two men are connected to this establishment."

"Their names?"

"Edouard Grabbin and Viktor Brandt. The latter is . . . *was* a German doctor."

"Not familiar with either, sorry."

"Perhaps I'm being dense here, but if this is a bar for women who prefer women, there must be some other reason men come here."

"You can't figure it out?" She was watching me carefully, assessing my judgment of her and her club. I imagined she did that a lot, and was pretty good at it.

"Well, I might be able to make a guess." I stood and went to a wall that was covered in photos of the club and its customers. Half the women in the pictures were dressed as you'd expect, hats, makeup, and pretty clothes. The other half seemed to be adhering to . . . if not a uniform, then a dress code of sorts: masculine suits and tuxedos, cigarette holders and short hair. And, of course, a monocle in one eye.

"Your guess?" Lulu pressed.

"It seems to me that this is a safe place for women to . . . commune together." I walked slowly back to my chair and sat. "I have no issue with that, but it occurs to me that if women need somewhere to meet, somewhere to drink and be merry—"

"And be free of judgment, most importantly," she chipped in.

"Of course. But if women need that, I'd surmise men do, too."

"And a very clever detective you are."

"So it's true, you host men here?"

"Once a month," she said. "This is first and foremost a place for women to meet and be safe, to express themselves. But I became aware that for many men, men of a certain class, the places available to them were not particularly salubrious."

"Hence the tickets."

"People have always been able to live with the notion that women can love each other," Lulu said. "Society has an easier time looking the other way with women, letting them live and love in relative peace. They have a harder time accepting that men want the same, too."

"The tickets let you control who comes and goes."

"They are a safety mechanism, yes." Her eyes twinkled with mischief. "But because we are a safe, clean, respectable place, they also bring me a hefty return."

"So it's not all charity then?"

"It's better than that. It's a win-win situation for everyone."

"Not these poor fellows. Do you keep a list of those you sell tickets to?"

"I do." Her back stiffened. "But there's no way in hell I'm giving it to you."

"I could come back with a search warrant. Better to let me look informally, wouldn't you say?"

"No, I most certainly wouldn't. My reputation would be destroyed if it became known I'd shown you that list." She grimaced. "And maybe worse."

"Some big names on it, huh?"

"If by 'big' you mean powerful, rich, and connected, then yes. It's not worth my life and livelihood, I promise you that."

"Ah, I see." I shook my head but couldn't help but smile. "Would I be right in thinking, then, that by the time I come back with a warrant, your list or lists will be ashes in the wind?"

"As I said before, you are a good detective." Her tone softened. "I would like to help, especially if these men were customers, but I just can't."

"A compromise, then. Take a look through your list and tell me if either man did, in fact, purchase a ticket. Can you at least do that?"

She thought for a good ten seconds, then stood. I repeated the names for her and sat and waited while she checked. When she came back, she didn't bother sitting.

"I have those two names on my list."

"What date were they here?"

"Saturday. This past Saturday. Grabbin and Brandt."

"Look, I know this is asking a lot." I stood and looked her straight in the eye. "A hell of a lot. But I have to speak to the people who were at that party. Some of them, anyway."

"No chance, Detective."

"Just hear me out. I have two murder victims, with seemingly nothing in common, until now. Both were at the same party, and frankly I don't give a damn if it was a homosexual party or a kid's birthday party. Both men were there, and that means it matters."

"It matters to you."

You have no idea how much. "Like you said, they were your customers."

"It's not happening, Detective. Imagine doctor-patient confidentiality, except when it's broken, good men are ruined for life. And maybe even imprisoned." She crossed her arms. "I've told you all I can, and all I will."

"Lulu, listen—"

"You can come back with warrants, *merde*, you can come back with thumbscrews, but these lips are sealed."

CHAPTER FOURTEEN

When Cyril Toussaint saw me that afternoon, after I'd told him who I was and why I was there, he wore much the same look on his face as Denis Berger did when I'd crashed his kinky party at the One-Two-Two. Part shock, part embarrassment, and one large part fear. He wasn't tied to a cross like Dr. Berger had been, nor was I inclined to kick him in the nuts for fun but, if it came to it, I might do it for information.

Nicola had found Cyril for me, and it'd taken her a long three hours of working the telephone and riffling through papers. I'd suspected he existed because of something that Lulu had said, the existence of all-male parties at Club Monocle. If it was purely a moneymaker for her, I thought it likely she'd not attend but have someone else oversee the actual running of the events. Well, that and the fact she was in possession of the wrong plumbing. I suspected there would be someone, a man, officially connected to the club who, even if he wasn't the one running the parties, would tell me who did.

I was right. Deep in the paperwork, poor Cyril Toussaint was listed as an investor in the club, and after a brief nose into his dealings with the police, I was sure I had my man. Specifically, he had no dealings with the police, not officially, because he'd had them quashed. Unofficially, he'd twice been manacled for seeking out male company in Montmartre—once he approached a detective and mistook him for a workingman, and once he was caught with his todger in the hands of a known prostitute who was more boy than man. Reports had been written, and then later when he'd exerted his influence they'd been rewritten such that the suspect's name was changed and the report was then filed in the wrong place.

A grubby fellow, then, our Cyril, but even so blackmail does not come easy to me. I'd been on the pointy end of an attempt myself earlier in the year, and while I'd not done anything as seedy as put my rising future in the hands of a teenage boy, my secret if revealed would have ended my career as surely as Cyril's would be ended. And, like him, I too might have ended up in jail. At least I was doing it for a good cause, unlike my blackmailer, who sought only a good story for his newspaper. Nevertheless, it was with a bitter taste in my mouth that I put on my sternest and most judgmental demeanor in search of information.

You see, Cyril Toussaint wasn't just an investor in Club Monocle, he was also a senior civil servant in the Department of Youth and Sports. And, as he and I both knew, if there's one thing that wouldn't look good to his bosses (and their new bosses), it was someone with his rank and position diddling hungry urchins in the back alleys of Montmartre.

Our chat began as I expected it to, with some bluster on his part. He was already red-faced but his cheeks reddened more as they puffed out his indignation.

"You have no right to come in here without an appointment and harass me."

I sat on the chair opposite him and kept my voice calm and reasonable. "Well, I am a policeman. There's that."

"Unless there is a crime in progress, you still need an appointment. My secretary outside—"

"Oh, but there is a crime in progress," I interrupted. "More of an unsolved situation, but really isn't that the same thing? Someone commits a crime and then does it again and again. . . . Seems like there'd be a need for a detective to step in and do something. *N'est-ce pas?*"

His eyes narrowed and he studied me intently. My calmness in the face of his rank and hostility unnerved him. He knew I had something on him, smart fellow that he was.

"What do you want?"

"I want to know . . ." I glanced over my shoulder and lowered my voice. "I want to know about a couple of people who were at Club Monocle last Saturday night."

"Club Monocle?" He feigned ignorance, and quite well, I thought. "Never heard of it. Is it some sort of gentlemen's club?"

"Yes, but not in the way you're pretending." I sighed dramatically. "You want me out of your office, right?"

"I do, of course."

"I promise, that will happen a lot more quickly if you stop lying and just tell me what I want to know."

"How dare you, I am not lying about any—"

I slammed a piece of paper on the desk in front of him, and that shut him up quick. He took a moment to scan it, and I watched the blood drain from his face.

When he spoke, his voice was weak and he wouldn't look me in the eye. "This was just a financial investment, I remember now. Yes, Club Monocle. Never even been there."

"Oh, you should go, it has a delightful bar and the woman who runs it is very helpful indeed."

That made him look at me. "What does that mean?"

"Although now that I think about it, she wasn't that helpful at all when it came to finding out who runs the monthly men-only parties. I had to do that legwork myself." Also untrue, Nicola had done all of it, but he didn't need to know that. "So, here's the situation, Monsieur Toussaint. I have in my office a couple of police reports that were misfiled and don't have your name in them."

Hairy eyebrows knitted together. "That *don't* have my name . . . ?"

"But they used to. And will again, if need be. After which, I will file them where they will be seen by . . . well, everyone."

His chair creaked as he settled back into it, and his final gambit was as feeble as it was unlikely to succeed. "You know, Detective, I have friends at the Préfecture, powerful friends. I could make your life very uncomfortable, or even—"

"But you won't, will you? Because once those reports make the rounds, and by the way they identify the arresting officer, who I'm sure could add some colorful details if necessary, you won't have a single friend in the world, let alone at the Préfecture."

I thought I could hear the wind whistle out of him like a deflating balloon, and hated myself for shoving him to the edge of panic.

"Listen, I'm not here to do you harm," I said. "I'm trying to find out who killed a man, maybe two men, and I'm at a dead end, if you'll excuse the pun. I've come across enough secrets in my time to know that not all of them need to be told and, as a man with a few secrets of my own, my tendency is to keep my lips sealed. You help me out, and by that I mean you answer every question fully and truthfully, then you have my word I will not speak of this again." I wagged my finger at him. "Don't think I approve of you taking advantage of young boys in back alleys, mind, but these days life is short and brutish enough without me adding extra misery to yours. Now, are we clear?"

He grunted and nodded, and his chin stayed down on his chest.

"Good. So, fair to assume you know everyone at these parties?"

It was a poor question, and as soon as I asked it, I knew it gave him an out.

"Not everyone, just some of them."

"Thing is, Cyril, it takes one lie, one *suspected* lie, for me to walk out of here and ruin your life. So I'm going to give you two names and I better believe every word that comes out of your mouth." When he nodded again, I continued. "Two gentlemen by the names of Grabbin and Brandt were at the party on Saturday."

"Yes, I can confirm that."

"I don't need you to fucking confirm that, I already know it for a fact."

"What then?"

"Do you know either of these men?"

"No. Honestly, I don't, I promise. Brandt I'd never seen before that night, and Grabbin, I've seen him at the club a couple of times but never spoken to him. He's not very friendly, unless you look a certain way."

"Young?"

"No, not that. Rich. He seems like a snob."

"Makes sense. Now then, did these two men know each other?"

He looked at me, both eyebrows raised in surprise. "Oh, yes, absolutely. I assumed that's why you gave me both names, because you knew that."

"But if you'd never seen Brandt, how can you be so sure that he knows Edouard Grabbin?"

"I mean, it was obvious, the way they interacted."

"You mean they were . . ." I pulled a face, unable to find the right word.

Toussaint actually smiled. "Lovers? Good heavens no, quite the opposite."

"Meaning?"

"I had to throw them out. They were all but fighting."

My turn to be surprised. "Fighting? About what?"

"Not to the point of fists, but remember where they were, an elegant club where people come to get along, not argue. Anyway, I don't really remember the details, just a lot of yelling. Something about a hotel in Vincennes, I think."

"Are you sure it was Vincennes?"

"Yes . . . wait, no. Rennes. Maybe Rennes."

I sat back, thinking. *There's the city of Rennes, again, connecting both men.* "Did you happen to catch the name of the hotel?" I asked.

"I didn't. And maybe it wasn't a hotel but a hospital, but that doesn't make much sense. I'm sorry, there are a lot of martinis consumed at these things, and I really wasn't wanting to listen to their drama."

"Understood. Anything more stand out to you from their argument? Any other little detail?"

"*Non*, I'm sorry. I can't think of anything else."

"Well, that's something though. Viktor Brandt and Edouard Grabbin fighting at a homosexual bar, about a Rennes hotel."

"Excuse me, Detective, but that's the second time you've said that wrong."

"Said what wrong?"

"His name."

"Whose name? What are you talking about?"

"The first time I thought you'd just confused him with someone else, but you said it again. Edouard Grabbin."

"Yes, that's who I'm talking about. Him and Viktor Brandt."

"*Non, monsieur.* It wasn't Edouard Grabbin fighting with that German. It was Jean Grabbin. Dr. Jean Grabbin, as he was quick to tell people. Like I said, seemed to be something of a snob, that one."

CHAPTER FIFTEEN

Thursday, December 5, 1940

The snow was falling when I stepped out of my apartment building the next morning, which surprised me because ten minutes ago, coffee cup in hand, I'd looked out of my window and seen nothing more than clouds in the sky. But already the cold streets were welcoming the heavy flakes, the cobbles and sidewalks slowly tucking themselves under the second winter blanket of the year, this one heavy. I pulled the brim of my hat to stop the flakes tickling my nose, but the occasional one drifted into one eye or the other, or slipped down the back of my neck to make me shiver.

I was on my way to the Préfecture, even though this was also supposed to be a day off, because when you're chasing a murderer it doesn't much matter what day of the week it is. A trail gets colder by the hour, and doesn't take time off for weekends or holidays, let alone the odd day off. And, of course, I had a deadline of my own thanks to some highly unreasonable Boche.

Strangely, Jean Grabbin had not posted a notice of his brother's death in *Le Temps* newspaper, so I'd had to make a few phone calls to find out where and when he was to be buried. The funeral was set for eleven o'clock in Bagneux, about five miles from the center of Paris. Nicola had managed to wrangle a car for me, god knows how, but thank heavens because I had no desire to bicycle ten miles on a wet Thursday. Public transportation was maybe an option, but also maybe not these days, with so many resources being redirected by the Germans to the Germans you never knew until it showed up whether a bus or train might appear. Even if it did, odds were good you'd spend an hour breathing in some wretch's body odor, and *then* walking five miles when the train or bus conked out.

I was also grateful for the car because my sturdy shoes continued to become less and less robust in the sole region. An old insert from a pair of dusty, worn-out shoes had replaced the cigarette packet for now, but that wouldn't be a permanent fix so I'd stopped by a cobbler on rue de Lille to see about shoring them up. I'd balked at his prices, and even found myself a little outraged at the cobbler himself, assuming him to be gouging poor slobs like me, but he explained: everyone was walking more, so more shoes were wearing out. More importantly, leather had become a scarce resource, commandeered for the most part by our protectors from the east, who did a fair amount of marching themselves. As a result, leather was expensive even when available, and he'd been patching up people's shoes and boots with everything from wood to cardboard. I apologized for my temper and promised to return with my own leather for him to use once my insert wore away and my socks started getting wet from the holes. Where a homicide detective was going to get leather I had no clue, but in that moment the idea of skinning a few Boche was quite appealing.

In front of the Préfecture, several uniformed *flics* eyed me uncertainly as I climbed into the car. To them, this meant I had status and power because access to a set of working wheels was a rarity and only those highest in the force could get their hands on a set of car keys. They probably wanted to remember my face so as not to run afoul of me in the future, which was fine by me. I was just glad they didn't know about my shoes.

I drove slowly, wanting to arrive once the funeral had already started, and noted that the streets were mostly empty, just a few people hurrying along the sidewalks looking for essentials while bundled against the cold. An old man slipped on some ice and I slowed down, ready to stop and help, but the butcher, whose store he'd just exited, rushed out and picked up him, setting him back on his feet like he were a tipped over wine bottle.

The cemetery that would house Edouard Grabbin for the remainder of eternity, or at least until the worms got him, was in a fenced-off area of a larger park that, in keeping with this low-income area, had not been well tended to. The dusting of snow prettied it up a little, but I knew as soon as it warmed up the pathways and the ground between the trees would turn into ugly patches of mud. From what I could see, the cemetery was the best looked-after part of the park—it certainly seemed to have a monopoly on what grass there was.

The parking lot was surprisingly empty, just a hearse and one other car. I put this down to the scarcity of motor vehicles generally, but I also didn't see any bicycles, horses, or any other modes of transportation.

Maybe Edouard Grabbin was as friendly as his brother? I couldn't think how else to explain the dearth of mourners, so shrugged it off and walked through the iron gate into the cemetery. Inside, I stopped and lit a cigarette, then looked up and counted five people gathered beside a grave about a hundred yards ahead of me. There was Jean Grabbin, the priest, and three other men whom I didn't recognize, two were white and one darker skinned.

In murder investigations I usually joined the outer ring of people at the grave site, lurking in the background to see who was there and who wasn't. The point is to be inconspicuous, to be the one watching and not the one being watched. With just five people in attendance that wasn't possible except from a distance, so I found a tree to lean against, hoping that the falling snow, the distance, and the words of the priest in his black cloak and matching hat would keep attention away from me.

After about fifteen minutes the priest wrapped up, and I watched as he turned to the other men, who all shook their heads.

Nothing to say, eh?

The priest then shook hands with the mourners and they all slowly trudged in my direction, Monsieur Grabbin walking alongside the priest and the darker man, who looked to be Indian, the other two men following behind. As they got close, I took off my hat.

"Monsieur Grabbin, my condolences," I said. "Do you have a moment to speak?"

Grabbin paused, but barely. "No, I'm sorry. I'm late for an appointment."

"An appointment today, of all days?"

He grunted and kept moving, climbing into the front passenger seat of the only other car in the parking lot, while the priest got behind the wheel and their companion got into the back seat. The snow had let up, but a bitter wind threaded through the cemetery and reminded me to put my hat back on, so I did. When the priest drove off, I decided to chat up the two fellows who'd kept the Grabbin brothers company. I hurried after them.

"Gentlemen, excuse me."

They stopped and turned to face me. I was surprised that one looked a little drunk, and the other a lot drunk.

"Yes, what do you want?" the drunker one slurred.

I introduced myself and they both stiffened, straightening themselves as if I were there to arrest them for being drunk at a funeral.

"What was your relationship to the deceased?" I asked.

"What are you inferring?" This time I got spittle and a wagged finger from the drunker one. "There was no *relationship*."

"No, I didn't mean . . ." I took a breath and tried again. "How did you know him?"

"Know who?"

I turned my gaze to the slightly-less-drunk mourner. "Sir, how did you know the dead man?"

"Oh, he's deaf," the drunker man said, patting his friend on the shoulder. "Lost his hearing in the war." He jerked a thumb behind him. "The one we had before."

"We surrendered too fast for it to have been this war," I said. Lately I'd been unable to keep to myself that I was less than happy about the rapid capitulation, especially since in the previous go-around I'd had mud for three meals a day, and slept in the stuff, all while being shot at and shelled.

"I didn't mind us giving up," he said with a shrug. "Didn't want to have to do all that again. Got my pension and a place to drink it, that's all I need."

"Fair enough."

"What did you want again?" He punctuated the question with a burp.

"The funeral you were just at. How did you know the dead man?"

He looked over toward the cemetery as if to remind himself where he'd just been. "Oh, that. Didn't know him at all."

"You didn't—"

"Never met him." He sounded almost proud.

"You do this for a hobby, attend funerals?"

"That's not a hobby, no sir."

It occurred to me that maybe Grabbin was a veteran and these two idiots felt somehow duty bound to attend a fallen comrade's funeral.

"I told you, never met the *mec*," he said, when I suggested the veteran connection. "No idea if he was a soldier or not. Don't even care."

I'd arrived at the crossroads of cold and impatient, and let my tone reflect that. "Then why the hell were you at his funeral?"

"That man." He pointed in the direction the priest had driven away. "The tall one. Not the priest, the other one." A solid hiccup this time. "He gave us each ten francs to be there."

"You were paid to attend?"

"There we were minding our business and our cups, and he

offered us all that money to stand by the graveside for thirty minutes. If you add it up that's . . . a lot."

"He found you in a bar and paid you?"

"*Oui, monsieur.* And we're heading back there now, to spend it all." With that he turned and wandered slowly away, alternately supported by and supporting his slightly-less-drunk friend.

I lit another cigarette and felt the warm smoke cut through the chill in my chest. I walked back into the cemetery and watched as two men stood beside Edouard Grabbin's grave, sliding their shovels into the mound of dirt they'd taken from the ground. It was almost like a dance, the slow, steady rhythm of two people swaying back and forth to the gentle hiss of metal slicing into mud, followed by the low drumbeat of wet earth hitting wood.

I shook my head as I pondered. These may be strange times, but a funeral with just a priest, a brother, and two drunks? Not even a funeral director in sight. Just the local gravediggers plying their grim trade with shovels, with that steady rhythm born of being the last living souls to render service to a dead man.

Movement behind them, at the far side of the cemetery, caught my attention and I squinted to see who or what it was. It took a moment to register, despite the size of the person I was looking at because, I suspect, the last time I'd seen this fellow he'd been manacled to a cross getting his gonads booted by a pretty lady in tall boots.

I started toward him, but apparently one visit with me had been enough. He turned and strode in the opposite direction, and I could see he was making for a little black Renault on the street beside the park. Part of me wondered if he'd fit inside it, but the rest of me wondered why he was watching over a complete stranger's funeral.

It's not like he's some drunk in a bar in need of cash, I thought.

I walked slowly back to my car, pondering his presence and second-guessing my immediate suspicions. He was a doctor, like Edouard and Jean Grabbin, so maybe there was a simple, explainable rationale for him to be there. And it's no surprise he didn't want to speak to me, if for no other reason than the embarrassment that I knew one of his extracurricular pastimes. No one would want that thrown in their face.

On the other hand, I wouldn't be doing my job if I didn't ask him directly.

CHAPTER SIXTEEN

It had been my experience as a detective that, more often than you would think, the most obvious and clear-cut of cases are anything but. The death of Edouard Grabbin looked like it was about to drop out of the file marked *Easy to Solve* and into the one entitled *Oops, Not So Fast.*

That was particularly distressing to me because it meant extra complications drawing me away from my investigation into the now-dead, as opposed to merely missing, Dr. Brandt. As I walked back to my car I even wondered if they were somehow connected, which I definitely didn't want and for two very good reasons: first, if so, I couldn't just ignore the odd funeral attendance I'd witnessed and thereby ignore the Grabbin case until I'd solved the Brandt case. Which was an exceedingly attractive plan. Second, if the deaths of Brandt and Grabbin were connected it meant I had to solve *two* cases to save my neck, a doubling of an already monumental task.

I cranked the engine to life and winced as the gears grated, then pulled out of the parking lot and headed back for Paris. I figured since I had the use of the damn thing, I might as well drive to the only place that seemed to be central to my investigations, and the only place I knew to look for Dr. Berger. Well, not the *only* place, but I doubted he'd head back to the One-Two-Two for another ball kicking so soon after the first. Even masochists needed recovery time, I assumed.

"To the hospital, we go," I muttered to no one but me and the clanking automobile that would take me there.

The snow had stopped falling and as I made my way out of Bagneux, I was treated to a road free of danger, chugging along between trees and buildings powdered with white snow. There I was, in a car, no Germans in sight, not even a roadblock to ruin the moment, sailing along at a good clip as if nothing had changed, as if nothing in the world were wrong. For that brief minute or two, snug inside the car, my thoughts turned to Christmas and what Nicola and I might do for a meal this year, a silly thought because we always had a delicious cheese fondue and lots of *eau de brandy*, cherry for me and pear for her, to wash it down. Which, of course, is when reality hove back into view, because what were the odds of us getting a good, dry Gruyère cheese and some Emmentaler to go with it this year? I tried hard to enjoy the landscape for the rest of the drive but my mind had been turned sour, to the point that I realized fondue was the least of my worries. I needed to solve one, possibly two, cases to even make it to Christmas Day.

Dr. Berger must have been a slow driver because, despite

his head start, we arrived at the hospital at the same time, him entering about twenty steps ahead of me. I decided to follow him to see where he went, confront him in his own space where he'd initially feel more comfortable but would quickly face embarrassment if a certain policeman were to make a scene. So, with me trailing behind, the big man passed through the lobby, turned right down a long hallway, and then climbed two sets of stairs. At the top he turned right again and I peeked around the corner to see him disappear through the second door on the left. I followed.

The door led to what might have been a lab, with three rows of waist-high, solid-wood benches containing sinks but bearing more stacks of paperwork than test tubes or burners. On either side of the lab were two glass-paneled doors with nameplates on them. One of those doors stood open and just inside was Dr. Berger, looking out at me with wide eyes and a dropped jaw.

"I hope your mouth stays open, sir, because I have some questions for you."

"You . . . you can't be in here."

"No one stopped me."

"You have to leave." His eyes flicked toward the door, and I got the impression he was more afraid of someone else coming in than me remaining. *But who might that be?* I wondered.

"I will. As soon as you tell me why you were at the funeral of Edouard Grabbin."

"Funeral of . . ." It was in his eyes, the panic of his mind working overtime trying to figure out what to tell me. I've seen it many times and the length of the pause depends on the intelligence of the man just about to lie. And it is always a lie. "I . . . went to pay my respects."

"From the far side of the cemetery?"

"I don't like funerals. And I wasn't dressed properly."

"Why not? Why didn't you bother to dress properly if you knew you were going to a funeral?"

"I didn't know. I mean, I hadn't decided. It was last minute."

"How did you know Edouard Grabbin?"

"I didn't."

I sighed dramatically. "You are wasting my time. I have a feeling that this conversation might be a lot more productive at the Préfecture." Lord knew how I was going to get him there if he didn't want to go, though. The man was a behemoth. Maybe Mistress Lau could come by and drag him there by the balls. He might even go willingly that way.

"No, I can't."

"Yes, you can. Look, if you didn't know Grabbin, who the hell were you paying your respects to?"

"I knew his brother, Jean. I was paying them to him."

"Ah, so you were being supportive of Jean?"

"Oui, exactement."

"But from a distance, where he probably couldn't even see you."

"Yes, I told you, I—"

"I know, I know, you don't like funerals and you had the wrong pants on. How do you know Jean Grabbin?"

"He used to work here." His tone, confident and sure, told me he'd moved from shifting ground to the truth.

Nobody has mentioned that. Merde, there's that connection I didn't want.

"What did he do here?" I asked.

"A doctor."

"What kind? Was he actually practicing medicine or did he shuffle papers around in a lab, like you?"

"He was . . ." Back on shifting ground. "A doctor. He practiced, but I forget which specialty."

"But you were friends."

"Not friends, colleagues. Acquaintances."

"Why did he leave?" This one I knew the answer to, Grabbin told me himself he'd retired.

"He was fired."

On the other hand, maybe I didn't know.

"Why?"

"How should I know?"

"Oh, come on. You were colleagues, people at workplaces talk. Was it because he was Jewish?"

"I don't . . . Yes, maybe. That sounds right." He glared at me. "Right, enough questions. Now you can leave. I have work to do."

"What about his personal life?"

"What about it?"

"Did he have a wife, children? Hobbies, maybe?"

"He was older, maybe he used to have a wife and children, but I never saw them." His brow furrowed. "He had an older brother who died a while back, though. Last year maybe."

"Two dead brothers, that's bad luck."

"It happens. Like I said, he was older. Are we finished?"

I wanted to leave on my own time, so I changed tack. "Speaking of hobbies, does your colleague Andreas von Rauch know about your extracurricular activity?"

He stiffened. "*Non.* Of course not."

"No? You think he'd mind? I mean, the Germans seem to be a

pretty domineering lot, particularly when it comes to us French. He'd probably approve."

"Dr. von Rauch is a very moral person." Berger looked at the floor. "I am fairly certain he would *not* approve."

"You admire him, then?"

"Of course. He is a brilliant man, and from a fine family."

"Indeed he is. Makes your collaboration much more palatable, I'm sure."

"'Palatable'?" I, apparently, had struck a nerve. "I am here because I want to be here. I believe in the cause, in what they are doing."

"And what exactly are they doing? What are you doing?"

"That is not your concern," said a voice behind me.

I turned and was surprised to see Andreas von Rauch. He wore a dark blue suit under a camel-colored wool coat, which he was in the process of taking off, and he had a smile on his face.

"And by that I simply mean our work is highly classified. As important, and therefore secret, as anything else that happens in the hospital." His smile broadened. "So important that even a respected member of the Paris police shouldn't be able to just walk in. How did that happen?"

I jerked a thumb at Berger. "I just followed the big guy in. Had some questions for him."

We both turned to Dr. Berger and if you imagine something large and manly suddenly wilting into something smaller and almost drooping, then you have the same image (and the correct one) that I did.

"I didn't realize he was—" Berger stammered.

"No matter," von Rauch said, waving the problem away with

an amiable waft of his hand. "No harm done. Did you answer the detective's questions?"

"I did, yes."

"Excellent, I'm delighted to hear that because our friends in Berlin were wanting the reports we promised them. You can pull them together right now and get them to the station." He looked at his watch. "The train leaves in just under an hour, so if you don't mind taking care of that, I would be supremely grateful."

"Yes, of course." Berger nodded and withdrew into his office, closing the door behind him.

Von Rauch turned to me, still smiling. "Let me walk you out; we can chat some more."

CHAPTER SEVENTEEN

The more von Rauch talked, the more I wanted to nose around and see what they were up to. Not because I suspected criminal activity there, just because I was nosy. That's an affliction many cops suffer from—if you don't become a *flic* because you have it, chances are you'll catch it pretty sharpish and get a full-blown case soon after you join the force.

Von Rauch had different ideas, of course, and true to his word he steered me out of the lab-cum-office into the hallway, and back the way I'd come. All the while chatting merrily.

"You know, I'm somewhat ashamed that I know Paris so little," he said. "The more time I spend here, the more I enjoy it."

"Especially since you have a friend here?"

"A friend?"

"The princess I saved." I wanted to know about their relationship and, if I could, steer him away from her. He seemed decent enough, but I didn't want senior German military personnel in my building making house calls to a mutual friend who lived right beneath me.

"Oh, yes," he said with a laugh. "I don't know her well; it's as much a family thing as a personal one."

"And probably some awkwardness with the whole invasion of her country." I wasn't sure myself if I wanted to irritate him or make him laugh. Both would have been a good outcome. As it was he looked slightly peevish.

"I would hope she'd understand that families such as ours, hers and mine, serve our respective nations as honorably and faithfully as we can. My being here is . . ." He cast around for the right words. ". . . making the best of a bad situation."

"Well, Paris is one of the better assignments, I'm sure."

"Indeed, and now that some of its best qualities are back on display, well, it just gets better and better."

"Best qualities?"

"Yes, the arts!" he said it like I was a moron, which maybe I was but no one needed that pointed out to them.

"I thought you were talking about the restaurants, the food," I explained. "And that sure as hell hasn't returned to normal. Unless your normal was to stand in line for hours to pay for a wilted cabbage leaf."

"Oh? I assure you, it's still at its finest in some places. You should dine with me at the Hotel Lutetia."

"No, I really don't think I should."

"Whyever not?" He looked genuinely surprised at my refusal.

I didn't want that look of surprise to turn into one of offense, so I gave him the secondary reason.

"You're a witness, or a potential witness, in my case. It wouldn't be proper."

"Ah, yes, I see. Of course. Perhaps once you've solved the case?"

"There's an assumption. But if so, maybe then. You don't know many other people in Paris?"

"Only Germans, and I do so like to practice my French." He snapped his fingers and smiled. "I should pay the princess a visit."

My skin started to prickle but a grunt was all I could manage. I certainly wasn't going to encourage it. We'd reached the exit and he kept walking with me, but stopped when we got outside. He lowered his voice and said, "May I ask what you needed from Dr. Berger?"

"I don't think so, no."

"It's just that he works for me, and if there's something I need to know, well, I'd like to know." He was being so polite about it, I wondered if there was an Englishman living somewhere in his past. "I know you wouldn't normally, but I feel this is a little different."

"How so?"

He pursed his lips, something I'd seen him do before when thinking. "I have great respect for you, Henri—may I call you Henri?" He didn't wait for an answer. "But you have to acknowledge the slightly awkward shift in the balance of things, yes?"

"Things?"

"Power, I suppose I mean."

"You mean, your lot taking over our country?"

"You basically handed it to us," he said, chortling, and my blood pressure spiked. I briefly wondered what the penalty for murdering a German doctor might be, but the answer was obvious, and distressing, enough that I kept my hands by my sides. "But yes, I do mean that. Berger, well, he's helping out and is a French citizen, so he's the lowest of the three of us. You'd have no reason to let him know anything."

"Glad to hear it."

"But I, on the other hand . . ." He adopted a pained expression. "Well, I'm a senior German official and while I'd never wish to pull rank, I think we both know it could be done."

I didn't have time to dance around like a pair of newlyweds so I told him, "I saw him at the funeral of my murder victim."

"Dr. Brandt?"

"Oh, you think Dr. Brandt was murdered?" I had a smile on my lips, but I was watching him carefully.

"I assume so. He wouldn't have committed suicide and an accident seems far-fetched. *Non?*"

"Maybe, maybe not. But I was talking about Edouard Grabbin."

"Ah, the Jewish doctor. What did Berger say was his reason for being there?"

"He was supporting the dead man's brother."

"Well, that's kind of him. I prefer he ask permission before he takes excursions, of course, but in this case that sounds like an act of kindness one can overlook."

"He doesn't strike me as being overly endowed with kindness," I said. "Is that how you see him?"

"You'd be surprised, Henri. Surely you see it every day, the depth and breadth of people. They seem one way but are also another. He's a fine doctor, a loyal colleague, and a reliable and, so it is now evidenced, kind man."

"That's what Siegfried said about Hagen, wasn't it?"

"My dear Henri!" Von Rauch clapped his hands together in delight. "Is that a reference to a certain opera named *Götterdämmerung*?"

"Indeed. And you don't have to look quite so impressed, some of us know a thing or two about the arts."

"Exactly my point! And while *Götterdämmerung* has its moments, I have to say no, there are no magic potions nor spears in my world. In any case, as I mentioned once before," he lowered his voice again conspiratorially, "some of the German works are a little bombastic for me. Wagner is a genius, of course, he's just not the genius I admire the most or relate to."

"So Berger would be Macbeth to your Lady Macbeth?"

"Nothing so grand, my good detective. And, after all, we work in pursuit of science, we do not seek power for its own sake as did Lady Macbeth."

"Her husband didn't much care what her motives were, did he?"

"He may have, if science had been one of them."

"What is the science you seek, exactly?"

Von Rauch laughed. "You are a fine detective, I can see that. Like a hungry dog, you take a bite and do not let go."

"Not at all, this is pure curiosity. Like you, I am interested in new things." *Not exactly a lie*, I thought. *But not exactly the truth right now.*

"Do you play chess, Henri?" Von Rauch caught me by surprise with that question.

"Not really. More of a backgammon player."

"An American game, no?" The edges of his smile fell away.

"From Persia," I said mildly. "No idea if it's popular in America—is it?"

"I don't know why I associate it with that country." Von Rauch pursed his lips again. "Perhaps because, in comparison to chess, it's a less sophisticated game. I mean, any game based in part on the roll of dice is inherently luck based and therefore less sophisticated, no?"

"I wouldn't say so. I'd argue there's more challenge, and thereby sophistication, in winning a game when part of it is out of your control."

"Perhaps," he said. "One thing is certain—it's easier to make excuses when you lose."

"I feel like we're starting to talk about something else now."

"We can return to opera, if you like?"

"Or your colleague, Dr. Berger."

"What else is there to say? As I've told you, he's a hardworking scientist. A good colleague, a reliable employee, and a believer in the work we're doing."

"Your work, yes . . . some would call that collaboration."

"Henri, listen to me." Von Rauch took a small step toward me and lowered his voice. "I implore you. It is time to see that we have won, and you have lost. The battle is over. Dr. Berger is doing what you should be doing—a job. Working with us, not against us. There is no profit in doing otherwise, and I do not say this to threaten you, Henri, I promise—there is only pain in continuing to oppose what we're doing here. You gave us Paris, you gave us France, and we are here to stay. Forever."

He stepped back, gave me a pitying smile, then turned on his heel and walked away.

And yet, that sure sounds like a threat to me, I thought.

•   •   •

I set off in the car for the Préfecture and reluctantly handed over the keys. That hunk of metal was one hell of a time-saver, so I was sorry to see the back of it. I thought about the cafeteria inside the Préfecture, but soon decided on a late lunch at my apartment. Not because the food was any better but because I wanted to avoid Nicola. Frankly, I was sick of arguing with people, doubting and second-guessing people, and the last person I wanted to joust with was her. But I knew if I saw her I'd have to say something about her new beau's lying to me about his schedule. Before I did that, I wanted to think, figure out what it meant. And since I did my best thinking walking and alone, it made sense to wear out some more shoe leather going to a place where I'd be on my own for an hour or two.

One of the things I wanted to think about, one of the people, was a certain *flic* by the name of Daniel Moulin. It was plain that he'd been untruthful with me, but I wanted to see if I could sort out in my own mind exactly how, and of course why. It seemed to me that he had just two reasons to lie. One, he was simply trying to cover his tracks and make it seem like he was doing work that he wasn't. In other words, nothing more than a cop padding his overtime hours to make a few extra bucks. Not something I could approve of, or even ignore, but not something that, these days, would get him fired.

The second option was the one I liked less: that he was

actively trying to mislead me and derail the investigation. The only reason I considered this was his appearance at the cathouse at the same time I was there. It could have been a coincidence, and I can see why he'd lie about being there, but . . . coincidences didn't just make me nervous, they made me look harder at the evidence. And in his favor, there was no real evidence that he'd want either Grabbin or Brandt toes up in a wooden box.

But there was no escaping the fact he'd inserted himself into this investigation very effectively, and lied to me at least once and possibly twice. And I didn't like having to look in front of me for clues to catch the killer, look behind me at the murderous Nazi waiting for me to fail, and then look over each shoulder at my colleagues feeding me horseshit while I worked. I was a detective, not a damned barn owl.

My musings carried me all the way to my building, but they were put to a stop the moment I passed my neighbor's door because it swung open as if she were expecting me.

"Henri!" She didn't wait for a reply but steered me into her apartment like a pilot boat redirecting a freighter. I didn't even get a chance to object. "Come in, perfect timing."

"Is it?" I didn't say anything, of course, but I was a little taken aback by her appearance. Mimi was always, without fail, well put together, dressed perfectly for every occasion, and with her hair and makeup as if done by a professional. As I looked at her now, she was by no means underdressed or scruffy, but she looked thinner and a little less than perfectly coiffed. I wondered for the first time if the food we regularly got from her was being delivered to her detriment. Maybe she was doing for us, but doing without in return. The thought humbled me.

Her humor, always at my expense, was as full and lively as

ever, though. "Taking a half day, are we?" she said with a sparkle in her eye.

"Are you joking?" I tried working myself into a righteous indignation, which was often the only way I was able to overpower this woman's immense personality. But my outrage hissed out of me like air from a balloon when I saw who was on her couch, and I immediately doffed my hat. "Madame Virginia Hall."

"Detective." She smiled and wagged a finger, which somehow made me weak at the knees. "I thought we agreed you'd call me Virginia."

"Indeed, we did. Virginia, very nice to see you again."

"You, too, Henri. How goes the investigating?"

"Very frustratingly." I turned to address Mimi. "But I gather you know a potential witness of mine."

"I do?"

"A certain Andreas von Rauch."

"Andreas, good heavens. Yes, our families have—"

"Been friends for decades, yes, he told me."

"How on earth is he connected? Surely not as a suspect."

"No, he's a colleague of my missing doctor."

"Ah, yes, he's a researcher. Brain things, if I recall. Quite the old-school gentleman."

"He's certainly a gentleman," I said, but Mimi caught my tone and, apparently, didn't like it.

"I know it's not said out loud anymore," she said a little huffily. "But there is such thing as class and—"

"You're not going to say 'breeding,' are you?"

"No, it's not in the blood it's in the upbringing. Men like Andreas may not be perfect but they know right from wrong and act accordingly. No matter what you might think of his foibles."

"That presumes his version of right and wrong aligns with mine."

"On the big moral questions, I very strongly believe it would."

"I prefer seeing to believing," I said.

"Do you have some specific concern, Henri? Or is him being German enough for you?"

"It most certainly is right now." I shook my head. "But nothing else I can put my finger on or articulate."

"Police speak for 'no.'" She looked a little too satisfied with herself for that response.

"So do you actually like him?" I asked. "Over and above all this class admiration you have for each other."

"Well, I don't know if I'm allowed to like him anymore," Mimi said. "But truthfully, he's an educated, intelligent, and very nice man. So, label that as you will."

"Don't worry," I said dubiously. "I will."

"Don't be like that," Mimi said. "Sit down, I have something to ask you. Well, tell you. Two things, in fact."

"Mimi, I don't have a lot of time, really." I stayed standing. "What is so important?"

"First, I was telling Virginia here about your misophonia, and she found it fascinating."

"Oh, you were? I hope that's all you told her."

"Oh, we both know there's plenty more, and far more interesting things, I could divulge." Mimi said it with a grin and a wink.

Virginia Hall straightened up and her eyes widened at this news. "Oh, is that so?"

It most certainly was so. Mimi knew everything, but as annoyed as I was she'd blabbed about my misophonia, I couldn't believe she'd say much more.

Mimi laughed, and I grumbled, "What ever happened to patient confidentiality?"

Mimi waved that concept away with one hand. "That's for patients who pay. It's also for recognized conditions, which yours is not. Anyway, Virginia had a great idea, something that I thought I could add into a paper I'm writing about the condition."

"You're writing a paper about it?"

"Yes, I didn't tell you?"

"No, you haven't mentioned that. I trust you don't mention my name?"

"Of course not, Henri. And if I didn't tell you, it's because you've been busy, as you keep reminding me."

"The world burns, but Princess Marie Bonaparte is writing a paper about misophonia." I shook my head but couldn't help but smile. I couldn't really complain—in the last war, I was sleeping, eating, and living in mud, whereas in this one I had a warm bed every night and hot food every day. What right did I have to judge her?

"The world continues to turn, Henri," Mimi said firmly. "When this is all over, medicine will still need its advances, science will still need its research."

"Stop it," I said, holding up my hands in surrender. She was starting to sound like Andreas von Rauch. "What is your point?"

"That you need a hearing test."

"My hearing is fine."

"Right."

I cocked my head. "Then why in the world would I need a hearing test?"

"Because it might be much better than fine."

"Mimi." I took a breath and controlled my blood pressure.

"I really am pressed for time. Please, I beg of you, explain briefly and simply what the hell you are talking about."

"Virginia wondered, and I agree, whether part of your sensitivity to sound might be that you have exceptional hearing."

"Considering I spent the better part of a year having shells explode beside my head, that seems unlikely," I pointed out.

"But that's why we're doing the test. We need to see how your hearing measures up, to rule it out or in. Either way, your hearing level is relevant to your sensitivity to sound. That makes sense, yes?"

"I don't want to do a hearing test."

"Why on earth not?"

"Because I'm not a lab rat."

"No one said you were, Henri."

"You don't have to say it, you just have to treat me like one. You know, by arranging for tests without asking my permission."

"Henri." Virginia Hall fixed me with a look that I couldn't resist, one that I'm pretty sure she knew I couldn't resist. "It will take maybe ten minutes, and I promise we will arrange everything so there is no inconvenience to you at all."

"Apart from ten minutes of my time." And those words sounded as pathetic coming out of my mouth as they looked in retrospect. Virginia didn't even both responding, she just smiled, knowing she'd won the game, set, and match for Mimi. I dragged my eyes away from her face, refocused them on my watch, and cleared my throat.

"There were two things you wanted to tell me." I looked at Mimi. "The second one was what?"

"About the children."

My stomach dropped. I didn't have time for this but I had

Mimi, Nicola, Virginia, and a nagging sense something was actually going on working against my desire to ignore the issue, in favor of working the murder cases.

"Let me guess. Another child was taken away?"

"No," Mimi said. "One of the ones taken before made contact."

"What do you mean 'made contact'? That sounds very dramatic."

"It was." Her eyes dropped, and then her head did. She took a breath and looked up at me again. "A boy, Alain. He's twelve and the last one to disappear. He telephoned, I don't know how, but he managed to get through to a number we'd given all the children in case they were taken."

"What did he say?"

"Not much. Not much at all."

"He just managed to say where he was," Virginia said, her voice soft and sad. "The city he was calling from, anyway."

I don't know how I knew, or why I knew, or if I knew at all. It may have been nothing more than a lucky guess. But only one city came to mind when she said that, and so I said it out loud and watched as their eyes widened and they both nodded, letting me know that I was right.

"He was calling from Rennes, wasn't he?" I asked.

CHAPTER EIGHTEEN

Friday, December 6, 1940

The next morning, Mimi's door opened just as I was coming down the stairs. A head poked out and looked up at me, and it wasn't the head I expected.

"Miss Ha— Virginia. Good morning, how are you?" I doffed my hat and, frankly, rather enjoyed the look of surprise and embarrassment on her face.

"Henri, *bonjour.*" She stepped onto the landing and closed the door behind her. "I was just leaving for work."

"It's early."

"I enjoy Mimi's company," she said, her head high and her eyes holding mine. "So we stayed up late talking and she offered me her spare room."

"She does like to talk, I can vouch for that." Whatever embarrassment she had felt was gone, and I couldn't care less where she slept. Well, that was not entirely true, as it'd entered my mind that I myself might enjoy a long and late night with Virginia Hall. *Is that out of the question?* I wondered for a second, before reassuring myself with another thought. *Too soon to say, let's not rush to judgment.*

"I'll walk with you for a bit," she said, and we started down the stairs.

"I'd like that. In the old days I'd have offered to buy you breakfast, but we'd spend until lunch finding somewhere that was both open and that had something worth eating."

Outside, she walked close to me in the dark, and I liked it. For a moment, until I realized she had an ulterior motive.

"You know, I started making some calls about those missing children," she said, her voice low in case the few passersby, or a large pair of ears at an open window, might hear. "I really think there may be something to it."

"Then you will be delighted with my morning agenda," I said with a smile.

"What do you mean?"

I had no reason *not* to go to Rennes, and five reasons I did have to: two train tickets, plus Mimi, Nicola, and Virginia. Well, six reasons if you included avoiding talking to Nicola, which I most certainly did. I'd intentionally focused conversation on my misophonia, the suggested hearing test, and the missing kids, simply because I still hadn't decided which of my two reasons for Daniel's lying was most likely. And while talking to her, or especially him, might have resolved that question I wasn't ready to do either. Easier right now to focus my efforts on a place that seemed to be calling to me from every direction: Rennes.

"Seems like if there's actually something happening," I said, "then it's not just happening here in Paris."

"Agreed," she said. "Does that mean . . . ?"

"I don't even need a ticket," I said cheerfully. "Police credentials work very well these days; people are particularly respectful of authority. Well, mostly."

"You're going to Rennes now? Oh, that's wonderful. Mimi will be delighted. Thank you, Henri."

"Just doing my job."

"Will you let me know if you find anything?"

"I'll even let you know if I don't."

Her smile was genuine and those watchful eyes seemed to sparkle in the low light, and while Mimi had the advantage of a spare room, I bet she'd not made her laugh. She leaned forward and gave me a peck on the cheek.

"Good luck, Henri. And thank you."

I watched her walk away, that carefully masked limp barely evident, and wondered why I was abandoning my usual type, small and pretty and not too much between the ears, for a strong American woman with a wooden foot. Unable to answer my own question, I set off for the Montparnasse train station and turned my mind to the business at hand.

A growing sense of foreboding pressed in on my chest as I walked. My change in mood wasn't helped by the start of a steady drizzle that dampened my face and turned my hat and coat into heavy slabs of concrete that weighed me down physically as well as mentally. Despite Virginia's delight, and my initial response to it, now something about leaving Paris, even for a day, seemed like a bad idea. Objectively speaking I didn't have the time, I knew that for sure, but more than that I felt like there were machinations in place that would keep spinning and whirling without me there to figure them out, making the case harder and harder to figure out, pushing the solution further from me.

Stepping into the cavernous station didn't help my mood, either. Normally, the press of bodies, the activity and excitement of travel, would lift my spirits, but the place felt more like a mausoleum than a place from where trips and adventures were launched. I'd never seen it so empty. And those who were here looked like they would rather not be.

When I reached the main concourse, a few men in dark suits and coats stood looking up at the large board showing arrivals and departures, the cities and times changing occasionally with a quiet *chck-chck-chck* that I usually found reassuring, but today seemed somehow sinister. Maybe it was the uniformed soldiers looking at me suspiciously through the clouds of cigarette smoke they were puffing out, or maybe it was the fact that everyone, including me, was looking at everyone else with darting eyes, but I needed a strong cup of coffee like never before.

Of course, the little café was ringed with gun-toting Boche, and I didn't fancy elbowing my way through them so I crammed my ticket into my pocket and went to my platform to wait in the cold morning air. The on-time arrival of my train did nothing to assuage my foul mood, because I knew it was down to good old (or new) German efficiency that it was there on time, and it'd be German efficiency that would have me leaving Paris and arriving in Rennes on time, too. An on-time train might seem like something to be thankful for, but a grumpy Frenchman needs something to grump about, and when he doesn't get it, well, what the hell is he supposed to do then?

Sure enough, the train rattled out of the station on the dot of eight as the schedule said it should, but instead of my mood darkening, the sway of the carriage, and perhaps the fact I was the only one in it, somehow made me begin to feel a little happier. I was a city man, for sure, but in happier times on occasion took an excursion to the countryside, usually with Nicola but sometimes with a willing *copine*, for a picnic or a visit to a winery or grand château. I liked to see the history of my country, breathe some fresh air, and get the grit out of my hair, my lungs. Not for too long, it didn't do to replace grit with pollen and ants, but a long weekend suited me well enough. I felt that little surge of the spirits then, as the train chugged past industrial lots and took me away from gray and featureless factories, giving me glimpses of blue sky overhead as we clanked west out of Paris, where even the grayness of the weather couldn't hide the greenness of the land.

I settled back in my seat and tried to formulate a plan for when, an hour and thirty minutes later, I got to Rennes. I knew that both of my corpses, Edouard Grabbin and Viktor Brandt, had visited the city, I assumed in some kind of homosexual assignation together. Which meant, with another assumption, a hotel. Presumably the one they'd been arguing about. They'd want somewhere close to the train station, somewhere that their money would be more important than their presence together. Nowhere expensive, nowhere they'd be remembered or recognized.

I hoped to hell they were wrong about that last bit.

As for the disappearing kids, I had a vague notion how to go about that. If there's one man who knows about the comings and goings of his town, no matter the size of it, it's the stationmaster. Failing that, I could check at the nearest hospital, since the other thing I knew for sure was that all three of the kids who'd been requisitioned like so much equipment had been disabled in some way.

And so, plan in place, I let my head lean against the worn padding behind it, and let my gaze fall into the deep green of the lush fields flitting past my rain-streaked window.

•   •   •

As it was the stationmaster's help I needed, it was less than ideal it was him that woke me up in Rennes. They had a station boy to clear the train but he'd seen the grip of my pistol poking out of my jacket and gotten scared. The stationmaster, a ruddy-faced, short man with onion breath, didn't look much less scared when he leaned into me and poked my shoulder with his whistle.

"Monsieur. Monsieur, you need to wake up. You are in Rennes."

I straightened my crumpled self and blinked some life into my eyes. "Yes, of course. Thank you."

He stood back and removed some of his breath from my comfort zone, a smile on his face now that he knew he'd woken a sleeping Frenchman and not a German. Either one could be grumpy, but one was more likely to be dangerous if so.

"You are a policeman?"

"Yes. And I think I need your help."

"Of course, whatever I can do. Perhaps you can come to my office, though, we need the train to be empty."

"Bien sûr." I got up and followed him, noting for no particular reason his gait. Despite being unusually short, he had oddly long legs and strode with the elegance of a tall man, such that I had to hurry to keep up. I wondered if, in a former life, he had perhaps been a spider. A cheerful one, though, especially since his office

turned out to be the left-luggage space. He perched on a particularly large leather trunk and spread his arms wide.

"Can you believe someone would ship this thing and not come
to claim it?"

"There is a war on, you know," I reminded him.

"Even so. A person's entire life could fit in here."

I didn't want to point out, I shouldn't have had to point out,
that in war people often lost their lives and so had no use for large
trunks in which to store a life's worth of possessions. So I just
agreed with him.

"There are two matters you can help me with," I said. That
seemed to please him greatly, so I continued. "Have you noticed
an influx, albeit a small one, of children coming in from Paris
being accompanied by . . ." I thought for a second about how to
phrase this, wanting to use words that would resonate with a
man like this. "Accompanied by men who seemed more like ad-
ministrators than parental types."

He didn't think for long, and his eyes rotated slowly upward
to meet mine. "Are you talking about the crippled children?"

"I am indeed." I gave him an encouraging smile. "You are very
observant."

"*Non, monsieur*, not particularly."

"But there have only been a handful, surely."

"From Paris, perhaps. But they have come from other cities,
from the countryside, too." He stared at the ceiling in thought.
"Thirty in all. Maybe more."

"Is that so?"

"It is so, yes." He smiled, looking immensely pleased with
himself. Which was perfectly reasonable, since I was immensely
pleased with him, too.

"Do you know why they are here?"

"Not officially, no."

"I'll take unofficially."

He leaned into me, and I saw a conspiratorial gleam in his eye. I also braced myself for his breath as I noticed his body odor and the thin layer of grime that caked his skin. What struck me in that moment wasn't the oddness of those things, because they weren't, not anymore. The oddness lay in me not minding, partly because I suspected I was less than spotless myself. The nation that had invented the finest perfumes, colognes, and soaps had not only been deprived of those luxuries, but was making do without their most basic counterparts. Our lives had shifted to a parallel track where what was once unacceptable was, just five months later, normal. Body odor and grimy skin. I tried to focus on what this man was saying.

"They say there's an ammunition factory here. They're using the kids to make bullets."

"That so?"

"*Oui*. Kids because they have little hands, quick and nimble fingers. And they like the disabled ones because they're easy to take, if they're wards of the state. And also, well, you know." He gave me a knowing look, but I had no idea what he was trying to convey.

"I really don't. What are you trying to tell me?"

"Well, it's against the rules of war, isn't it? To use kids like that as slave labor."

"I'm sure it is, yes. What's your point?"

"That's the irony of it. Because they're disabled it's not like they can escape and tell anyone, can they?"

It was a sickening irony, but not one I could argue with. "Do you know where this factory is? Or where they might be being kept?"

"That's the odd thing. No one seems to know where the factory is." He shrugged. "I've asked, on the quiet of course, but no one knows."

"I'm not surprised. Something like that, using children as slave labor, it makes sense they'd keep it secret. Plus an ammunitions plant—they'd definitely not want the location to be discovered. The British would be sure to target it if they found out."

"Ah, yes, I didn't think of that." He leaned back a little, and I was glad of the fresher air. "You might check the old hospital, about half a mile down avenue Foch. Due east."

"Why do you say that?"

"I walk past it to get here, just a lot of activity there, Germans. And the place was supposed to have been closed down. It's obvious they're using it for something and it's not suitable for medical purposes, so I wonder if it's some sort of dormitory or something for those poor children."

"Thank you, I'll check it out."

A shadow crept across his face. "Please, do not mention my name at all."

"Do not worry. I don't think I even know it."

"Oh, how rude. I didn't introduce myself, my name is—"

"Monsieur," I interrupted. "I know you only as someone who works at the train station. If you wish to remain anonymous, perhaps that's how we should leave it."

"Of course!" He slapped himself on the side of the head and grinned. "What am I thinking?"

The truth was, of course, you'd have to be completely blind or have a total and complete inability to describe your fellow human beings for this fellow to remain anonymous should the Nazis go to work on you with pliers or a blowtorch, but if it made him feel better I was all for the pretense.

He snapped his fingers. "You said there were two things I could help you with."

"Right, yes. The second is a little more, well, awkward."

"Awkward?"

"Delicate."

"Delicate?"

To stop him repeating every word I said, I went ahead and told him what I wanted, which I probably should have done in the first place. "Where in Rennes would a man go . . . where in Rennes would *two* men go if they wanted to spend some time together but didn't want to attract attention?"

"You mean, like for dinner? Because these days it's hard with ration cards and—"

"No, I don't. At all."

"Oh, you mean . . ." He craned his neck and looked behind me, as if expecting to see someone standing there. "Funny, you don't look like the type, and I didn't see anyone with you."

"Not me, you dolt." Maybe I would find out his name and give it to the Germans. Without them even asking. "In general. Is there a place known for being discreet? A club or a hotel?"

"For people like that?" He straightened himself to his full height of just under five feet. "I can assure you, I most certainly wouldn't know."

I stood and picked up my hat. "Thank you for your help." He put out his hand but I was already on my way, my mind on the long day ahead and my eyes looking for the exit and the signs for avenue Foch.

•   •   •

I found the run-down hospital easily enough, thanks to the make-shift repairs the Germans had made. Specifically, the oversize black-on-red swastika flags that hung across the front of the building, and flapped in the breeze on its roof.

Only the Nazis can make a dilapidated building look worse, I thought. They'd also staffed the place with a few more soldiers than I thought necessary for a mere children's dormitory, but maybe they cared more about the little ones than I imagined they would. I passed the building on the opposite side of the street, stopping to light a cigarette as I eyed the main entrance and pondered my potential approaches.

On the one hand, I could show my police credentials and make everything official, which the Germans typically loved. The one thing you could say about the Boche is that they respected authority and if you had the right badge, pass, certificate, or piece of paper, then you had access. Trouble was, I had no clue what piece of paper I needed to get into that building, and being a Frenchman anything I presented was automatically worth less than a German document. And once an official attempt at entry was made, my cover was blown and, if refused, the most I'd ever learn about this building was by standing in the street lighting cigarettes and looking through windows from afar.

My best bet, it seemed to me, was to make a surreptitious entrance. Find a side door and wander in with an innocent look on my face and my credentials close to hand should someone stumble across me and take umbrage at my presence. I set that plan in motion by ducking into avenue du Colombier, a smaller street that ran alongside the hospital and looked to have been where deliveries were once made, maybe the emergency entrance even. Now it was busier than I wanted it to be, but the ratio of German uniforms to plain clothes, nurses, and white coats was more to my advantage than at the front of the building so even though I slowed, I kept going. I caught my break when I spotted a young nurse wheeling a large man toward a ramp. I could see she was going to struggle, and the clipboard she had in her right hand was only going to make things worse, so I hurried over to her and gave them both my disarming smile as they got to the bottom of the ramp.

"Allow me, please," I said.

"Oh, that's very kind, thank you," the nurse said. The man turned his head my way a little and grunted.

"You know, I thought they'd shut this place down," I said as we made our way up the slope.

"They opened up the ground floor as a clinic," she said, then lowered her voice. "They didn't want us locals mixing with their soldiers in the main hospital."

"I bet they kept our doctors, though, eh?"

"The good ones." She frowned. "I come to make sure the two they sent over here don't start drinking until after lunch."

We were coming up to the entrance, and I was suddenly worried the two sentries by the front door were paying more attention than they should be.

"That's good of you. Say, I'm looking for a friend inside, but I'm not sure they want me poking about. Would you mind saying I'm helping you?"

"Happy to. Always glad to poke those bastards in the eye when I can. Is your friend injured?"

"Sort of." I wished I hadn't lied to her. If she came here often, maybe she'd seen something, knew something. But we were at the door and out of time for explanations.

"He's my assistant," the nurse said to the guards slowly in French. "I have a bad back, can't push."

One of the German soldiers translated for the other, and they both looked dubious. "He's not dressed like an assistant," the first one said.

"My regular didn't show up for work," my new friend said. "One of you probably arrested him. Or shot him. Look, I'm paying this one by the hour, so if you don't mind, I'd like him to get on with it."

They reluctantly moved aside and I wheeled the heavy man in as she held the door open for me. I thought I heard her whisper "assholes" as we went in, but it might just have been the *whoosh* of the door shutting.

The first floor was devoid of walls or furniture, presumably cleared out before some kind of planned demolition. Now, it was one large space that had been turned into a joke of a clinic. The patients and their caregivers waited on the east side of the building, to my right, and were called into makeshift examination rooms, except they weren't rooms at all. They were six square spaces made of sheets that may have been clean, but were gray and worn nonetheless. They afforded minimal visual privacy and, because we couldn't see what was happening inside, everyone listened extra hard and heard everything. This wasn't the place to come to discuss your anal warts or ask how to get rid of your secret lover's genital pustules.

Luckily for me there was enough hustle and bustle, enough distractions, that I was able to wander away from the waiting masses toward where the nurses were bringing in the meager supplies of bandages, which also happened to be where I spotted the door to the staircase. It was unlocked and opened at the first tug and, since no one yelled at me to stop, I went through and made my way slowly up, treading as lightly as I could.

The door to the next level was missing, so I peeked around the jamb but it was plain there'd be no point exploring. The place was a mess, and if anyone had set foot there in the last month I'd have been shocked. Spilled paint cans, split pieces of wood, piles of mattresses, and a musty smell tinged with old cigarette smoke, or new cigarette smoke and old armpit odors, that encouraged me not to linger. I headed up to the next floor, wondering if I was wasting my time, trying to think of a reason why one floor would be utterly abandoned and the next useful to someone.

Of course, I reminded myself that my mind didn't work in the same way as these fucking Germans' and that the sooner I stopped expecting it to, the better. I was still surprised when I found myself peering through the thick glass panel of the door on the very next floor, not able to see anything in particular but wondering a couple of things. First, why there was a door at all, and second, why it was freshly painted.

I pressed down on the handle and felt it give without so much as a click, which suggested to me it'd been newly installed. *In an old building like this, shouldn't it creak or catch or . . . something?*

I pushed the door open and stepped into a long hallway, one that stretched in both directions. The only other things I could see were doors, eight in all. Four to my right side, two on each side of the hallway, and the same to my left. *Very symmetrical,* I thought, *very neat. Who does that remind me of?*

The sound of footsteps coming up the stairs behind me set my heart to racing and I looked around for somewhere to secret myself. I moved to my right, and tried the first doorway but it was locked, I scurried to the next one and tried the door handle but again it was locked.

A third attempt saw me sliding quickly into what at first seemed like a storeroom. Filing cabinets lined the wall to my left and straight ahead, and I was curious to see that they looked new. I opened one drawer and it was empty, so I opened four more until one of them held just one file folder. I plucked it out and examined the front. It had a boy's name, Christophe Deluth, with his date of birth: August 12, 1930. I opened the folder. A photograph of Christophe was stapled to the inside of the folder's cover, and showed a child with a badly disfigured face. He had almost no nose, and his chin and cheekbones were far bigger than they should have been. He looked like someone had melted his face, stretched it around randomly, then handed it back. I felt sorry for him, and his wide-set eyes radiated sadness.

"Are you in this hospital, Christophe?" I whispered. A quick scan of the first page indicated he was, indeed. Admitted three weeks earlier, not for his facial disfigurement but for an unspecified mental condition. His address was listed, too, the kid was here all the way from Bordeaux. *Fairly certain they have hospitals there still. So why here?*

I looked through the remaining pages, but stopped cold when I came to the penultimate one, entitled AUTOPSY REPORT. It contained his measurements and details you'd expect, but what I didn't bank on seeing was the handwritten note that read: *Tolerance to pain—surprisingly low.*

What the hell did that mean? I looked for a manner and means of death but in that space the word TRAUMA was all that was typed. Not how exactly, just the vaguest possible word that described a thousand ways to die. The final page was untitled and handwritten in German, very poorly, and while I recognized a few words I couldn't string enough together to make sense of what I was reading. Maybe something about the brain. Didn't *Gerhin* mean "brain"?

I put Christophe's file back as I'd found it and opened up every other drawer, hoping to see something more definitive. I found six more folders in all, and each one looked like the first. That is to say, each contained a photo of a child with either mental or physical (or both) conditions, details of their condition, where they were from, the briefest of autopsy reports, and a scratchy, handwritten page that I couldn't properly decipher but that I was fairly sure had something to do with the child's brain.

As I put the last folder away and slid the file drawer closed I was still confused about what it all meant, but the rising sickness in my stomach was suggesting that something very wrong indeed was happening here. I was no doctor, and my German was more than rusty, but it seemed like none of these kids came to the hospital with life-threatening conditions. Yet they were all dead. My mind resisted the obvious, and hideous, conclusion but settled firmly on one thing: Mimi and Virginia had been right to be concerned about those missing kids. And that meant a huge shift in my own thinking: I wasn't just looking for a missing Boche and a murderer, I now had to find out exactly what the Germans at this hospital were doing. And maybe even stop it.

All seemed quiet outside the room, which I confirmed with an ear pressed to the door. After a good thirty seconds, I quickly opened it and stepped into the hallway, scanning both directions.

I'd just started to move toward the staircase when a door opened right behind me, and a German nurse stepped out. I knew she was German because she wore the stupid hat they made their nurses wear, and it matched the hideous mustache she'd not bothered to shave off, one that, even if a French woman had been so hirsute, she'd have had the decency to take a razor to. I didn't know if it was the lip hair or the head covering, but something had made her both bold and, well, the word "plucky" came oddly to mind, and she squared up to me and said something rapidly in German that I didn't begin to grasp.

"*Ich bin verloren,*" I said, which I hoped meant *I am lost*, but from the way she looked at me meant *I am a Volkswagen*. At that moment the door to the stairway opened and I saw a large man who, I gathered, didn't like the look of me talking to Nurse Grizzly. He said something I didn't catch, but he said it while wearing a German uniform and with one hand on his sidearm, so I listened as hard as I could, and repeated my lie to the nurse about being lost.

He broke into a trot and my protestations fell on deaf ears and by the time he got within ten feet of me his gun was in his hand. The nurse quickly stepped past me and took up her station behind his left shoulder. I was left standing with both hands in the air hoping like hell he wouldn't shoot.

It was at that moment a small boy on crutches appeared in the doorway of the room right next to me, turning us all into statues. Except our heads, of course, which slowly turned toward him. We took in the sight of him and he looked right back at us, at me first as I was closest, but he looked away because there was nothing about me to say who I was or what I was doing there. His glance at the nurse was brief, I presume, because he knew her and why she was there, and he could see that, despite the tension of the moment, she was unhurt.

Of most interest to me was the way he looked at the German. There were a dozen feelings and emotions tumbling through his mind and running across his face and through his eyes and I flatter myself that I read just about every one. The clearest and most obvious was fear, which I saw when the blood drained from the boy's face, although I could hardly fail to notice the speed with which that happened. But I noticed, too, the way his eyes narrowed and his lips tightened, which suggested the boy had spirit, and knew this soldier enough to hate him. And as we all stood still, I saw the lad shift his weight onto what seemed like his good foot, his left, adjust his grip on his crutches, and then take a look behind me.

Is he thinking of hightailing it? I wondered in that fleeting moment. *Really? A boy on crutches against a Boche with a gun? I like this kid!*

And then I saw the look in the soldier's eyes and the smirk that played on his lips, and I knew why the kid hated him. Those eyes were cold, dark, and empty, and the smirk was a promise to himself of something hugely unpleasant. Unpleasant for someone else, that is. I'd seen that look before, and always on the faces of the kind of men who enjoyed sinking their bayonets into the chests of teenage boys crying for their mothers as they lay wounded and bleeding in No-Man's Land, or into their backs as they crawled with torn and broken limbs, desperate to get to the safety of their trenches. Those devils, like this one, lived for war. Not so they could fight, no, the only men who fight in wars do so because they are told to by other people, and they only go along with it because they are too scared not to, or stupid to know better. No, men like this live to mop up around the edges like rats around a garbage dump feasting on rotten scraps. Worse than rats, though, because rats do it to survive and pricks like this one enjoy it.

The boy seemed to make up his mind, and in just the way I thought he would. With all his weight on his good leg he swung the crutch in his right hand up toward the German, swiping at his gun and knocking it from his hand. The kid then shoved his way past me and swung himself down the hallway as the soldier clasped his arm in pain, swearing.

"Alain, *non!*" The nurse scurried after him.

The German stooped to pick up his pistol, but I put my foot on it.

"*Sie können kein Kind erschießen,*" I said, hoping I'd found the right words to say *You can't shoot a kid!*

Still bent over, he swung a fist at my leg, landing a punch hard enough to make me move it, those black eyes now blazing hatred at me. He stood up, the pistol at hip height but leveled at my stomach. We both looked down the hall to see the boy, with the nurse right behind him, disappear through a doorway at the end that looked like a fire escape. I turned back to the German but when he spoke, it was in French. And that made sense when I took a second to think about it—he was a guard in a French hospital keeping an eye on French kids.

"He won't get far, he's a cripple on stairs. That half-witted nurse could stop him."

"Maybe, but he got the better of you."

"For a second."

"That's all he needed."

"He won't get far," the Boche sneered. "And it will be all the worse for him that he tried."

I didn't doubt it, looking at that spiteful visage and remembering the look on the boy's face earlier.

"Why is he here?" I asked.

He looked me up and down, and I could see his interest flipping from the kid to me.

"*Non*. Why are you here?"

"I got lost. I was helping downstairs and was looking for a bathroom. I got lost."

"You're a bad liar."

"Is there one on this floor?"

"One what?"

"A bathroom. All the doors were locked, and I still haven't found one."

"You're not looking for a bathroom. Why are you nosing around up here?"

"I told you."

His eyes narrowed as he considered his options. I hoped pulling the trigger wasn't one of them, and to my immediate relief a noise behind me took it off the menu. The fire escape door opened and an orderly in medical scrubs had our little escapee in a firm grip and was scooting him back along the hallway toward us. The nurse was trailing in their wake clucking and chirping like a distressed hen, and when I looked at the Boche a grin had settled on his face. He looked like the hungry rat that he was.

"There. Not far at all, just like I told you," he said quietly.

The orderly came to a halt by the door and, unless I was mistaken, put his body between the German and the boy.

"He changed his mind about leaving," the orderly said.

"I'm sure he did," the Boche snarled.

"I'll put him back in bed." The orderly didn't wait for an answer, steering the kid past the slavering Boche and into the room. The door swung shut, no doubt meager and temporary protection, but enough for the moment.

"He'll get his," the German said. "And I'm guessing you will, too. Who are you?"

"I should probably leave." I pointed to the way I'd come. "I was helping a nurse with her patient, they're probably done by now and need my help getting home."

"I asked you a quest—"

"He's a big fellow, needs my help getting in and out of—"

"Answer me!" he bellowed

I had about three seconds to think.

Three seconds to decide which way to play this.

Play one: bullshit him. Make up a name and try and talk my way out of this, which in that moment I felt had a low probability of success, and a high probability of failure. Failure in this situation, with this man, would not be pretty, of that I was fairly certain.

Play two: an appeal to authority. This man was a bully, and the only thing bullies accede to is power and authority. I am a policeman with a badge and a gun, working a case and here on official business. That is to be respected. At least in theory. This being a war, and one we'd just lost, turned everything upside down, but it was a better bet than me trying to bullshit, so I decided, in those three seconds, it was the better play. I just had to hope he thought so, too.

I drew myself up to my full six-feet-something height and spoke slowly and clearly.

"I am Detective Henri Lefort of the Paris police, murder squad. I am here investigating the disappearance and death of a German doctor, Viktor Brandt. I would therefore request that you holster your weapon and give me you full cooperation."

He looked at me for a moment, smiled, and said, "What a load of bullshit." Then he punched me full in the face.

CHAPTER NINETEEN

I woke up in a dark room, my wrists and ankles bound. Which was about all I knew for certain, other than that I was lying on my side on the floor. On one that had no carpet.

Fortunately, and I mean that loosely, my wrists were tied in front of me, so I was able to lever myself into a sitting position, and that's when I noticed the pain in my jaw. I worked it a little and while it hurt, the slow rolling movements I was able to pull off told me it wasn't broken.

The rope around my wrists was expertly tied such that my feeble attempts to get free merely resulted in the bonds becoming tighter, so I didn't bother messing with my ankles. Instead, I blinked and tried to get my eyes used to the dark but the most I could figure out was that I was in a room that was roughly a square that had windows on just one side that had been boarded up. I had no idea what floor I was on, or if I was even in the same building where that Boche had knocked me out. Which made me wonder what he'd done next. . . . I patted myself down as best I could, and . . . *Merde.* My gun and police credentials were missing.

I dragged my sorry self to what I assumed to be the nearest wall and propped myself against it like the sack of potatoes I was. I couldn't think of anything else to do but wait. Someone, at some point, would want to talk to me about why I was there. Surely.

It may have been thirty minutes, or maybe an hour, but eventually I heard voices and footsteps. My heart started beating faster, which it had learned to do on its own accord lately when my ears picked up the sound of these particular footsteps. German boots, you see, make a fairly distinctive sound, or maybe it's the way the men wearing them are taught to march. Either way, when you're downwind of a pair of them coming your way your body has a way of wanting to warn you to show a clean pair of your own heels. Unfortunately, mine were strapped together so I'd just have to hope that for once the owner of these jackboots was coming in with a friendly smile and some good news. Maybe an apology and a late lunch.

A key went into a lock opposite me and when the door swung open I turned my head and closed my eyes against the light that filled the space around me. When I was finally able to peer through cracked eyelids, I saw two men in black SS uniforms standing over me. One was tall and wiry, the other was short, stocky, built like a boxer. And he looked like he wanted to punch me.

"I am Sturmbannführer Paul Ziegler." The short one spoke in French. "What is your name?"

"You have my police credentials, you know my name."

"How do we know you didn't steal them?" Surprisingly good French, as it happened.

"Why would I do that?"

"For many reasons. To snoop around here, for one."

"Why would I want to snoop around here?"

"You ask a lot of questions for a man tied up on the floor."

"Well, I am a policeman." I gave him my most disarming grin.

"So you say. Why are you here?"

"I am investigating a case."

"What case?"

"A doctor went missing, then turned up dead. I was asked to look into it."

"In Rennes?"

"No, in Paris."

"Then I ask you again, why are you here? In this hospital, in Rennes?"

"It's a long story, but I should let you know that I was assigned this case by a man named Stefan Becker. One of your lot."

Ziegler muttered something in German to his friend and a moment later I was on my feet and then off them again, only to find out why my hands had been tied in front of me: the rope was being looped over a hook in the ceiling that the darkness had hidden from me. My toes just about touched the floor, so I had to stay completely still to maintain my balance, once I'd found it.

"You are better at asking questions than answering them," my inquisitor said. "Let me help you with that."

"Wait! This Gestapo man, Stefan Becker, you should talk—"

He disagreed, however, and let me know by sinking his fist into my stomach with enough force to bring my knees halfway to my chest. He walked slow circles around me as I gasped for air, and I must have taken a full three minutes to unwind enough to get a toe back on the floor to stop myself swinging from the ceiling like a chicken in a butcher's shop. Sweat beaded my forehead and my wrists burned from the rope but more than anything I wanted to avoid another blow from that man's fist.

"*Monsieur, s'il-vous plait.* I will answer your questions. I just wish you would understand I am working to solve the murder of one of your colleagues."

"I don't have any colleagues who are . . . *were* doctors in Paris."

Right. Every Nazi for himself.

"Understood. I am here because the dead man came to Rennes. I think with another man." *Merde. This is where it gets awkward.*

"Another man? To do what?"

"I'm not sure. That's why I came here. To find out."

"What do you suspect? You must have some idea."

"I thought perhaps it was some secret assignation."

"'Secret assignation'?" He looked genuinely perplexed. "This other man, he was French?"

"Yes. Also a doctor."

"So you think they came here to the hospital for what? Some kind of spying, is that what you're suggesting?"

No, but thanks for the lifeline. "Possibly, yes. I just don't know, Herr Ziegler."

"When was this?"

"About a week ago."

"That recently." He shook his head emphatically. "Then you are lying." Without warning he hit me again, right under the solar plexus, and every molecule of oxygen left my body. I thought I was about to die on that hook, not just fail in my mission but actually be beaten to death, all because I couldn't talk some sense into this *mec*.

"Why do you say I'm lying?" I eventually managed to gasp.

"We've had this place locked down for two weeks. I know everyone who makes it past the first floor." He grinned, but there was little mirth in it. "Which is why you're here."

"Then they went somewhere else. I don't know where. But please—" He raised a fist and I winced and withdrew into myself as best I could, but he didn't hit me again.

"Tell me about the person who was murdered."

I tried to get my mind straight but my ribs and stomach felt swollen and bruised, and my arms ached.

"Can you let me down, please. I won't try to get away. You have my word."

Ziegler smirked. "I don't need your word. Try anything and I'll shoot you in the gut and leave you here to die. Know what it's like to die from a gut shot?"

"I fought in the last war."

"So, you do." He nodded to his silent partner and they lifted me off that damned hook and unceremoniously dumped me on the floor. Which, under the circumstances, I didn't mind in the least. "Killed some Germans, did you?"

"Not enough." My bad habit of speaking before thinking, but he just smiled.

"So, this doctor who was killed. The name?"

"Brandt," I said. "Viktor Brandt."

He tried not to show it, but it was like I'd rung a loud bell in the room. Ziegler glanced at his friend, just a flick of the eyes, and muttered something I didn't catch.

"Tell me what happened to him," Ziegler said.

I told him what I knew, leaning heavily on the facts and dancing around my suspicions about his romantic inclinations because from what I knew Germans went big on shows of moral indignation and having been suspended from that hook in the ceiling once I didn't fancy setting this SS character off by outright labeling his fellow countryman a homosexual. The problem was, Ziegler wasn't an idiot and I'm not a good dancer so he spotted my clumsy attempts at a waltz right away.

"You think he and that Grabbot man—"

"Grabbin."

"Grabbin, whatever, you think the two of them came here to have a secret rendezvous, is that it?"

Much to my surprise, he was amused, not annoyed, but I glanced up at the hook anyway, just to make sure I wasn't getting any closer to it without me realizing.

"You want to tell me why I'm wrong?" I asked.

"You're the detective, not me. But I'll tell you one thing: if that's your theory, I don't hold out much hope for you solving the case."

He slid a long thin knife from a sheath on his belt and, as I held my breath and stared at the blade, cut the rope from my wrists and ankles.

"*Merci*," I said. "You seem to know Viktor Brandt. What can you tell me about him?"

"*Moi? Non.* I never met the man." He sheathed his knife just as someone knocked on the door. Ziegler went to it and cracked it open. He exchanged words with someone in German, some-one who handed him a paper bag. He then came over to me and dropped the bag in my lap, and my balls told me there was something fairly heavy in there. "It seems you are who you say you are, and you are doing what you say you are doing."

"Imagine that."

"Oh, it's quite a rarity these days, believe me," Ziegler said lightly.

I looked inside the bag and saw my gun and police credentials inside. "Ah, my old friends."

"Indeed. Now then, take your old friends and get out of here, if you please."

"I was hoping that before I do you could tell me where the hell I am."

"You're in the same building you trespassed in. Sixth floor."

"You're sure you don't want to tell me what you know about Viktor Brandt?"

"The only thing I'm sure of is the choice you face. You can take the stairs out of here, go straight to the station, make your way back to Paris on the next train and not come back. Or, you can stay here in Rennes and continue to investigate, but if you cross my path one more time I will hang you back up on that hook and beat you to death with my fists."

"I see." I took my gun from the bag and tucked it into its holster, then put my credentials away in my inside jacket pocket. "In that case, if you would kindly point me toward the stairs I would be most grateful."

•   •   •

The train station was busier than when I'd passed through a couple of hours earlier, and I was thankful for that because for some reason I didn't want to see the smug, irritating face of the stationmaster. What I did want to do was have a cup of coffee, lick my wounds, and spend a few minutes thinking about what to do next. My train didn't leave for forty minutes so I had time to do all three, and I managed to find an empty chair away from the clusters of German soldiers who seemed to populate all of the train station cafés these days.

The first thing I thought about was those children, the sad and scared faces of half a dozen boys and girls who'd come to Rennes alive, but died in that hospital. At least that was my assumption, given my experience there and the way the place emanated evil. I resolved to talk to my boss about it, get a larger investigation going, because not only was I just one man but I was a man who was extremely unwelcome at the Rennes hospital. That decision made, I turned my mind to the other reason I came to the city.

Despite the pummeling, I'd gained some interesting information from my Nazi friend Ziegler, but I didn't know what to do with it. You would think that, in a murder investigation, gathering new information would be a good thing, something valuable. Mostly it is, but sometimes it's not. Imagine a mechanic working on a broken engine. It's helpful when someone hands him a tool, yes, but when someone hands him the wrong tool, or a broken tool, he then has to figure out what to do with it. Put it down? Use it in some different way?

So it was with the information I'd gleaned from Ziegler: that he knew Viktor Brandt. More than that—Viktor Brandt had something to do with the hospital. I was certain of that for two reasons. First, Ziegler wanted me out of there fast, and for good. Why? Because, I believed, he knew that if I stayed and asked questions, I'd find people who knew Brandt. Second, Ziegler was positive Brandt hadn't been at the hospital with Grabbin that week. If he *had* been there, Ziegler would have known. But how would Ziegler know that if he wasn't familiar with Brandt, and Brandt wasn't familiar with the hospital? Or maybe Ziegler had flat out lied to me.

Either way, Brandt and the hospital are definitely connected, I thought. *But how, and why? By those children?*

I sipped my coffee, trying to ignore the thinness of it. Café owners were doing what everyone else was doing at home: reusing coffee grounds to make three, four, and five cups of coffee. The Boche got the fresh grounds, while saps like me got the soggy leftovers. The spoils of war aren't just gold, art, and land. The victorious get the smaller spoils, too, the coffee and the butter, the silk hosiery and the shoe leather, the paper and the pencils.

I dragged my wandering mind back to the present. The machinery of this case was still broken and the ill-fitting wrench that had been handed to me by Ziegler had value, even if I couldn't see it yet.

Wait a minute! I thumped the table and my watery coffee jumped up from my cup and then back down into it, as if too weak to even make it out onto the table. I realized I was looking at this wrong. Brandt and Grabbin weren't homosexual lovers. Or maybe they were, but that's not why they were in Rennes. They were here for the same reason the children were.

I needed to ask Stefan Becker about that ammunition factory, get some answers from those damn Germans and not let them stonewall me. If they wanted to know who killed their man, they needed to work with me, not against me.

But first I needed to find out more about Edouard Grabbin, and that meant a visit to his brother Jean. This time I wouldn't take no for an answer. I needed to know what the hell was going on at that funeral, how the dead man knew Brandt, and exactly

THE DARK EDGE OF NIGHT

what his job was at the hospital. Also what happened between him and Brandt at Club Monocle. And if I had to stand on the retired doctor's neck to get some answers, well, then that's what I was going to do.

After all, in this investigation my own neck was very much on the line, and so far I'd been lied to by my own junior officer, knocked unconscious, hung from a hook, and pummeled by an SS officer. It was more than clear by now that I was playing a dirty game, one where no one else was following the rules, so if they weren't, why should I?

Time for me to roll up my sleeves and not worry too much about how dirty my hands got.

CHAPTER TWENTY

It was late afternoon by the time I found myself in front of Jean Grabbin's building. Heavy clouds lumbered across a darkening sky above me, both matching my mood, and none of it boding well for Grabbin's neck should he decide not to cooperate. My dark humor wasn't helped by the recently repainted hospital wagon that almost flattened me as it pulled away from the curb on Grabbin's street. I was sorely tempted to use my service revolver to remove the brains of the reckless driver, but he must have sensed my fury because he was already ducking out of the line of fire as he roared past me, so all I could do was throw some choice curse words his way. And while I might normally appreciate the irony of my almost-demise under the wheels of one of Paris's few remaining functioning ambulances, the weather and my recent experience of dangling from a hook suffocated any hint of that.

The door to Grabbin's courtyard was open, which annoyed me because apparently even good luck was annoying me now. I sidled up to the front of his home and tried peering through the windows to see if he was in, but they were too grimy and it was dark enough inside so I saw nothing. I banged on his door loud enough to wake the dead and waited impatiently.

A minute later I banged again, even louder, and kicked the base of the door when he failed to respond. The glass panel in the door responded a little more promptly, but then again my elbow was more persuasive than my fist, but the key was missing from the lock so I had to smash out the other glass panel and the wooden cross beam between them, and then drag myself through the top half of the door, to get myself inside. All with my gun in my hand in case Grabbin heard the ruckus and came at me with a frying pan.

He didn't, however, so once I'd collected myself I put on a few lights and started poking around. I didn't find much of anything in the kitchen, nor the living room, but from the state of the fireplace it looked like no one had been home for at least a day. The ash was piled high but there were no embers still glowing, and in my experience that took twenty-four hours, maybe a little longer. And it was definitely cold in there. I pulled my coat tighter around me and made my way to the back of the apartment, where a bathroom separated two bedrooms.

The bathroom itself was tidy enough, and from what I could see contained enough medicine, lotions, and potions to sustain one man. If Edouard had been living here some of the time I might have expected to see more, but then again maybe Jean had thrown everything of his out already.

If he'd been that quick to bury his brother's body, why would he hang on to his brother's cologne and toothpaste?

I checked the bedroom to my left, pushing the door open with my foot and holding my gun in front of me. It was empty and, once I saw inside, I guessed it to be the smaller of the two bedrooms, and therefore Edouard's when he lived there. But, like the bathroom, there was no evidence anyone had lived in it recently.

Hurriedly cleaned out again? Odd for sure, but consistent with the quick funeral.

I spun around at the sound of footsteps and raised my gun, my grip tightening, my senses heightened.

"Monsieur Grabbin?" I called out. "This is Detective Lefort, Paris police. Are you in here?" I moved forward slowly, the low light in the apartment playing tricks on my nerves. "Monsieur Grabbin, are you here? Don't play games, I am armed and I don't want to shoot you by mistake."

The footsteps again, heavier this time, but now I could tell they were right above my head. I took a deep breath and calmed my fast-beating heart. I lowered my gun, but not all the way because I still felt like something was wrong here.

The hallway floor creaked under my feet as I made my way to what had to be Grabbin's bedroom door, which was fully closed. I don't know why, but I knocked gently on it, as if there was a chance he was engaged in some act of lovemaking or other delicacy I ought to respect, and I needed to give him a moment to extricate himself from. But it wasn't that, not really. When you've done this job as long as I have, no, not even this job. When you've been around death as long as I have, when you've seen it coming, seen it pass by and take people, then you learn to recognize the shadow it leaves, the vacuum it creates. I knocked on that door not so Monsieur Grabbin could prepare himself for who was on the outside, but so I could prepare myself for what was inside.

I was not wrong.

I opened the door slowly, the porcelain knob cold in my hand, and at first all I saw was a large bed against the far wall, neatly made up with a tautly stretched blue bedspread and two plump white pillows, pristine against a dark bedhead. The room had one window, a surprisingly large one for a ground-floor apartment, and it would have been dark inside but for the rising moon that was framed by it.

It was a surreal image, the moon in the window, which was maybe why it would later make me think of a painter's easel, capturing light so brilliantly and casting it carefully over what I saw next, which was also surreal. The body in the corner on the other side of the bed, which I saw in rough strokes, but clear enough that I could make out a bald head and a blue shirt. Two open, staring eyes looking at me across the room, I could see those eyes wide with recrimination, as if wondering why I hadn't come earlier, why I hadn't come in time.

He'd been shot twice in the chest, I saw that as I rounded the end of the bed. His eyes seemed to slip away from me as I got closer, as if he couldn't bear to look at me anymore. I bent over him and touched his cheek and his papery skin was stone-cold, not that I expected anything else. Generally speaking, I was skeptical of anyone claiming to be able to tell how long a man had been dead unless they'd heard his heart stop beating and sat there with a stopwatch. There were too many factors to consider, too many assumptions, and once a man had gone cold it was nothing but a fool's game. The best you could do was find out when he'd last been seen alive and hope the killer had been stupid enough to stomp on his watch or put a bullet through the family's grandfather clock.

With that thought I looked at Grabbin's wrist. His watch was still ticking merrily away, sadly, unlike his heart. I touched the blood on his jacket, trying to make as much sense of this as I could, and it was dry so I knew he'd not been killed particularly recently. And look at that—he was wearing a jacket, in his bedroom. That told me something, too, I just wasn't entirely sure what yet. I looked over the rest of his body, from the damp cuffs of his trousers to the mud caked on his shoes, and I began to have a very vague sense of what might possibly have happened. Not *why*, I had no idea why, but if I was asked about a sequence of events that fit the physical evidence in front of me, I could probably just about manage that. I poked at the blood around the bullet holes, not just on the clothing but closer to the wounds, which had also dried, so I could properly begin at that guessing game I so derided.

I did that because I didn't know what else to do.

Maybe one more sweep of the apartment? I thought, tiredness suddenly hitting me hard. *Then get the reinforcements in.*

I walked around the bedroom, nosed through a chest of drawers and a closet, finding nothing. The spare bedroom turned up nothing as well, perhaps because I hoped it would. The living room, too, seemed as normal as a single man's living room could be.

Grabbin's bookcase caught my eye. Not for any reason other than I think you can tell a lot about a person by the spines they line up on a bookcase. Jean Grabbin's taste ran narrow, staying with his professional field and nothing that grabbed my eye or suggested anything particularly sinister. The only books that weren't expressly medical were ornithological, which I found somehow charming. Equally charming was the way the old man had meticulously arranged the books, not by author or subject as a librarian might have done to make them easier to find. No, these had been stowed by size and color, so that when you stood back and looked at the bookcase, the spines almost flowed together in a pleasing drift of undulating and gently changing color.

The only slight interruption in that flow was a thin, box-shaped folder that looked like some I'd seen at doctor's offices and hospitals to keep medical files. It was three-quarters along the top shelf and matched the color sequencing of Grabbin's filing system quite nicely, it only caught my eye because it wasn't a book. Also because nothing else in that place had caught my eye, and I was getting desperate.

I reached up and pulled it down, resting it on a side table so I could open it up and have a look at its contents. I was right, it was definitely for medical documents. The first set were, perhaps unsurprisingly, for his brother, Edouard. I looked closer and blinked, trying to clear my mind, unsure of what I was seeing. I started at the top of the document, his death certificate, and reread his name to make sure I was getting this right. The date of birth was correct, too, as best I could recall. The address was correct, too, the place his body had been found.

But two things on this form confounded me. The first was how he died, which was listed on this document as "natural causes." The second was the fact that the certificate, which clearly hadn't been issued recently, bore the date of, and had been officially stamped on, April 12, 1940.

According to this, Edouard Grabbin, the man who'd been found freshly murdered less than a week ago, had been dead for more than six months. And now the only man who might explain what the hell was going on, at least the only man I knew of, was propped up in the corner of his bedroom, dead as a doornail and staring into infinity with two bullets in his heart.

Of course, his killer probably had a fair idea of what the hell was afoot, but I didn't know who he was, where he was, and presumed he wasn't about to stick his head through the door and offer any insightful hints to set me on the righteous path to solving this case. Murderers are rarely that helpful, in my experience.

Almost as confounding were the other death certificates sitting beneath the one belonging to Edouard Grabbin. They were of three boys aged nine, twelve, and fourteen, all from Paris and, as best I could tell, none were relatives of Grabbin's. They were also much more recent, days old, in fact.

And they bore stamps I'd not seen before, heavy red lettering: *A-T4.*

What the hell does that mean? And who were these boys? I wondered if there was some connection to Rennes, but there was nothing on the certificates about the city.

I needed to look around more closely this time, because if Jean Grabbin had these he may have kept something else. Moving much more slowly than before, I scoured the ground floor of his apartment. Not only did I have a good reason to be looking—well, several good reasons—but I didn't have the pressure of worrying someone might be lurking inside ready to jump me. Grabbin's jumping days were done, poor fellow, and while I needed to report his death I also needed to make sure that if there was something to find here, I found it before the many heavy-footed *flics* of the Paris police stomping through this scene messed the place up.

It was close to the front door that I finally found something that aroused my suspicions. It was the floorboards around an armoire. I'd opened it up to find it completely empty, which itself seemed strange, considering how many books and other odds and ends Grabbin had throughout the apartment. While pondering why he'd want an empty armoire, I'd poked at it with my toe absentmindedly and, looking down, seen how scratched up the floor was. I put my hands against the piece of furniture and rocked it back and forth, and with some effort managed to move it a little.

Was it left empty so he could do that? That explains the scratched-up floor . . .

I didn't have any better ideas, so I huffed a little and puffed a little more until I'd pushed the damn thing aside, and to my great satisfaction revealed a doorway.

Well, well, well . . .

I tried the handle and it opened inward without so much as a squeak. A well-used doorway, I concluded, with a staircase leading down to a cellar, which was a rarity in buildings like this, but by no means unheard of.

I started slowly down the steps, hoping there was a light down there because the meager light from the upstairs apartment barely made a dent in the stairway. By the time I got to the bottom, my eyes could barely see past my nose, which itself was busy dealing with the odor of damp, and the smell of something else. Formaldehyde, perhaps? Maybe mixed with bleach. . . .

At the base of the stairs, I paused to let my eyes slowly adjust to the pitch blackness. Beside me, a table slowly took shape, and on it I saw a box of matches. When I lit one the flame revealed a block of wood bearing a row of four stocky candles, which I lit, one by one. Like a chain reaction, the lighting of these showed me half a dozen candelabras sitting on sturdy benches set against the brick walls of the cellar, the only method of lighting down here.

As I lit them all, my breath puffed out in clouds in front of me and I was suddenly aware of how cold it was down there.

I became suddenly aware, too, of three wooden boxes on the low wooden table in the middle of the room, wooden boxes that looked a lot like coffins, each covered with a white sheet. A candle in hand, I moved toward one of the boxes and paused for a moment, then lifted the sheet and looked down on the pale, dead face of a young boy. I felt the blood drain from my own face as I stared down at the gray, dead child, his eyes half open still. I couldn't tell how he'd died but someone had operated on his skull and crudely, very crudely, sewn his scalp back into place. With a rising sense of dread and horror, I pulled the sheet back over him and checked the other two boxes, seeing the same thing. I had to take a moment to steady myself, pull myself back into the moment, and so I soothed myself with slow breathing, the way Mimi had taught me to deal with my misophonia.

Slowly I regained my composure and reminded myself why I was there, my mission all the more important after this hideous discovery. Knowing I'd found the bodies that belonged to the death certificates, I stood in that cold, damp cellar shaking my head, none the wiser, and asking myself the same question, over and over.

What in the name of all that's holy is going on here? Is Jean Grabbin . . . Was Jean Grabbin some kind of sick child murderer, kidnapping and killing children in his secret dungeon?

Except murderers don't bother with death certificates. I made my way upstairs and looked at the official documents again, at the causes of death. Like Edouard Grabbin's, they said, "Natural causes." I wondered if this meant they were unrelated to the Rennes children, whose stated cause of death was "trauma."

None of this was making sense, but I couldn't sit around here and pontificate. I had to report Grabbin's death and the finding of these children. Seeing their actual bodies would strengthen my claim for a proper investigation into the Rennes hospital. Or so I hoped. I also hoped that someone at the Préfecture would know what A-T4 meant.

As I trudged up the stairs I pondered the matter of Edouard Grabbin. If he died in April, which would explain why he'd not written in his diary for eight months, then who the hell did they bury yesterday? Assuming there was anyone in the casket at all . . . My head was swimming at all the loose ends. I'd never seen an investigation like it, where every time I made a discovery it made the case *more* confusing. I took a deep breath and decided that the best thing to do was to go home and sit down with the person I trusted the most, to go over what I knew and didn't know with Nicola and decide how to proceed after talking to her. It wasn't just that she was the smartest person I knew, though she was, she also brought out the best in me.

With that plan in mind, I made my way to the small police station that was between Grabbin's apartment and mine, and sent a very unhappy young *flic* to stand watch and make sure the dead man's home was not further violated until I returned in the morning. That done, I set off at a tired but contented clip for rue Jacob, where I was sure of a warm meal, a full glass of wine, and a patient ear.

And maybe, if I was lucky, a signpost or two to send me in the right direction toward solving this damn case because I was more than aware of the ticking clock and the grinning Gestapo ape who'd be more than happy for me to fail and see me swing for that failure. Those bastards had tried that little ruse before, though, and had come up short, so I set my jaw and quickened my step because if anyone was going to swing it was the bastard who was littering my city with bodies, *not* this poor, tired sap trying to find that killer.

CHAPTER TWENTY-ONE

The aroma of soup hit me the moment I walked in the door, and nothing had ever smelled as good.

"There's half a sandwich to go with it," Nicola said. "I had to choose whether to add the ham to the soup or the half sandwich, I hope I chose right."

"Judging by the smell, you did. *Merci*, I'm famished." I shot her an anxious look. "Nothing crunchy in there?"

"Yes, some celery. But I ate mine already, so you're safe." She put a hand on my face as I ladled the thin, lumpy broth into a bowl. "*Cheri*, you look terrible."

"You'd look terrible if you'd been hung from a hook and punched in the gut."

"The gut? Then what happened to your face?"

"That was another one of them. He went first then two others hung me from a hook and punched me in the gut."

"You need to learn how to fight, Henri."

"Thanks for the sympathy."

"I made you soup and a sandwich, that's better than sympathy."

"Half a sandwich."

"Don't be ungrateful."

I smiled and kissed the top of her head, because I really wasn't. "Do we have wine? That's better than both."

"Actually, we do. Mimi dropped off a whole case earlier."

I groaned. "Oh no."

"What do you mean, 'Oh no'?"

"A whole case? That means she wants something in return."

"Henri, you're terrible. She's a good friend who—"

"No, no." I wagged a silencing finger. "A bottle or three, she does that because we're friends. A whole case? She wants a favor."

"She hasn't asked for a thing. Not one thing."

"*Merde.* That's even worse."

"How can that be worse?"

"Because it means she wants the favor from me." I collapsed back in my chair. "And I'm too tired for that, even if I had the time. Which I don't."

"I still say she's just being nice. And even if not, you can always say no, it's not like she'll ask for the wine back." She popped the cork from a bottle and poured me a glass.

"She can't if we drink it all."

"True." Nicola laughed. "Are you working tomorrow?"

"Always. Can we talk about the case? I need to pick your brain."

"Of course, you know I love to help."

"*Merci.*"

I dug into the sandwich, almost inhaling it, sending the vegetable soup after it with equal gusto as we talked. Not great manners, I knew, and if someone else with misophonia had been in the room they'd have choked me to death.

"I don't suppose you've see the symbol 'A-T4' stamped on anything? It's German, I saw it on some death certificates and need to know what it means."

"Never heard of it," Nicola said. "But I can ask around. That's the kind of thing Mimi or Virginia might know about."

"You're best friends now, the three of you?" I asked, smiling.

"Hush up and eat." She ignored the barb. "And drink more wine."

"Good idea." I took a sip and immediately felt calmer, more relaxed. I thought about where to start, but the realization rose within me that I needed to talk to her about Moulin, too, because the fact was, with his lies and his role in the investigation, he could be considered a suspect. As ridiculous as that sounded, as she'd find it, she needed to know what he'd done and what he'd said. Especially if she was going to be of any use to me. The idea of telling her now, of this close, collegial conversation turning into an argument was almost more than I could bear but it was a talk we had to have and the truth was, I was running low on time. "*Merde,*" I said, by way of strengthening my will.

"What's wrong?"

"We have to talk about Daniel Moulin for a moment. I know, I know." I held up my hands when she gave me her exasperated *What now?* expression. "I'll just say what I have to say, all facts and no commentary, and if you hear me out then I will listen to what you have to say without interrupting, and we can take it from there. Yes?"

"Yes." She took a large sip of wine, some might have called it a gulp, but gave me her full attention.

"Thank you. And some of this you know, some you don't. On Tuesday, Daniel's day off, I went to the One-Two-Two, following a witness. I wasn't expecting to go there, it was something I did in the moment. I saw Daniel there, I am sure of it, and he saw me and made himself scarce so I couldn't confront him. Later, when I asked him if he was working that day, he said he was working overtime. But I checked, and everyone who works overtime now logs it, and he not only hadn't logged any overtime, no one remembers him working. Which means he lied to me about it. I can't think why he would do so, but when I think about how he suddenly appeared that first night when we were at the crime scene and made himself useful, basically made himself a part of the investigation—"

"Henri, you can't possibly—"

"Just listening, remember?" Nicola bit her lip, but nodded. "I can't imagine he has anything to do with any of this, but I've never had a case like this, never had a case so unusual. Look, I'm not asking you to suspect him, all I'm asking you to do is not to discount him because you like him. I'm asking you to look at what I just told you, and keep an open mind. Can you do that?"

She held my eye for a moment and I could tell she was trying to figure out what to say. In the end she took another drink of her wine. I put my plate and bowl on the table between us, and did the same.

"Henri. He's a good man. He's not involved, he's not a murderer, that's ridiculous." She smiled, and it was almost as if she pitied me. "I promise, I will keep an open mind and if it turns out he did it I will be the first to slap handcuffs on him. But he didn't."

"You're not a police officer, you can't put handcuffs on anyone."

"I can if they ask me to."

"Nicola, for heaven's sake!" I could feel myself blushing.

"Hey, you're the one frequenting the One-Two-Two, and I hear that place can be very kinky."

"First of all, I don't *frequent* the place, I was there one time on business, conducting an investigation—"

"I wasn't judging, Henri." Her straight face contrasted with the playful twinkle in her eyes. "I know a man has his needs and it's been a long time since you had a girlfriend. I just don't need to know the details—"

"Will you stop? I was there to interrogate—"

"If that's your story, Henri, call it whatever you like."

"All right, that's enough, I'm not talking to you anymore." I turned my head away, trying to hide my own smile. How one person could make me laugh and irritate me so at the same time, I never could figure out.

"Fine, I'll stop. Tell me about the case. We can talk about your sex life, such as it is, another time."

"That will be a very short discussion," I said with a grimace. "But you heard what I said about Daniel. I'm not sure you're taking me seriously. He lied to me."

"Henri, everyone lies. You and I are lying to him about who we are. Does that make us murderers?"

"We have a damn good reason, and you know that."

"And maybe he does, too."

"What could it possibly be?"

"Look, Henri, everyone has secrets, too. You do, I do, we do. The witness you followed to the One-Two-Two sure as hell does, right? And none of those secrets have anything to do with being a killer. Sometimes you have to trust people, allow them to have their secret lives, trust that they're not out to do you harm, that you don't have to know everything."

"We've had this conversation before; I don't know him well enough to trust him."

"Maybe the problem isn't that you don't trust him, maybe it's that he doesn't know you well enough to trust you. At some point, one of you has to be the bigger man. One of you has to reach out and take that leap."

"You want me to tell him. Just sit him down and tell him everything I did, who I was, and everything that happened? That's insane, Nicola. Tell a man who's lied to me, who's snuck around behind my back, the one and only thing that could not only destroy my career but land me in jail?"

"Then don't, Henri. I'm not trying to tell you what to do. I'm just saying that you can't expect him to trust you if you won't reciprocate. You always think you're the one with the biggest secret in the world."

"Yes, as a matter of fact I do. And it's a secret I'm keeping for us both, remember."

"Well, your secret, *our* secret, is getting old and gathering dust." She reached out and patted my knee. "And the world's changing, Henri. New secrets are needing to be kept. Big ones. Dangerous ones."

"I have no idea what you're talking about."

"I know." She smiled, and the kindness in her eyes melted my heart. "You're a good man, Henri. A stubborn, cantankerous mule of a man, but a good one. Let's leave Daniel out of this for now. Tell me more about the case."

That sounded good to me. "You have a pencil and paper handy? You might want to write some of this down."

Nicola reached over to the table beside her, prepared as ever, swapping out her wine for the paper and pencil. "Talk to me."

•   •   •

We stayed up late, taking our time over each point, taking our time, too, over the bottle of wine. Just talking it out helped me sort through a few things, and for the remainder of the night we left the subject of Daniel Moulin alone. Not just because I wanted to avoid an argument, and not for any particular evidentiary reason, but because I needed to focus on what was important in the investigation—apart from saving my own neck, of course.

As we talked into the small hours of the night, Nicola and I agreed: one of the first things I needed to do was find out who the hell had been murdered in that apartment, because if he'd been dead since April it certainly wasn't Edouard Grabbin.

I had a sneaking suspicion I knew who it was, but I needed to confirm that suspicion. And to do that, I needed my boss to sign off on Form 3467-R.

"You think he will?" Nicola asked.

"I don't know. Why wouldn't he?"

"I bet he'll need permission from the Germans."

"Of course he will. He needs permission from them to take a leak."

"Not true," she said. "Just to shake it dry afterward."

I laughed, choking on the last of my wine. "Open another bottle?"

"You sure? Don't you have to get up early?"

"Come on, tomorrow's Saturday. The weekend."

"As if that means anything anymore."

"It must to someone."

She nodded slowly. "Just not to us."

"Come on, let's open another bottle. We have more to discuss."

CHAPTER TWENTY-TWO

Saturday, December 7, 1940

Chief Louis Proulx looked at me incredulously across his desk. It was nine o'clock in the morning on a Saturday and I was at work, but more astonishingly I had filled out an official police form, the *correct* official police form, and had done so without complaint and with total attention to detail.

"There are too many things for me to say, Henri, I scarcely know where to begin," he said, holding the single sheet of paper up as if it were a medieval scroll, and he a scholar ready to examine it.

"I have an idea. You forget the histrionics, and just say yes."

"I just say yes?" He stared at me earnestly. *"Tu rigoles."*

"Why would I be joking? My neck is on the line here, remember?"

"Henri, Edouard Grabbin was just put in the ground. I just signed a form saying his brother could do that. Now you want me to sign a form saying you can dig him up."

"Right. Except it wasn't Edouard Grabbin. And even if it was, it's not like his brother is going to object."

"Because you found him dead last night."

"Correct. Along with three children."

"This is insane."

"A lot more so for me than you." I pointed to the form. "So, if you don't mind . . ."

"It's not a question of me minding." He put it on the table and picked up the telephone. "It's a question of permission. And not mine." He dialed a number and asked to speak to Stefan Becker, the mention of whom made my skin crawl. Proulx listened for a moment, said, "Please, it's important," and hung up. Then he looked at me and said, "He will call me."

"When?"

"They didn't say. No doubt when he's good and ready. In the meantime, tell me who you think is buried there if not Edouard Grabbin."

"I don't know. I really don't. But I have a feeling it has something to do with what the Germans are doing in Rennes, maybe that bullet-making factory. Which, by the way, they are keeping very secret."

"Of course. Any munitions factory is top secret; if the enemy finds out it only takes one bomb and the whole place goes up. A single hand grenade has been known to take out a factory." He leaned forward conspiratorially. "Have you heard about the groups of French citizens getting together? Calling themselves *Partisans*?"

I nodded. "I have heard them called the *Resistance*, but stay well away, Louis. If you and I have heard of them, you know the Gestapo have. Whisper those names too loudly and the wrong ears will pick up on your words and, trust me, sooner rather than later you'll find yourself hanging from a hook wishing you'd minded your own business."

Proulx sat back in his chair. "Hey, I'm not saying anything else. I'm just a humble and hardworking policeman trying to do a job and stay out of trouble." He lowered his voice. "I'm not saying I wouldn't look the other way in certain circumstances but . . . I have a Préfecture to run and murderers to catch—"

"Oh, you do, do you?" I said with a smile, and he smiled with me.

"I'm with you every step of the way, Henri. Right behind you, at least."

"And way behind me, should I screw up and that Gestapo dog Becker comes looking for me."

The phone rang and the smiles slipped from our faces, as we both wondered at the timing, should Becker be on the other end of the line. He was. Proulx was serious as he made the request, and even more serious as he tried to argue my case. When he hung up, his face was grim.

"He said no. Digging up bodies is a bad look, especially fresh ones, and the Germans don't want us doing it. I'm sorry, Henri."

Anger rose inside me. "He doesn't want me solving this? Is he intentionally trying to sabotage me?"

"Look, wait a minute. How about this scenario—it's Edouard in the grave. Killed by his own brother, which is why he was so quick to bury him. Out of guilt. Guilt that ate him up, leading him to shoot himself. Suicide."

"Suicide?"

"Couldn't live with himself."

"So he shot himself twice in the heart."

"Ah. Minor detail."

"And did he also kill Viktor Brandt and those poor kids?"

"Brandt, maybe."

"And why did he do that?"

"Who gives a damn, Henri?" Proulx slammed a fist on his desk. "Jesus, Henri, what did that phone call just tell you?"

"That Becker wants my neck on the guillotine."

"*Merde, non,* you idiot. This isn't about you! That phone call told you that he doesn't give a damn about the truth. So make up a story that fits the facts. That way Becker is happy and your neck doesn't get anywhere near the guillotine."

"And that's how we do our jobs nowadays? Men die, *children* die, and we just sit around making up stories about how?"

"It is if it means we stay alive. It is until we're able to do them properly."

"That's not right, Chief, and you know it."

"There's a war going on out there, Henri. Hundreds of people are dying every day, and no one's bothering to ask who killed them, or how, or why. Because it doesn't matter. They're dead. And now you're going to risk your life . . . for what? Why exactly?"

"For the same reason those poor bastards are dying every day, Chief."

"And what reason is that?"

"It's what I signed up for. This is my job. And if I don't do this, what the hell else am I going to do with my day?"

I stepped out of his office and headed for mine. Nicola was at her secretarial station in the open part of the office, so I asked her to bring me a cup of coffee so I could update her. My colleagues didn't know about my aural condition, my misophonia, they just knew I got cranky around noises, so they'd let me have my own space, for which I was grateful. I sat back and propped my feet on my desk, wondering why Becker was so intent on hijacking my case. Maybe it was as simple as making the Boche look bad, but why did they care if the French police dug up a recent grave? I supposed they *were* in charge of everything, and god knows the paranoia runs strong with that lot but still . . .

Nicola tapped lightly on the door and came in with a cup of what the Paris police criminally misrepresent as coffee. It was bad enough before the invasion, but now it ought to come with a health warning.

"So, what happened?" she asked, perching on the desk beside my feet.

"Unsurprisingly the Germans got involved."

"I am surprised, actually. What does it have to do with them?"

"Well, it's their city now, and I'm supposed to be investigating the murder of their dead *mec*."

"But it's not him in that grave. Is it?" Our eyes met and she could see what I was thinking. "You think it might be."

"I do. I can't even say why. It's just this feeling."

"What are you going to do?" she asked.

"Two things. First, I'm going to pay a visit to the doctor who did the autopsy. Most SS have a tattoo, so while it wasn't noted on the report, I want to see if the doctor remembers seeing one on the body. I doubt it, but it's worth asking."

"And the second thing?"

"You know that store on rue Galvani, the one that sells left-over equipment from the last war?"

"Yes, but it's closed. The Germans took everything from it."

"*Merde*, of course they did. Is there anything they haven't ruined?"

"What is it you need?"

"I spent a year digging trenches in 1918. With the right tool, I can dig one in the dark, in my sleep. With the right tool, I can dig a trench in the pitch black, with a glass of Bordeaux in one hand and not spill a drop. Give me the right tool, and I can—"

"*Bien*, Henri, you need a shovel, I get it." She paused and looked at me. "You're really going to do that?"

"I was denied official permission. That, to me anyway, is not the same thing as being told I may not do something."

"Very well." She pursed her lips. "Then as well as soup and a half sandwich tonight, I will find you a shovel."

"Make sure it's the right kind. It has to be sharp-edged and slightly tapered, narrow, too, because with the right—"

But she was already closing the door behind her, I could only assume adequately briefed and confident in my abilities when it came to digging trenches in the dark.

•   •   •

Before I could do any digging, though, I needed to go back to Jean Grabbin's apartment and take care of that crime scene, see what else was to be gathered there. I grimaced as I slugged back the almost cold coffee and shrugged on my coat, then walked out of my office to find Nicola.

"I just called for the wagon to go collect your new corpse," she said. "Hope that was all right. It won't be for a few hours."

"Perfect, that'll give me a chance to see him in situ one last time."

I looked up as Chief Proulx appeared by her desk. He had a

soft spot for her, in a fatherly way, as most of the men in the unit did.

"*Bonjour*, Nicola."

"*Bonjour*, Chief Proulx. Can I get you some coffee?"

"God no, not until the war's over."

"Hey, Chief, do you mind if I borrow Nicola this morning?" I asked.

"Where are you going?"

"To finish up what I started last night. See poor deceased Monsieur Grabbin."

"The new one," he said grimly.

"Well, you won't let me dig up the old one."

"Funny. And no, I need her here. What's left to do there?"

"Search the place," I said. "Again. And interview any witnesses."

"Were there any?"

"I doubt it. Probably find myself interviewing the body."

"Well, if that's the case you won't need anyone to take notes, will you?"

I gave him my harshest glare, and for good measure shot Nicola a doleful look over his shoulder, but it had no effect because she was busy trying not to laugh. I'm sure she didn't fancy a long cold walk just to watch me search a dead man's apartment, especially since the dead man, along with three dead children, was still there.

My mood wasn't improved much by the fresh air and brisk walk because I'd not had a chance to properly fix my shoe problem, and by the time I got to Grabbin's place my feet were both wet and sore. The *flic* standing guard was happy to see me, though, so I let him go home in exchange for two of his cigarettes, one of which I smoked on the doorstep before going inside. I would have smoked the second one, too, but my fingers were freezing and I figured the wagon would be coming for Grabbin's body before too long.

A methodical plod through the back rooms of the apartment brought me nothing more than the slowly rising smell of Grabbin's dead body. The cold of a Paris December did its level best to delay the inevitable but my delicate palate, no doubt developed nicely by Mimi's fine taste in wine, was too sophisticated these days to miss the sweet smell of newly rotting flesh and the unmistakable stench of death. The more you're around it, the more unmistakable it is, sadly.

The front rooms weren't any more revealing, and a closer study of the death documents was as mystifying as before, and I chided myself for leaving them there overnight. It may have been the proper protocol—it's hardly the thing to do to take evidence home—but the way this case was going it seemed like a big risk to not secure them, even improperly. But no one seemed to have been there, so I breathed a sigh of relief over that, at least.

I'd brought a sturdy flashlight and with that and daylight seeping into the cellar, I was pleased to see a good deal more than I had the previous night. Not particularly happy to get a better view of three dead children, but that couldn't be helped.

The place was musty and cold, colder than upstairs, and perhaps for those reasons didn't smell as strongly of death despite the three little bodies that lay in front of me. Or maybe it was because I was trying extra hard to push them from my mind, I'd become pretty good at pretending bad things didn't exist these days.

I lit a few candles for background illumination, and shone my flashlight slowly around the cellar to see what was what, where I should start looking. The one thing I'd not noticed before was a wine rack, which unsurprisingly was bare save for two empty wine bottles.

Not everyone has a Mimi to keep them stocked with the finest Bordeaux, Sancerres, and Chablis, I reminded myself.

But also, who keeps empty wine bottles in racks? I did a quick scan for wine-making equipment but didn't see any. I walked over and took one bottle out and inspected it. Clean and new, and empty, so I put it back. The other one was also clean and new, but had something inside it, a piece of paper. I held it upside down and shook it, but it got caught in the neck and wouldn't drop out, so I stepped back and threw the bottle low and hard against the wall. The shards glittered in the beam of the light, and I stooped to pick out the scrap of paper, smoothing it against my trouser leg.

On it was written:

Étienne D says: RVABDBVAT4 in R—<u>need 3</u>

There it was again, A-T4. Along with a bunch more letters that, of course, made my life more confusing and not less. And who the hell was Étienne D?

I looked at the paper again but was distracted by a noise from upstairs, one that sounded like footsteps. And to my practiced ears, it sounded like the footsteps of someone trying to be quiet— slow, deliberate, with the wooden floors making more noise than the steps themselves. I doused my flashlight, moved quickly to the nearest lit candles, and blew them out. Then I slid into the darkest corner and waited, slipping my gun from its holster, my eyes glued to the stairs. Those same footsteps crept above me, crossing through the apartment, presumably making sure it was empty, picking up the pace as whoever it was gained confidence. I gained some of my own and blew out the rest of the candles, sinking the cellar into total darkness. I positioned myself in another corner, kneeling behind the wine rack so I could stand up and have a full view of the cellar. There was no way for him to stumble into me, or sneak up behind me, assuming he came down here.

And then, finally, he started down the cellar stairs. A beam of white light poked its away ahead of him, and my heart immediately ticked faster and my thoughts raced.

The first of them was this: *Interesting, you came prepared. You know this place.*

I tried to control my breathing, tried to slow my heart thumping in my chest, but it didn't help that I had absolutely no idea who this person was, nor whether they were armed, or whether they were the killer. For all I knew, this could be Daniel Moulin on one of his secret escapades. Of course, it could be the killer *and* Daniel Moulin on one of his escapades, for all I knew about that *mec*.

He reached the bottom of the stairs and swept his light across the room, but not in a way that made me think he was suspicious of anyone being there, more that he was making sure it was empty. He moved quickly, assuredly, going to the back tables where the candles were. He put the butt of his flashlight in his mouth and I strained to make him out, but with the light shining away from him, being absorbed by the dark brick, he was no more than a black silhouette, and not one familiar to me.

He struck a match in order to light the candles I'd just extinguished, and then he froze. My eyes followed where his were looking, and I knew why he'd paused. A thin stream of smoke rose from one of the candles, telling him someone had been there, was perhaps there still.

I leaped up and switched on my flashlight, aiming it and my gun straight at him.

"Paris police, Detective Lefort, do not move!"

He looked slightly ridiculous, his eyes wide with shock and a flashlight poking out of his mouth, a match burning in his fingers. He also looked slightly familiar, but I couldn't immediately say from where; the darkness of the cellar and the brightness of my light were distorting how he looked.

He mumbled something I couldn't understand.

"Take that thing out of your mouth, drop the match, and then put your hands back up," I said. "We've already got three bodies in here, I don't want any more."

Slowly, his squinting eyes never leaving me, he dropped the burning match on the floor and took the flashlight from his mouth, then placed it on the table next to him.

"Who are you?" he asked.

"I am the policeman and the one with the gun. You know what that means?"

"Not much these days," he said, and suddenly I remembered where I'd seen him before. "Unless you're working for *them*."

"Them?"

"The Nazis."

"You were at Edouard Grabbin's funeral," I said.

"Not me. We Indian men all look alike."

"Yeah? Then how'd you know an Indian man was at his funeral? Weird that Jean would know two Indian men of the exact same height and build, don't you think?"

"Fine. It was me. So what?"

"Who are you?"

We both looked toward the stairs as someone banged on the front door.

"*Merde*," he said. "I'm not supposed to be here. Do you know who that is?"

"Probably someone here for the body." I shone my light over the children. "Bodies."

He swore again. "I can't be here."

"You're not going anywhere until I know who you are, and why you're here."

He blinked into my flashlight, and I didn't think I'd seen a man less intimidated by me, which was impressive considering not only my position as a detective but also the gun pointed at his chest.

"I'm a friend of Jean's. And now I have to go."

"Don't you dare move!"

"You said you don't want any more bodies." His voice was urgent. "If they find out I was here, I'm dead."

"Who? And who the hell are you?"

"I worked at the hospital." He started toward the stairs, and I did nothing to stop him. Mostly because my one and only option was to shoot him, and I wasn't going to do that. "My name is Étienne. Étienne Darden. If I'm alive this time tomorrow, I'll come find you."

He reached the bottom of the stairs and started up, just as the name Étienne Darden registered. Étienne D.

"Wait!" I called out after him. "Who was in that grave? Who did you bury as Edouard Grabbin?"

But he was gone.

CHAPTER TWENTY-THREE

I desperately wanted to rest before my upcoming nighttime adventure, but I also knew I couldn't afford to. The clock was ticking, and whether my Gestapo friend was sizing me up for the hangman's noose or Madame Guillotine, it was about now he'd be starting to measure the rope or sharpen the blade. So whether I liked it or not, I had to go after Étienne Darden and find out what he knew. I was done at the Grabbin apartment anyway, and didn't much want to see the sad loading of Jean and the three kids into the meat wagon for their last ride to the morgue. Funny that, if you like black humor—dead and completely unaware of the privilege, they got to ride in one of the few motorized vehicles left in Paris, while me, a murder detective temporarily alive and in a race against time, had to hoof it to the same place, the hospital morgue.

My first stop there was to Dr. Davide Villefranche, who'd conducted the autopsy on the body buried as Edouard Grabbin. But as soon as I laid eyes on him, I knew it was a waste of breath. Rather, as soon as he laid his breath on me, I knew it was a waste of time. He couldn't even remember doing the autopsy, let alone remember whether the dead man's body had sported an SS tattoo, and the glazed eyes and sweet smell of metabolized alcohol that saturated his body and breath told me he wouldn't remember anything he did that morning, either. Frankly, I was impressed he knew which end of a scalpel to hold, though I don't suppose even a drunk makes that mistake too often. I thanked him for his time and was about to make my way to the service stairs, when I had a thought.

"Do you know Étienne Darden?" I asked.

"Of course. He's been here years."

"What does he do here?"

Villefranche stared at me blankly. "Who are you again?"

"Police. I'm investigating a murder."

"Who was killed?"

Damned if I know. "Mind if I ask the questions?"

"Oh. I suppose not." He rubbed a sleeve across his nose. "What do you want to know?"

"Étienne Darden. What does he do here?"

"I think he got fired." He scrunched his brow as if deep in thought. "I'm pretty sure of it. Like a week ago. Few days maybe."

"Who fired him?" He gestured toward the gods, or maybe it was just administration. "And what for?"

"He got into it with one of the doctors. A fight."

"Which doctor?"

"They fired him, too."

I felt like a dentist, what with all this teeth pulling. "Which doctor?"

"Grabbin. Jean Grabbin."

"What were they fighting about?"

"It was here, actually. Right here. I didn't understand it."

"Please, it's important." I put a hand on his shoulder. "It's really important, no matter what it was, no matter how odd it seemed."

"I thought I heard Darden accuse Grabbin . . ." Villefranche shook his head. "No, that makes no sense."

"Tell me. Whatever it was."

"It sounded like he accused him of taking children."

"Why were they down here?"

"How would I know?"

I thought for a moment. "You didn't tell me what Darden's job was."

"He was a porter. He did a bit of everything, really. But his title was porter."

"What does a porter do?"

"Move patients. Unpack equipment and supplies. Generally take people and things where they need to be."

"And he's worked here a long time, knows everyone."

"Yes, for sure."

"And did you tell me who fired him?"

"I don't know. I assume the Germans."

"Why do you assume that?"

"You've seen him, yes?"

"Ah, his skin color."

"I can't tell if they like the Jews more or less than people like him, but either way, he was always going to lose his job. Plus . . ."

He went quiet for a moment, and I waited for him to finish. "They don't like it when people ask questions. When people know more than they like. Darden was one of those people. That's why he confronted Grabbin."

"Because he found out something Grabbin was doing?"

"I suppose."

"And do you know what Grabbin was doing?"

"No," Villefranche said emphatically. "And I don't want to know."

"*Bien*, well, thank you for your help." I turned to go.

"The strange thing about it is," Villefranche said, almost to himself. I turned to listen. "A few days ago I was leaving work. I saw them out back, talking."

"Why is that strange?"

"Think about it." He leaned toward me, and my eyes watered from his breath. "They have this big fight, Darden makes these terrible accusations involving children, and they're both fired from the jobs they love. Then they're back here, whispering into each other's ears like they're best friends. How do you explain that? Doesn't make sense to me."

"Nor to me. None whatsoever." I leaned away into some fresher air. "Do you happen to know where Darden lives?"

"*Non*, sorry. Try administration. Or ask Jean Grabbin, since they seem to be best friends again."

"Thanks. I think administration is my better bet."

●   ●   ●

Étienne Darden was my next problem, and that was mostly because I didn't have an address for him. The hospital couldn't find it in their records, though I'm pretty sure I know how hard they looked. But in a way I was relieved—I simply didn't have time or energy to go to wherever he was and drag answers out of him. I needed to go home, eat, and rest up before my exertions of the evening. I'd hoped Nicola had cooked something, but when I let myself into the apartment she wasn't there. I took the soup from the night before, reheated it, and took the other half of the sandwich and ate the same meal as the previous evening, still tasty just one day staler.

It was nine o'clock before I heard her familiar tread on the stairs, and moments later she came through the door.

"I was beginning to worry," I said, getting up. "Everything all right?"

"Just making sure you have all you need."

"The way you said that . . ."

"What?"

"Sounded strange. What do you mean?"

"I have a car and the equipment you need in the trunk. What else could I mean?"

"I don't know." I gave her a peck on the forehead. "Thank you. Sorry. You're an angel."

"Well, I signed the car out in your name, just so you know."

"Of course, you had to."

She gave me a tired smile. "I was tempted to put it in GiGi's name, if you must know."

"Dear GiGi. He can't wait for me to fail. Maybe I should swing by his house and see if he'll help me."

"You should." Nicola laughed, then squeezed my arm. "Digging trenches. You ever think you'd be doing that again?"

"Can't say I did."

"I'm sorry you are, Henri. Doesn't seem fair."

"That's all right. It's funny in a way."

"How so?"

"Mostly as a policeman I can do what I like, just show my credentials, maybe get a court order if I have to, and then get on with it. Do it in broad daylight no matter who's watching." I gave a wry smile. "But not digging, apparently. Then or now, digging is done only by the night, only under cover of darkness. Just like old times."

She gave my arm another squeeze. "You sure you don't want me to come?"

"We've been over this. If things go badly, one of us needs to be in the clear."

"I know, I just . . ." She sighed. "Did you eat?"

"I finished the soup, I hope that's all right."

"Of course."

"And the sandwich."

"Pig." She punched my arm. "I'll raid Mimi's apartment."

"Good idea. See what she has, I have a feeling I'll be wanting some breakfast."

"Any idea what time you'll be back?"

"Honestly, no. But I should be going."

●   ●   ●

As kids, a few friends and I would sneak out at night and go to a local cemetery to tell ghost stories and scare each other. The rustle of a tree branch or sudden hoot of an owl would send us into fits of terror, sprinting for the safety of the exit, only for us to creep back between the headstones and crosses, some crumbling and some newly marbled, to play our game of chicken all over again. The terror was real, of course, all the more so because our belief in ghosts and ghouls, while tenuous, had yet to be dispelled by the logic of adulthood and reason.

But when you've spent a year of sleepless nights watching over fields littered with the bodies of your friends and enemies, when you've sat at the dark edge of night listening to the groans of the dying, watched the sun set on their last twitches, well, then a neatly laid-out cemetery, with the long-dead tucked deep in the soil in their tightly sealed coffins, is no place to dread.

Unless it's a cold, wet night and it's your job to dig one of the bastards up all by yourself.

I did have two advantages, though. The first was that Nicola, as I should have expected, had procured precisely the perfect shovel—a sturdy handle, a tapered end, and sharp edges. Also, since the grave had been dug recently the soil hadn't settled and become overly compact. Nevertheless, my shoulders, arms, and back quickly reminded me how long it'd been since I'd done any real digging and three minutes into my task I shed my coat, already feeling the sweat trickling down my spine. Three minutes after that, I was taking my first extended break, wondering why the hell I'd not found a better way to identify the man in this grave.

Thirty minutes after that, I realized I had a serious problem. Not only was the soil filling in where I'd been digging, but I'd been stupid enough not to bring gloves, and my hands were rubbing themselves raw against the handle of the shovel. Pretty soon I'd have blisters, and pretty soon after that, I wouldn't be able to hold the damn thing at all.

I swore loudly and rammed the shovel into the soil, resolving to have a quick smoke to give my hands a rest and calm myself down.

It helped, too. A moment of quiet, the pain temporarily subsiding, both from my hands and my back, my dark deeds hidden from the world in that black place. I felt ridiculous in the moment, knowing I was doomed to fail. Fail at digging up this coffin, fail at solving this case. I had no idea who was buried here, or who'd killed whoever was buried here. I didn't even know whose body we'd found on the tracks, whether that was really Viktor Brandt or not. If I had to make one final gamble, I'd say Brandt was beneath my feet, but with throbbing hands, an aching back, and lungs filled with smoke and not enough capacity to dig however many more feet I had left to go, a guess was about the best I could do.

And something told me Stefan Becker wouldn't be particularly satisfied with that.

A sound behind me made me turn and look toward the parking lot. I squinted but couldn't see anything, or anyone. A lack of moonlight was good for my nocturnal mission, but less good for helping me spot who may have spotted me. I stood motionless for a while, my eyes scanning the dark cemetery, but didn't hear or see anyone. And then the darkness was broken by shadows moving toward me, six of them drifting between the headstones and markers, black figures evenly spread out, moving like they belonged to the night. I knew there was no point running. If they were here, they were here because they knew that I would be. Which meant they knew who I was and they could find me when the sun rose, or tomorrow, or the next day. Running would just delay whatever it was they had in mind. And if that was something unpleasant, or even permanently unpleasant, well, where better for that than a cemetery?

As they got close, two things became clear. One was that they had a leader, because they started to move closer to him. The second was that they were wearing scarves to cover their faces. They all had long coats, too, and unless I was mistaken each man carried a rifle under his coat. I wondered if this was Becker's informal firing squad.

The leader held up a hand for his men to halt, but he moved past the last of the gravestones and walked right up to me. My mouth fell open when he pulled down his mask.

"Jesus Christ," I said. "What are you doing here?"

"Digging is hard work, sir. I thought you could use some help."

"You thought so? Or Nicola thought so?"

"She *is* a very thoughtful person, sir, can't fault her there."

"I thought I told you to stop calling me 'sir.'"

"Wasn't that just off the job, sir?"

"We're digging up a grave in the middle of the night, for god's sake. I think this is off the job."

Moulin nodded. "You're probably right. On that subject, we should get straight to work." Moulin gestured to his band of men, all of whom shed their long coats to reveal not rifles, but shovels. One of them had the kind of useless, broad-headed tool that would break his back before making a dent in the ground, so I gave him mine and he grunted his thanks. They lined up on either side of the shallow ditch I'd dug and went to work with impressive energy and coordination. Moulin and I stood to one side, keeping watch.

"So, I can trust your friends?" I asked.

"You'll have to now. But yes, you can."

"I usually like to be given the choice."

"So I understand."

I shot him a look, but in the dark it didn't mean much. "So, who are they, your friends?"

"Probably best if I don't make introductions. And I should let you know, if the Boche show up, they'll scatter."

"Understood. You should, too."

"You'll be able to explain six extra shovels?"

"I'll think of something. Or I won't. I'm not sure it'll much matter at that point."

"I expect you're right."

We were quiet for a moment, then I asked: "What did she tell you?"

"Nicola? That I could trust you."

"With what?"

"With what I was doing at the One-Two-Two."

"Ah. So I'm not crazy, it was you."

"It was."

"And the overtime?"

"Yes, I lied about that, too, of course. My apologies, but it was necessary." He fell silent.

"Well? Seems like now would be a good time to explain."

"*Non.* It's not." He waved a hand toward the men, now up to their knees in the hole but digging like they'd just started. "It has to do with them, so until they are safe and out of my sight, I'd like to wait."

"Very well. But I am curious."

Moulin looked at me and I could see his grin, even in the dark. "I think you will enjoy my reason. Very much indeed."

"That so?" I lit two cigarettes and handed one to him. "Very curious indeed."

We stood in silence, apart from the rhythmic sounds of metal slicing into wet earth, and that earth being dumped aside. As they got deeper there was less room to work, so they had to take turns, slowing the progress. I started to wonder if I'd brought enough cigarettes, but then wondered if I should be smoking at all, each match strike was a tiny flare that could be seen, each cigarette a glow in the dark for some eagle-eyed night owl to spot and report. But I had to do something to keep myself busy, to calm my nerves.

And eventually we heard the *thunk, thunk* of shovels hitting something that wasn't dirt, and the two men taking that shift started scraping instead of digging, scooping the last of the mud and flinging it up out of the grave as Moulin and I dropped our cigarettes and walked over, my nerves suddenly jangling all over again.

"You want us to open it?" one of the men standing on the coffin said.

"Yes, may as well," I said.

He hesitated for a moment. "We don't know what you're looking for. Someone in particular, or just to know if there's anyone inside?"

"Gold, maybe," said one of the men behind him, and there was a murmur of laughter to break the tension.

"Someone in particular," I said. "If there's gold, it's yours to keep."

"*Bien*, we'll remove the lid." He aimed the edge of the shovel at the center of the coffin and rammed it hard, and I knew it wouldn't take more than a few blows. Like shoe leather, coffee, and tobacco, coffin quality had taken a turn for the worse in recent months and in many cases the material undertakers used wasn't much better than cardboard. And it was less than a splitting sound and more of a *whump* when the lid gave way, and the two men peeled strips of it away and tossed them onto the piles of dirt either side of the hole they were in. That done, the bystanders stepped in close and hauled one of their colleagues out, leaving one standing at the foot end, all of them peering down into the grave, their flashlights illuminating its grisly contents as I stepped between my anonymous helpers to take a look for myself.

"Can you unwrap him, please?" I asked.

The man in the grave knelt and pulled the grubby sheet away from the body, and I could tell right away the dead man wasn't Edouard Grabbin. Death made no man look better but this corpse, naked but for that sheet, had to have been in his forties at most, not his seventies as Grabbin would have been. The skin was too smooth, too unmarked and unblemished to belong to a man in his seventies.

"Look under his arm, see if he has a tattoo of his blood type," I said.

The man in the grave looked up at me, and I saw he wasn't a man at all, just a boy. "I don't want to touch him."

"I'll give you one franc if you find that tattoo," I said. "Left arm, above the elbow."

"I don't want to touch him," the kid said again. "But I'll do it for three francs."

To my surprise, Moulin stepped forward and growled at the boy. "You'll do it, and you'll do it for France. Now, get on with it."

He loomed over the surprised, and now cowed, kid, and we all watched as he stooped and gingerly fished around for the naked corpse's left arm. I'd not even considered that the young fellow might not have seen a dead man before, and began to feel guilty. But it didn't take long before all of our flashlights were aimed at a black tattoo showing the SS officer's blood type. There was no doubt, then, this man was Viktor Brandt.

CHAPTER TWENTY-FOUR

Daniel Moulin and I moved to one side.

"What do you want us to do now?" he asked.

"You can all go. I sure as hell needed help digging that hole, but I can fill it in myself." I looked toward the horizon, where the edges of the night had lightened, black giving way to gray. It surprised me that I'd been out here that long, but apparently time passed quickly when you were desecrating graves. "And there's no need to put everyone at risk."

"*Bien, merci.*" Moulin went back to his men and spoke to them in a low voice. Moments later, they started drifting away from the grave site, like spirits freed from the earth, disappearing into the darkness in all directions, singly to avoid the German patrols, and thereby escape whatever excessive ramifications they'd face for violating the curfew.

Moulin, however, stayed.

"You don't have to," I said.

"I know, but we need to talk, *n'est-ce pas?*" He leaned on his shovel. "I think we have questions for each other, and perhaps even a few answers."

I smiled to let him know he was right, about the first thing at least, and together we began heaping the heavy, wet soil back into the grave. Side by side we shoveled and scraped until my back screamed for me to take a break, and I felt like work could come second place to talking.

"They're long gone, your friends," I said. "Want to share your secret now?"

"I suppose so."

I lit two more cigarettes and gave him one. "She's right, you know."

"Nicola?"

I nodded. "You can trust me."

"Good. I hope you'll feel the same about me." He took a draw on his cigarette. "About the One-Two-Two. I was delivering some medicine to one of the girls."

"Medicine? They have a doctor who attends to them regularly."

"I know. Look, Henri, there is a rising movement here in Paris. *Non*, in France. People wanting to do something, to strike back."

"But that's danger—"

"Dangerous, I know. We're doing it in an organized way, a way that doesn't cause reprisals. Ways that upset and disturb. We're not killing, we're not blowing things up. We're making life unpleasant, making the Boche not want to be here. Making them want to leave us alone. Or if they're looking for someone, we can make that person disappear to somewhere safe. We're resisting more than we're attacking. These men who came here tonight. You know who they were?"

"I have no idea."

"They were schoolteachers and builders. One was a dentist, one was a mechanic. One a university student. The kid who wanted your three francs is a budding poet."

"Figures. They'll do anything for money."

Moulin laughed quietly. "And some of them will do anything for France. As you saw."

"What does this have to do with the One-Two-Two?"

"The girl I was taking the medicine to. She infects herself on purpose and passes it on to her German clients, infects them. But only with whatever can be cured when diagnosed quickly. I bring the cure."

"That's . . . remarkable. And brave." I couldn't help but wonder about the long-term effects of doing that, and had to hope there was a good doctor involved at some point. I also had to marvel at the lengths people were going to to oppose our invaders, and how many of the bravest ones were women. "Does Marcel Jamet know?"

"He does not. Not everyone is on board with what we do, and we don't know who will turn us in."

"Hence you bringing the medicine and not the brothel's doctor."

"Exactly."

"You're taking quite the risk."

"Infecting German pricks is well worth it."

"Not that," I said with a chortle. "I meant admitting to a policeman that you're infecting German pricks."

"Ah, yes. But look at it from my perspective." He grinned. "I just helped that same policeman dig up a body and violate curfew." He took another drag. "Also, I was assured he was trustworthy."

"Then perhaps it's my turn," I said, studying the end of my cigarette, as Moulin went back to work shoveling mud into the grave. "What has Nicola told you about how we know each other?"

"Nothing. I assume you once were more than friends, that it didn't work out, and you do better as friends." He stopped shoveling. "That happens. I don't mind."

"She really hasn't told you?"

"She hasn't."

"Then I will. Nicola is my sister. No one at the Préfecture knows, we couldn't tell them when I first joined, for reasons I don't have time to tell you right now, but we didn't and we've seen no reason to expose that lie as the years have gone by."

"Your sister." He was taking his time with the news. "I suppose that explains why you are so protective of each other. But why should it be a secret?"

"There is more to the story. A lot more. But you'd have to be married to her to get the rest of it." I dropped my cigarette in the dirt and went back to shoveling.

"Well, then I may have to do that."

"Not yet, Moulin. We have more work to do."

We were getting close to finishing, and I was getting close to being finished off, when Moulin must have noticed my tiredness.

"Have one more smoke, Henri. Stretch your back, I'll do the rest. And I have a question."

"Ask it."

"If this is Viktor Brandt we're covering up—"

"And it is. You want to uncover him and check again?"

"*Merde, non.* But who was the poor *mec* we thought was Brandt? The dead guy by the railway tracks? And what the hell do you think is going on here?"

"I've been thinking about all this." I looked again toward the horizon, and a weak winter sun had opened it up to allow enough light into the cemetery that I could see the expression on Moulin's face. He looked at once tired and curious. "Let's look at what we know, how it all fits together."

"You talk, I'll shovel and listen."

"Jean Grabbin is at the heart of it all. He must have killed Viktor Brandt in his brother's apartment, then disfigured him and staged his death to look like a robbery. Pretended it was his brother Edouard, who'd already been dead for months."

"Why would he do that? I mean, why would he kill him, and also why disfigure him?"

"I'll answer the second question first—because you can't just kill a German doctor. Even if it was self-defense, which would be the best-case scenario for Jean, there would be ramifications. Severe ramifications. And remember, both men had been at the homosexual club, so that's going to cause a problem for Jean if it comes out. Much better for him if it's a random robbery gone wrong, and it's his brother who gets quickly buried."

"That much makes sense. But why fake the death of Brandt? And whose body was that?"

"Once we started poking around, maybe it made sense to Grabbin that we found a body. Once we do that, and have a simple explanation for how he died, the investigation is over, right?"

"I suppose so. But whose body?"

"No idea," I said. "But I know who might."

"And who is that?"

"The one person who knew Grabbin, was friends with him, and also worked with him."

Moulin stopped shoveling. "Who?"

"Étienne Darden. You know who that is?"

"I don't think so."

"Well, you're going to help me find him because I need to talk to him. Now Grabbin is out of the picture, I think Darden might be the key to all this."

"I'll do what I can. But hold on, let's back up a little," Moulin said. "You've skipped over why Jean Grabbin would kill Viktor Brandt in the first place."

"I'm not sure exactly. But I think, no I'm positive, it has something to do with what's happening in Rennes. I know they argued at Club Monocle, maybe to do with some ammunition factory—"

"Now that's a mystery I can solve for you." Moulin started shoveling again. "There isn't one."

"What?'

"There's no munitions factory being built in Rennes."

"How do you know?"

"It's one of the things we've focused on. One of our intelligence missions. I promise you, there is no munitions factory being built there."

"All the more reason for me to talk to Étienne Darden then. He's the only person who can fill in the gaps for me."

"I bet our network can find him, we can find anyone."

"Who is this 'we' you keep referring to?"

"It's . . . a loose organization. The way it's set up, no one really knows more than two or three people. We have ways to pass messages and information but for our own safety, we don't know people outside our cell."

"I'll take help from where I can get it."

"Understood, but there's something you need to know." Moulin stopped for a rest, breathing hard. "If I'm to get you to this Darden fellow, they will need to know why."

"That's the point," I said, frustrated. "I found his name on a note in Grabbin's apartment, with some jumbled letters and numbers. I don't know what they mean, so I don't know why I want to talk to him until I talk to him."

"Just tell me what you're thinking, what you do know."

"I know that Grabbin and Brandt worked at the hospital. That's how they met. I think Grabbin learned something about what Brandt was doing, whatever he was doing in Rennes, and I think he confronted Brandt when they were at Club Monocle. I know they got into an argument there, bad enough they were thrown out. Whatever that argument was about, that's what got Brandt killed."

"How does Grabbin having three dead children in his basement fit into this?"

"I don't know, but I bet Darden does."

"Grabbin was some kind of murderous pedophile?"

"Well, I'm certain he killed Viktor Brandt and, as you said, he had three dead kids in his basement, so I don't know that you're making wild guesses at this point. Although I think there's more to it than that."

"The question is. What?"

"Indeed." I looked at the grave as the cool morning light cast long shadows around us. The soft gray outlines of the gravestones were like puzzle pieces laid out on a table, and in my mind they were slowly starting to move into shape. Not slotting together yet, but certain pieces were moving either toward or away from each other as the options narrowed and the facts as I knew them made one possibility clearer or a particular theory redundant. Also narrowing, though, was my time frame and it was clear to me, standing there in that cemetery, that the only piece of solid, helpful information I had—that the man in this grave was Viktor Brandt—had come about because I'd taken decisive action. I couldn't aimlessly follow clues or passively wait for leads to pop up. My head was on the chopping block and if I wanted to whisk it away from the shiny blade of Madame Guillotine, then I needed to get busy. And if that meant knocking together a few heads myself, then so be it.

"I think we're done here," Moulin said, scraping a last load of earth into place.

"Good work, I think you're right."

"What now?" He stretched his back. "Some sleep perhaps? It is my day off, after all."

"Your day off, good, that's perfect. And maybe sleep, but only once you've got me into contact with Darden."

He groaned. "Which means more work."

"Yes. But on the bright side, I have a car here, you don't have to walk home."

"But no sleep when I get there." He sounded like a sulky child.

"You're welcome. If it's any consolation, I'll be working all day myself."

"Doing what?"

"I'm going to a whorehouse."

He gave me a tired smile. "One that I know?"

"It most certainly is."

"Need company?" He slung his shovel over one shoulder and we set off for the car.

"No, it's your day off," I said. "But don't worry, I'll have a couple of friends there to keep me company. They just don't know it yet."

CHAPTER TWENTY-FIVE

Sunday, December 8, 1940

The first order of business, once I'd dropped Daniel Moulin at his place and cleaned up a little, was to root through some filing cabinets at the Préfecture and locate the address of a certain Violet Boulet, otherwise known as Mistress Cassie Lau, whose information was on file thanks to her profession. The second order of business was to drive over to her apartment in the Eleventh Arrondissement and bang on her door until she woke up. She opened the door with her hair tousled, wearing a fluffy robe and an unhappy look on her face.

"What time is it?" she demanded, glaring at me.

"It's almost eight o'clock."

"What the hell do you want at not even eight o'clock?"

"I need your help with something."

"Make an appointment, like everyone else."

"No, you don't understand. I need your help today. Now."

"I don't work on Sundays." She put her hands on her hips. "So, first you can apologize, then go away and make an appointment for next week. Where I work, *not here*."

"I'm sorry, I'm not being clear." I found myself getting tongue-tied, and could see why men who were into being dominated paid her to do so. I wasn't into it, wasn't paying, and was jabbering like an idiot. "I'm here on police business, like before. That murder case."

"So? Enough that you bother me with that at work, why do you have to bother me at home?"

"I need information from someone, and the easiest way to get it, is with your help."

Her eyes narrowed with suspicion, and I quickly laid out my plan. The kicker, and the part that had to be the most persuasive, was that it dealt a blow to the Boche. On the drive home, I'd told Moulin what I was planning and he'd mentioned that Lau was one of the workers at the One-Two-Two who turned a blind eye to his visits. We'd both assumed she'd therefore be open to helping out, but assumptions in this business can be dangerous.

When I'd finished, she thought for a moment. "I don't work for free," she said. "I have a special skill, and I assume you're getting paid to do what you do, so I don't work for free."

"I'll pay your fee," I assured her. "Anything else?"

"No. Except . . . You're still sure he's working with the Germans?"

"Yes."

"Against France?"

"I believe so. He's sure as hell not working to help us."

"Then pay half my fee and my services are at your disposal."

"Thank you. The only trick will be getting him there without making him suspicious."

She laughed at that, and her whole visage softened. She put a hand on my arm and shook her head slowly, as if I were a stupid child. "You don't know much about human sexuality, do you, Detective?"

"Well now, I think I know plent—"

"You don't. Not about my world, anyway, where sex, or a certain kind of sexual act, can be like a drug for some people. For our friend, it most certainly is. He craves it like a man in the desert craves water. I can guarantee you that one day after he's been to see me, no matter what I've put him through, he's dreaming of his next visit." She squeezed my arm. "Money and shame are the only things that keep him out of my elegant little dungeon. Believe me when I promise you that if I offer him a free sample, even with no notice, he will come running. You'll see."

We agreed to meet up at the One-Two-Two at noon to see if she was right. In the meantime, I went back home to put the other part of the plan into motion. Mimi, unlike Mistress Lau, was glad to see me and invited me in for a boiled egg and bread.

"If you can spare it," I said, my stomach already rumbling with anticipation.

"Would I offer it, if I couldn't?"

At that moment I heard movement behind me, and turned to see Virginia Hall standing there. I stood.

"*Bonjour*, I didn't realize you were here. I hope I'm not about to eat your breakfast."

"I have several eggs, Henri," Mimi said.

"Henri, what a pleasant surprise." Virginia gave me two *bisous* and the three of us sat at Mimi's kitchen table. "What were you two discussing?"

"I don't quite know. Henri hadn't explained the reason for his early morning visit," Mimi said. "Perhaps to escort me to church?"

We all laughed at that, and in the midst of the chuckling I shot Mimi a look to let her know that I was there on private business.

She smiled and said, "It's all right, Henri, anything you can say to me, you can say in front of Virginia. I promise. Let's just say she's . . . fully on our side."

"I see. So my secrets won't appear in her newspaper?" I said, with a smile.

"Not unless you want them to," Virginia said. "Believe me, I have other reasons to be in Paris, more than just writing. I won't elaborate but let me just say that I can be useful when it comes to giving your new occupiers the occasional black eye."

"Ah, good to know." I turned to Mimi. "Do you have a camera I can borrow?"

"I do. What for?"

"You remember last time?" I said with a wink.

"Oh, of course I do. It worked rather well, as I recall."

"This time I want to do it myself, though. Make it a weapon instead of a shield."

"Do what yourself exactly?"

"Preferably a small and easy-to-use camera. Easy to conceal."

"I've changed my mind, I don't want to know what for," Mimi said, standing. "I'll fetch it for you."

She got up and left, and I noticed Virginia eyeing me, as if sizing me up.

"What is it?" I asked.

"Do you need a small camera, or do you need a miniature one?" she asked.

"Small is fine. Why?"

"Just trying to be helpful." She smiled innocently, but the message was clear. *Just let me know.*

Mimi returned with the camera, which she put on the table beside me. She then turned and plucked the egg from the simmering pot, dropping it expertly into an egg cup that she slid in front of me, along with a thick slice of brown bread that she'd warmed up, probably to disguise its two-day-old status. As if I'd have complained.

"*Merci beaucoup,*" I said, and dove right in as the two of them chatted about their day, which, as best I could tell, involved going for a long walk and keeping their eyes peeled for soaps and silks. I asked them to add shoe leather to the shopping list but wasn't sure they took it in, and they barely noticed as I thanked Mimi for the food and slipped out and upstairs to let Nicola know what was happening. And, hopefully, to show me how to use the camera, as I'd forgotten to ask for instructions on the way out the door.

●　　●　　●

It's fair to say, I think, that some people enjoy surprises, and some people detest them. I didn't know Dr. Denis Berger enough to gauge his general view of surprises, say, of birthday gifts or sudden trips to the countryside, but judging by the look on his face when Mistress Lau let me into her salon, my second surprise visit was even less welcome than my first.

Of course, shackled to the same cross as before, he was no

better positioned to effectively protest, either, which was rather unfortunate for him. Particularly since his discomfort was the reason for my visit.

"Now then, if you'll give me just a moment to get this contraption set up," I said, glancing at Cassie. "Are you able to make it a little brighter in here, by chance?"

The gag in the doctor's mouth turned his words of protest into a jumble of grunts and moans.

"Yes, of course." She switched on two more wall lamps. "What a nice little camera."

"Thank you, I borrowed it from a friend. She promised that with just the right light, it will capture every wrinkle and fold." I held it up and squinted through the viewfinder. "Lovely. Well, perhaps not lovely, but what I need. Would you mind striking a pose beside our model here, Mistress?"

More wide-eyed protests—at least, I assumed they were protests—and in a moment the esteemed doctor, naked and harnessed, was photographed with his fierce-looking dominatrix. She even added a few welts to his chest and thighs for realism, as if anyone could doubt what they were seeing. All the while, Dr. Berger was groaning and writhing, and no doubt wishing he'd looked this particular gift horse in the mouth.

"I think I have the pictures I need," I said finally. "Now perhaps a few answers. Would you mind?"

"Not at all." Cassie Lau reached up and unstrapped the gag from the back of his head and pulled it free.

"Look, I don't know what you want from me," Berger started, "but for god's sake if you know who I am then—"

I didn't wait for Cassie to kick him in the balls, after all he wasn't paying her, I was and so figured I deserved some fun. I gave him a full minute to recover before stationing myself in front of him.

"First you listen," I said calmly. "I will ask you some questions, and you will answer every single one of them." He opened his mouth to speak, so I stepped back as if to kick him and he shut up immediately. "Good boy," I said. "But listen to this first. I now have pictures that I have no real desire to share. Pictures you most certainly don't want shared. So, if I hear any threats about who you are, who your friends are, any of that bullshit then all of those fine and powerful friends will soon find themselves knowing you a little better than you'd like. Are we clear on that point?"

He nodded, but didn't speak.

"Good," I said. "Now then. Tell me what you know about Jean Grabbin."

"Dr. Jean Grabbin?" he asked, his voice husky from pain.

"That's the one."

"I don't . . . I heard he died. I don't know how."

"In case my directions were unclear." I reached up and slowly put one hand across his throat and pressed, very gently. "I don't need you telling me shit I already know. I found him, so I know he's dead. Tell me how well you knew him, and why he was fired from the hospital."

"I didn't know him well at all, he was in a different department. I heard he was fired for stealing documents, patient files. But it was just a rumor, I don't know for sure."

"Who fired him?"

"The new administration."

"Oh, so that's what we're calling them, is it? Your Nazi bosses." I moved my hand away, suddenly not wanting to touch his skin.

"It's a job, just a job. You do a job, you're a policeman, I'm a doctor."

"And who are you healing, exactly?" I asked.

"It's research, I don't have contact with patients. It's valuable research."

"What are you researching, exactly?"

"Illness."

"Can I borrow that?" I pointed to a nasty-looking whip Cassie had looped over her wrist. "I don't want to risk breaking a toe."

"Of course. Aim for the inner thighs for maximum effect, he hates that." She laughed. "And by that I mean, genuinely hates it, not . . . you know."

"No, no, no . . . you don't have to, I'm answering," he stammered.

"You're right, he must hate it." I glared at him. "You're not answering, you just told me you're researching illness." I lashed him once on his right inner thigh. "What the hell else would you be researching? Be specific. Or just stop wasting my time and tell me what you don't want to tell me."

"But I don't know what that would be."

"Liar," I said, and evened the score on the other thigh, making him cry out in pain. "What does your research have to do with Rennes?"

"That's . . . that's where we get the samples from."

"Samples?" I felt it in that moment, the dread rising in my stomach, the horror and panic and the desperate hope I was wrong. "What fucking samples?"

"The tissue samples. For testing."

The little room started to tilt and I stepped back until I could feel the solid wall behind me. I took slow breaths until the waves of nausea subsided and I won the battle over my body, shutting down every normal, rational, human response while my mind took over and figured out everything else I needed to know.

"A-T4." I stepped toward him, and said it again through gritted teeth. "A-T4." What is it?"

His eyes were streaming tears, and I'd never seen a man look so afraid. Later, I'd wonder if there was a large measure of guilt and self-loathing in there, too, but right now I was providing all the loathing that room needed.

"Aktion T4," he whispered. "It's their name for the program."

"The program you're working on. You're killing children, aren't you?"

"No! No, I'm not, we're not!"

"You're taking children with disabilities to Rennes, killing them there, and shipping them back to Paris to experiment on them." Behind me I heard a sharp intake of breath, and I felt bad Cassie was there to hear this.

"No, I don't know anything about that," he protested. "They die because they're sick and then we do research to see what caused them to be disabled."

"I see," I snarled, "so they all just happen to die within a day or two of being snatched from their homes and taken to Rennes. Is that what you're telling me?"

He was sobbing now. "I don't know anything about that, I don't."

"You know everything about it, you murdering scum."

I wanted to punch him, to lash him, to kick him, but I couldn't. The horror of what he and his charming, sophisticated colleague Andreas von Rauch were doing was so far beyond what I could imagine, it was like they'd drained the life from me, too.

Any retaliation from me would be so weak, so pathetic by comparison, there was simply no point. I steadied myself under the horrified gaze of Cassie and tried to shove my jumbled thoughts back
into some semblance of order. Just because what they were doing
was horrific didn't mean they wouldn't get away with it. I wasn't
naïve enough to think that I could charge over to the hospital and
clap the irons on von Rauch and declare victory. Hell, the fact was
I didn't even know who'd finished off Jean Grabbin, though that
picture was clearing up. And this wriggling worm, pinned to the
cross, could make it even clearer.

"Why were you at the funeral the other day?" I asked.

"I don't know," he began, and I struck him across the face
with the whip, not caring that he screamed like a baby nor that
he'd be sporting a bright red weal on his cheek for a week. "Andreas told me to go! I was ordered to go, to keep an eye on you."

"On me?"

"He said he wanted to know if you were there. If so, I was to
stay, and if not I was to leave and go to an address."

"What address?"

"Please, don't hit me. I would tell you if I could remember. I
asked him to write it down but he said not to. If you give me a
moment, perhaps . . ."

"What part of the city?"

"The Seventh Arrondissement."

"I know exactly where you were to go," I said.

"You do?" The poor bastard looked relieved, so I whipped him
across the belly for good measure.

I stood there thinking for a moment. I was pretty sure I knew
what'd happened, but my next problem was this Aktion T4 abom-
ination. Even assuming I could nail Berger and von Rauch, which

was by no means a certainty, I was hardly in a position to take out a fully functioning Nazi program.

"This Aktion T4," I said. "Who is behind it?"

"Please, it's stopped. For now, anyway." His eyes slid away from my face, and I knew he was lying or trying to hide something. I raised the whip slowly and he squealed, "It is, it is, I promise."

"Keep talking," I growled.

"It has rules, like everything German. It requires three doctors to sign off on every . . . you know." He swallowed and his eyes got large, and we both knew he could no longer deny his part.

"On every time you murder a child."

"It's euthanizing, much more like euthanizing," he said weakly, but no one in the room believed it, least of all him.

"All three of you have to sign off," I said. "But since Brandt died, there've been just two."

"Right." He shifted, and it wasn't just physical discomfort.

"When does the new doctor arrive?"

"Tuesday. The day after tomorrow."

"You know who and when exactly?"

"No, but I can find out," he said hurriedly.

My mind flashed back to Mimi's apartment, to Virginia Hall and her reason for being in France. I remembered her mention of the miniature camera and her aside that whatever I had planned would only make it into her newspaper if I wanted it to. I thought, too, about the power that some people had, and the prejudices others carried with them, and about the power of public horror and I hoped to god it was as effective as I imagined it to be. In sum, I thought quickly and came up with a plan.

And I shared it with the other two people in the room because, as it turned out, I thought their participation would be crucial.

"Cassie, I have imposed on you a great deal, and I have one more favor to ask," I said. "I will pay for your time in full."

"What is it?" I was shocked at her voice, how soft, almost weak it was. She'd heard and apparently understood the gist of what was going on, what her client was doing, and it had shaken her to the core. She was pale and was looking at me, or maybe had just turned away from him.

"I need you to come to my apartment building tonight. Come at seven."

"Yes, just tell me where." Her tone became firm. "And you don't have to pay me. Not for this or for tonight. Just make sure I never see this man ever again."

Behind her, Berger whimpered and I silenced him with a look of contempt.

"You'll see him one more time, and that's tonight. After that, never again. You have my word." I moved toward him, enjoying the look of confusion on his face. "You're invited, too, Fritz."

"Invited?" he stammered. "To what?"

"A dinner party."

"What?"

"You heard me. And it will be the last dinner party you ever attend." I picked up the camera. "And remember what I have here, so don't even think about not showing up. In fact, you don't even want to be a minute late. Do I make myself clear?"

"Yes," he said, nodding furiously.

"Good." I stepped back and gave the murderous bastard one last kick in his impressive manhood just to make sure he climbed the stairs to my place with a limp.

CHAPTER TWENTY-SIX

It was a plan of sorts, of course, and, as hinted at, later on I'd have to admit that it wasn't the most carefully thought-out plan, and it probably had too many moving parts. And it wasn't even completely original; I had my previous scrape with an American journalist to thank for the seeds of this particular variation. But I'd learned in the last war that even when the odds are against you, if you charge full tilt, make enough noise as you go, and hope for the best as you do it, well, sometimes you can force things to go your way. And while I would be happy to take the credit for any success, those three elements—speed, surprise, and luck—were probably why the dinner party came together as it did.

Those things, and the help of some wonderfully devious women. Of course, they needed a little convincing at first.

"A dinner party?" Mimi stared at me. "Are you serious?"

"I am." I gave her my most disarming smile.

"Henri, you want me to host not just a dinner party, but do it *tonight*?"

"That is correct." I was in her kitchen again, and I looked around. "Is Virginia still here?"

"No, she went home. Why?"

"Because she's essential to the plan."

"Plan?" Mimi said, fixing me with a look that was a lot more than inquiring.

"Dinner. I meant dinner."

"I see." She frowned. "And who else have you invited to my home for this evening's little event?"

"I haven't invited them all yet. I need you to do that, too." I handed her a piece of paper. "I made a list."

"Oh, for heaven's sake." She leaned over the list. "I don't even know some of these people. How can I invite people I don't know?"

"Ah, yes. You see the three names on the top, those are the ones you take care of. I'll invite the rest of them."

"Let me see," she said, studying the piece of paper. "Virginia, Nicola, and . . . oh, what a wonderful idea, I'm so glad."

"Think you can manage?" I asked.

"Well, of course."

"Good. Oh, and by the way, two of mine won't be guests exactly."

"What do you mean?" Mimi looked at me, suspicion writ large on her face.

"They will act as servers. Carry the food, take away empty plates, pour the wine."

"I don't need servers at such a small dinner party, Henri,"

Mimi chided. "There will be, what, six of us eating? I don't need servers for that."

"Please try to remember something, dear Mimi. This dinner party isn't about you."

"Well, no need to be rude about it," she said huffily.

"I don't mean to be. But if this is to work, well, I'm asking you to let me take the lead for once."

"And do as I'm told, is that it?"

"You could put it that way, yes."

"Even as a child I was not good at doing what I was told. Oh, the spankings I got for that."

I smiled and thought of Cassie Lau. "We could arrange for that, actually."

"What are you talking about?"

"Nothing, nothing. I'm just asking, can you play along tonight?"

"Why can't you just tell me what you're up to?"

"I'd like to, and I'll tell you afterward." I looked her in the eye. "But you have to believe me when I say this: if you knew, there's no way you'd be able to act natural, act normal, tonight."

"I think you underestimate my acting abilities, Henri."

The truth was, she underestimated the evil at play. I was fairly certain she'd not let certain of the people on that list within a mile of her dining table if she knew the truth, but I wasn't going to dwell on the point.

"You'll know soon enough, I promise."

"All right, well, I suppose I better get busy. Luckily, I have a store of wine and cheese, but I'll need to get hold of some meat and potatoes, maybe a vegetable."

"It doesn't need to be too fancy; the point is to get them here and feed them something, not impress them."

"My dear Henri." She looked at me imperiously. "The point of a dinner party is always to impress. I refuse to host such an event unless I can be sure the guests will be talking about it for a week."

I couldn't help but smile at that. "You have my word, Mimi. They will be talking about it for a lot longer than a week."

"I do wish you would stop being so mysterious."

"Can't and won't," I said. "When you speak to Virginia, can you tell her to bring that miniature camera she talked about? And have her come early, I'll need her help with something."

"Setting up a miniature camera, perhaps?"

"Quite possibly. Now then, I must go." I took Mimi's hand and kissed the back of it. "Thank you for your help and understanding."

"You are welcome, Henri. The truth is, it's been a while since I've had guests and it will be nice to have a full table."

My heart sank on hearing those words, because this wasn't a dinner party; it was a deception, a game I was playing. A play, perhaps, but where some of the actors thought it was real. Mimi knew it wasn't, but she didn't know why. I couldn't tell her, not yet, but I had to let her know she was helping me put on a tragedy, not a comedy.

"Mimi, you have to know one thing. This dinner party, it's not . . ." I cast around for the right words. "It's not one we will look back on fondly."

Her words surprised me. "I know, Henri. I'm not stupid. But you're keeping me in the dark because you want me to pretend it's a normal dinner party. So that's what I'm doing. That's what we all do these days, take the nice moments and pretend they're real for as long as we can." She gave my hand a squeeze. "You spend so much time living with the bad, Henri, you need to do that more often. Pretend. Enjoy the fleeting moments of good."

"Maybe after tonight."

"I hope so." She raised a hand to stop me leaving. "I have a note for you. It was delivered to Nicola but she's gone out and wanted me to give it to you if I saw you."

"A note?"

"Apparently it's important." She went to a side table, where she picked up an envelope and handed it to me. I opened it on the spot and smiled.

"Ah. I know that road, good."

"What is it?"

"It's where a friend of mine lives. A friend of mine, and a guest of yours. Must dash."

I gave her two quick kisses and let myself out of her apartment. I wanted to run upstairs and fill Nicola in on my plan, but since she wasn't home I re-scribbled her name into Mimi's column. I still had the car, thankfully, because the address was in Montmartre and would have been a long walk. And I needed every spare moment in case Étienne Darden wasn't at home in his apartment. I had to find him, convince him to tell me what he knew, to fill in the pieces. And I was pretty certain he was on the right side of all that was going on, which meant I didn't get to use the rougher methods of interrogation that had been so effective with Denis Berger.

And that meant being nice even if he didn't want to cooperate, which was something I could do well enough in normal times. I just wasn't sure I could do it with the knowledge that children were being targeted, and also with the specter of an executioner looming behind me.

•   •   •

I decided against knocking on Étienne Darden's door, thinking he had more reasons to not open it than to do so. Instead, I stood quietly on the third-floor landing and listened. His was an old building, one where sounds traveled—I'd already heard voices of occupants of the apartments I'd passed to get to his. So I was confident that if he was home, I'd hear him moving about.

That confidence waned after fifteen minutes, not because I heard nothing but because the building was so creaky I couldn't tell whether the noises were coming from behind his door or somewhere else. In the end, I did what I should have done from the get-go and banged loudly on his door. I was about to knock again when I heard footsteps behind me, and I turned to see his surprised face as he rounded the corner. We stared at each other for a split second, and then, before I could say a word, he turned and ran.

"Wait, stop!" I shouted, but of course he didn't because no one in the history of policing has ever stopped when a *flic* has yelled that, but still we persist in doing so. I cursed, and took off after him.

He was quick but I'd learned after twenty years of chasing criminals that your best bet is to go flat out from the beginning and not pace yourself, like rookies often did. That's because if you made the person you're chasing panic, there was a good chance they'd bang into someone or take a spill before they had time to gather their wits and plan their escape route. And that's exactly what happened to Étienne Darden. When he heard me clattering at top speed down the narrow wooden staircase behind him he panicked and upped his speed to one he couldn't sustain, not upright anyway, and I had the pleasure of watching him lose his footing and tumble face-first down the last flight. He was still on the first-floor landing when he hit, and he pushed himself to his feet but his left ankle declined to cooperate and the look he gave me told me I could slow down and catch him at my own speed, which I did. He'd not even made it to the front door of the building.

"That was fucking stupid," I said. "Now you have to walk all the way back upstairs with a twisted ankle."

"Upstairs? You're not arresting me?"

"For what?"

"I don't know. You're a policeman, why else are you here?"

"How about we go back upstairs, where you can stop asking questions and I can start. How does that sound?"

"And then you arrest me?"

"No. I am almost positive that nothing you say today will result in me arresting you."

"What if I don't want to talk to you?"

"That would be very unfortunate," I said, intentionally ambiguously, because even though I had no intention of, say, twisting his other ankle, there was no reason that possibility couldn't float in the back of his mind. "Let's get you upstairs, eh?"

He winced and swore all the way, but we got there and when he collapsed into a leather armchair I sat on the sofa across from him. The apartment itself was tiny, just this room with a kitchenette, a small washroom by the main door and as far as I could tell no bedroom. I was probably sitting on his bed. But it was clean and tidy, and had more than its fair share of books.

"Like reading, I see."

"Keeps me sane," he said, rubbing his ankle. "And it's about the only thing you can do these days that won't get you killed."

"Even a simple staircase can be dangerous these days," I said.

"Very funny." He gave me a doleful look. "Why are you here?"

"To get some answers."

"I didn't kill Jean."

"Why would you say that?"

"I was at his apartment on Saturday, he was dead. Makes sense you'd blame me."

"Did you have a reason to kill him?"

He laughed bitterly. "I'm a dark-skinned man at the scene of a crime, what other reason do you need?"

"You were friends with him?"

"We became friends, yes."

"After a fistfight. Strange way to become friends."

"You seem to know plenty," he said. "No need for me to tell you much of anything."

"Wrong. There's plenty I don't know."

"Well, there's plenty I can't tell you, and even more I'm not willing to."

"Why wouldn't you help me catch the person who killed your friend?"

"Why do you think?"

"I have no clue, I really don't."

He laughed again, then shook his head. "My god, you really don't. You know they're going after the Jews first, right?"

"I mean, yes, I know they are targeting Jewish people but what does that—"

"I said first. Look at history, Detective. It's always been the same: some band of conquering marauders takes over a country and tries to mold it into their own image. Or the image of how they see themselves. Except with the Nazis it's not a country, it's the whole world."

"Not yet."

"It will be. But that's not my point. My point is, I don't look like they want me to look. So pretty soon, when they realize Jews are getting thin on the ground they will be looking out for people like me."

"What does that have to do with helping me catch Jean Grabbin's killer?"

"It means I have no plans to stick my neck out and make myself visible. No plans to speak out against people who have every reason, every desire, to make me disappear."

"You're talking about the people behind Aktion T4."

His eyebrows shot up in surprise. "You know about that?"

"I know something about it, yes. But not everything, that's why I'm here."

"That's . . . different then. Who told you?"

"Denis Berger."

"That weasel?" Darden's eyes flashed with anger. "How did you manage to get him to turn on his new masters?"

"I can be very persuasive under the right circumstances."

"I hope you made him suffer. That bastard deserves to swing for what he's done."

"If that's true, then I'll see he does. But I can't do it without your help."

He looked at me, long and hard, then slowly shook his head. "I'm sorry, Detective. I would like to. And in the old days I know you could have helped me out, guaranteed my safety, but these days, that's not true, is it?"

I didn't speak for a moment. I didn't know what to say because he was right. Finally, I nodded. "You're correct. I can't protect you from the Nazis. I can just ask you to do the right thing. To get justice for your friend and help me stop this evil they are perpetrating. Isn't that enough?"

"The moment I tell you what I know and you write your report, which I know you have to do, then I'm dead. We both know that's true. I have one life and I'm the only one around to protect it, and I didn't sign on to be a hero. That's your job."

"So you'll do nothing, just sit in your apartment and read your books while children are being murdered."

"I didn't say I wasn't doing anything. I just don't plan on doing anything with my name written on it." He smiled wryly. "My father used to get annoyed when I'd get in trouble for doing small things. He was a big character, and he said if you were going to ignore the rules then don't bend them, break them. If you were going to make a splash, then soak everyone around you."

"Meaning?"

"Meaning I don't plan on dying because I signed my name to a piece of paper. That is *not* how I intend on leaving this world."

"Not even to stop children being murdered?"

"I know it's selfish, Detective. But if it means me being murdered, I'll trust you to find another way."

"And if I can't?"

"Then think badly of me, I'll deserve it." He wagged a finger. "But remember this. It's not me killing them, and it's not you. It's the Nazis. They're doing this to us, and that's all there is to it."

"Just tell me this. I found a piece of paper at Grabbin's place." I turned my mind back to the writing on it. "It said, 'Étienne D says: RVABDBVAT4 in R—need three.' What does that mean?"

He thought for a moment, then asked me to write it down, which I did. After studying it, he smiled and said, "It's the initials of those involved. Andreas von Rauch, Denis Berger, Viktor Brandt. But written backward."

"And it's true they need three doctors to sign off on . . ." I grimaced. "To keep the program running."

"Yes." He looked at me, sadness in his eyes. "I know you think I'm a coward, and maybe I am. But I don't know how else to stay alive. I'm sorry."

I got slowly to my feet, knowing he was right. He was my only witness but once he filled in the gaps, named the Germans behind Aktion T4 for a formal report, he was a dead man. And I was powerless against the new regime, against the SS and the Gestapo, who could snatch him up and do whatever they wanted with him whenever they wanted. I started for the door and had my hand raised to open it when a thought struck me and I turned back to him, a surge of hope rising in my chest.

"There is a way," I said.

"A way for what?"

"I can protect you. If you give your statement and sign it, I can keep you safe."

He shook his head. "The police have no power against—"

"I'm not talking about the police." I smiled as I pictured Daniel Moulin and his band of gravediggers. "Have you heard of this new movement across Paris, across the whole of France? It's called the Resistance, and one of the things they do is get people who are in danger to safety."

He cocked his head to one side, clearly interested. "What would that mean for me, exactly?"

"I'm not sure. I'd have to talk to some people."

"America," he said wistfully. "I've always wanted to go to America. But I'll sign your statement for Switzerland. I'd settle for a view of the Alps."

CHAPTER TWENTY-SEVEN

Étienne Darden's fridge was empty, so we sat across his small dining table sipping from glasses of water he'd poured from the kitchen sink. Mine was lukewarm and a little salty, and I cursed the Germans for managing to ruin even the tap water.

"Just so we're clear," he said, tapping the blank piece of paper that sat between us, "I'm not signing anything until your people promise me safe passage."

"We're short on time, Étienne." I produced a pencil from my jacket pocket. The truth was, *I* was short on time, but he didn't need to know the distinction. "We have to do this now."

"I'm not signing until I know I'm safe."

"A statement is no good to me unsigned. It's nothing but an anonymous piece of short fiction."

"I'll tell you now, you write it down, I'll sign later."

"Fine, we'll do it your way." And just like that, I had another guest to my dinner party. I started asking him some basic questions just to identify him—his full name, place and date of birth, job and length of employment at the hospital—and finally got to the meat of it.

"How long have you been friends with Jean Grabbin?" I asked.

"Less than a month, not even two weeks. I've known him for years, of course, working at the hospital, and we were always friendly, but we became friends more recently."

"How did that happen?"

He grinned. "It started with a fight."

"I heard about that. Tell me more."

"I was a porter at the hospital, as I said. That means I pop up anywhere I'm needed." He shook his head slowly. "You wouldn't believe some of the things I've walked in on."

"I probably would, given what I do for a living."

"Fair enough, maybe you of all people would. Anyway, I walked past the morgue one night, close to midnight and saw a light on."

"Why were you there?"

"I park my bicycle behind the building. There's a rail I can lock it to, and it's the only place I've not had the damn thing stolen from. Plus, it's out of sight of you-know-who. Damned Boche would requisition it as quick as they could adjust the saddle."

"True enough. I presume the morgue was supposed to be dark and empty at that time?"

"Sometimes it's operational at night, especially these days. But the blackout cover had obviously failed, so it wasn't that I was surprised someone was in there, I just didn't want them to get in trouble for not being blacked out."

"Very kind of you."

He shrugged as if everyone in the world would have done the same. "Anyway, I went in and there was Dr. Grabbin, all by himself. Well, *not* all by himself, which is the point of the story, I suppose."

"Who was with him?" I leaned forward, riveted.

"A child. A dead child. I was shocked at first, and he looked so guilty. I knew he was up to no good and the only thing I could imagine was that he was . . . you know."

"My god, surely—"

"And, to reinforce my worst fears," he quickly went on, "he had this large bag; he was putting this child's body into it. I was horrified."

"I can imagine."

"Well, the thing is, I didn't really give him a chance to explain. I just grabbed him and dragged him out of there and beat him until two of the security guards stopped me."

"Did you tell them what he was doing?"

"I couldn't." He rubbed the back of his head. "They saw a man with darker skin punching a doctor so they assumed I was mugging him. They stopped me by clattering my skull with their nightsticks. I still get headaches from it."

"So what happened?"

"We both got terminated. Me for attacking him, and him because someone higher up didn't trust what he was up to. At least that's what he told me."

"You were seen later together, days later, talking."

"He found me and explained what he was doing."

"Which was what?"

"He'd noticed these kids being brought into the hospital. Seen them being kept in a secure ward and then quickly taken away, maybe a day or so later. Then they'd be back, but dead."

"So he was taking their bodies to try and figure out how they died exactly?" I asked. "But he wasn't a pathologist, was he?"

"No, he wasn't. And that's not what he was doing. Not at all."

"Then what?"

"Did you know, he had a daughter?"

"I didn't, no." Nor did I see the relevance, but I humored him just the same.

"He had a wife and a daughter. When the girl, Abbie was her name, was eight years old she got sick. Some lung disease, he told me the name but I don't recall it. Anyway, after that she was basically an invalid, needing constant care and always around. Could never go out with friends or do anything that a normal kid could do."

"That's sad." *And still irrelevant.*

"They got to be very close, Jean and his daughter. Then one day she was feeling better so his wife took her out on a little boat on the Seine, while Jean was at work. He never found out exactly what happened, the details of it, but somehow the boat tipped over and both his wife and daughter drowned."

"Oh, I wasn't expecting that ending."

"Can you imagine going on a boat in the River Seine without being able to swim?" He shook his head disapprovingly. "I never said that to him, of course. Anyway, to make it even more tragic, they never found Abbie's body. The wife, yes, but not his little girl."

"Oh, I think I see now."

"He was returning them. The children. He didn't have the skills or knowledge to figure out how those kids died, and he was powerless to stop it obviously, but the one thing he could do was return them to their loved ones. That way they could have what he never had: someone to say goodbye to. A grave to visit."

"I judged him harshly," I said.

"I did, too. And he wasn't an easy man to like but he had his reasons for how he was. As you now know."

"Did he tell you about Viktor Brandt?"

He looked at me for a moment. "Does this have to go in the report?"

"Probably. I need to solve this case, no matter who did it."

"He told me. He said he and Viktor immediately had an interest in each other, had been out once together, then when Jean realized something was going on with the department Viktor worked in, they had a huge falling-out. They'd had one tryst at Jean's late brother's apartment, just to be away from prying eyes, and Jean had Viktor meet him there, to talk. Jean never got into the details, but I think Viktor laid out the whole thing, even tried to get Jean on board. Jean was horrified, sickened to his core. He used those exact words to me."

"And so he killed Brandt?"

"After Brandt threatened him. Once he realized Jean wanted nothing to do with this program, or with Viktor himself ever again, Viktor told him to keep his mouth shut or he'd end up in one of those work camps we keep hearing about. Apparently his personality changed in that moment, he went stone-cold, scared the hell out of Jean."

"And that's when he killed him."

"Yes. He said he didn't know what else to do, how else to protect himself. He knew he couldn't keep quiet, and of course that meant he'd obviously be identified as the person leaking information."

"And he staged it to look like a burglary gone wrong because he knew a dead German, especially a high-ranking one, meant reprisals."

"Exactly."

"What about the body on the tracks, who was that?" I asked, scribbling all this down furiously. And hopefully legibly.

"A homeless veteran who'd just died. Don't worry, Jean didn't kill anyone else."

"How did he get the body from the hospital to the tracks? That's a lot of work for one man."

"Yes, a lot of work," Darden said. He held my eye as he spoke his next words. "It's almost as if he had some help."

"Ah, yes." I put my pencil down. "That makes more sense. Some help, of course. I don't suppose you would know anything about that, would you?"

"Not a thing," he said, with the most innocent of smiles on his lips.

•　•　•

My stomach rumbled with hunger as I drove through the winding streets of Paris back toward the Seine, the river that had taken Jean Grabbin's wife and daughter from him, but also the river that had somehow led to the parents of these dead children having them home one last time. Tragedy did strange things to people. I'd seen that firsthand in my job and in the last war. It could destroy part of you but also bring to life something else, some deeper part of you. For Jean Grabbin, that was a streak of decency, of kindness, that he otherwise kept under wraps.

I felt bad waking Daniel Moulin—he'd made it clear how tired he was—but when I banged on his door he was fully dressed and sipping a cup of coffee.

"Would you like some?" he asked.

"Is it actually coffee?"

"Not really. I wouldn't really recommend it. Just a habit at this point."

"Thanks, I'll manage without then."

We sat in his small living room, and I told him what I'd learned from Denis Berger and, more pressingly, from Étienne Darden.

"So Grabbin wasn't the child rapist we thought," he mused. "Quite the opposite."

"Right. The next question is, can your people help Darden?"

"Probably, but it's not as simple as that."

"It is to me. And it is to him."

"Of course, but I'm not the one who decides these things. I told you how it works, a loosely associated network of cells, no one knows anyone, all that secret stuff."

"Daniel, without his statement these bastards might get away with all this. You must know someone who can make a decision about helping him. And quickly."

"As a matter of fact, I do." He sat back and eyed me. "But Henri, I'm really trusting you on this. No one can ever know his identity."

"You have my word. Who is he?"

"His name is also Jean, perhaps fittingly." He raised a finger to reiterate the seriousness of what he was about to tell me. "Please, Henri, if you keep just one promise to me, it must be this one."

"I'll keep them all, Daniel, but especially this one. Who is this Jean fellow?"

"His name is Jean Pierre Moulin. And he's my big brother."

I imagined my eyebrows stretching over the back of my head, such was my surprise. "Ah, so he got you into all this in the first place, did he?"

"He gave me a choice."

"Good. Can I talk with him?"

"That will be up to him." Moulin looked at his watch. "There's a café on the corner; you walked past it coming here."

"I noticed, yes."

"Have lunch there. If he wants to meet with you, he will come by. If he's not there by the time you finish eating, he's not coming."

"He's close by, then." I stood. "Thank you. And I'm hungry, so this might work out perfectly."

"Just to warn you," Moulin said. "He'll want something in return."

"Like what?"

"I don't know, but he doesn't do favors. He trades services, and in my experience he'll ask more of you than you're asking of him."

"What happened to just doing it for the right reason, for France?"

"Whatever he asks of you, it will be for France, I can promise you that much." He stood up, too, and I followed him out of the building, where he went left and I went right. I dug my hands deep into my pockets against the cold, and as I walked I hoped his brother would see me, and hoped almost as much that the café had something worth eating.

Chicken soup, as it happens, which went down a treat, as did a half-carafe of the house wine. Rough stuff, but so were the times and so I didn't mind the burn at the back of my throat as much as I would have seven months earlier. I ate slowly, of course, as if the rate I spooned the broth into my mouth would somehow affect Jean Pierre Moulin's decision to see me.

When I put my spoon down for the last time he still hadn't arrived, and I thought about ordering another half-carafe and drowning my sorrows, but I had too much thinking to do for that. I knocked back the last mouthful and reached for my hat.

"Just one course, monsieur?" A figure appeared and helped himself to a chair across from me. He was a handsome man in his early forties, at a guess, wearing a black wool coat with a dark scarf wrapped around his neck, and a hat much like mine perched on his head. He took it off and smoothed his slicked-back hair with one hand, as his dark eyes seemed to penetrate me. He looked like a movie star, but had an air of ruthlessness, even danger, about him.

"Looking after my figure," I said. "It's good soup, I think there's actual chicken in there."

"Rare these days."

I lit a cigarette and offered him one, then lit his. "Thank you for coming."

"My brother speaks well of you," he said. "A man to be trusted, he seems to think."

"Those also rare these days?"

"Not so much that they're rare." He blew out a plume of smoke. "The problem lies in confiding in someone who's not. A single spilled secret these days means your neck, and a fairly unpleasant time for a week or so beforehand."

"So I've heard. Trying to avoid a little neck-stretching myself."

"The Boche have you working for them, my brother tells me. Solve the crime or suffer the consequences."

"That's about the gist of it."

"And you think I can help." He had a wry smile on his face, as if the idea was preposterous.

"You can. I need a witness to sign a statement, then go somewhere safe."

"Won't you need him to testify at a trial?"

"I don't think it'll come to that," I said. "In my experience, the Germans don't like trials, especially when the evidence looks bad for them. No, I think my signed statement will get me most of the way there."

"And he won't sign unless he's promised safe passage." He sat back and stared at me again. "Daniel told me."

"Those were his exact words." I tapped the ash from my cigarette. "Daniel told me you'd want something in return."

"I do. Two things, really. Information from you and action from him." He smiled. "The two are related."

"What exactly are you asking for?"

"My understanding of this Aktion T4, the one your friend is going to tell you all about, is that it requires three doctors to sign off on each . . . well, let's call it what it is: murder. Am I right?"

"Yes. Right now there are just two of them."

"Thank heavens for that." Moulin took a drag and stared out of the café's window for a moment. "So what we need from you, or him, is information about who and when the new doctor arrives."

"I already know that. On Tuesday."

"Ah, you must not have told Daniel, he didn't know. Tuesday, eh? That's good enough."

"Good enough for what?"

"For us to prepare your friend to carry out his part of this deal."

"And that is?"

"He will assassinate the newly arriving doctor of death." He stubbed out his cigarette. "That's the condition. He does that, we help. Otherwise, he's on his own."

I looked hard to see if he was joking. "You can't expect a man like that, a hospital porter, to assassinate a German in broad daylight. It's suicide! Not to mention the repr—"

"It's war, is what it is, Detective. And I'm not here to negotiate." He rose and shook my hand. "Let Daniel know by nine o'clock tomorrow morning. A minute late, and the deal's off."

CHAPTER TWENTY-EIGHT

It was a pared-down affair, as Mimi apologized to the guests as they trickled in. That may have been the case in terms of the amount and range of food, but not as far as the excitement I felt. Or maybe it was terror. Perhaps a mix of the two. Either way, I knew several things had to go exactly right for the evening to be a success, and none of those things had anything to do with the food and wine.

The first thing had gone right. I'd taken Virginia Hall up to my apartment, on the pretext of choosing an appropriate bottle of port, and told her what I knew and what my plan was. And, of course, how essential she was to it. Doing so was a gamble for sure, but there was something professional about her, almost clinical, that suggested she'd be able to know the truth and fake pleasantness this evening. It helped, too, that she wasn't the host and didn't have to lead the evening by the nose, as Mimi would. I also guessed that her journalism background, and her clearly nefarious other reasons to be in Paris, would give her enough strength of mind, and will, not to throttle von Rauch and Berger at first sight.

She'd been shocked, just as I was, but she rallied quickly and an angry glint in her eye backed up her words that she was on board with all of it. She'd then spent fifteen minutes going over the delicate mechanisms of the camera, impressing me with her knowledge and, despite the circumstances, she aroused feelings I'd not been familiar with in a while. Maybe it was her demeanor, so assured and confident, but I knew for certain it was also the subtle but rich perfume, one that you could barely notice unless you leaned into her, which I found myself delighted to do on several occasions.

The first to arrive were Étienne Darden and Cassie Lau, who I also briefed in my apartment. Nicola had found what passed for waiter's clothes, basic white over black, and they took turns changing in my room. When we were all ready, me in a suit and Nicola in a red dress, we trooped down the stairs and I introduced them to Mimi and Virginia. But only after giving Mimi credit for the transformation of her apartment. The wartime harshness had been smoothed away by candlelight, several vases of spindly and slightly fading flowers, and an immaculately set dining table, replete with china plates, several bottles of good Bordeaux, and snow-white napkins.

"It looks like an expensive restaurant," I said, looking around. "And smells like one. What's on the menu?"

"You'll find out," Mimi said after shaking hands with her new waitstaff and steering me to one side. "Now then, I want the full story."

"Not until after, remember?" I said.

"You said nothing about telling me after it's over," she said crossly.

"I'm fairly certain I did." I gave her my most innocent smile, but the truth remained: I didn't trust her to know the truth and be able to maintain a dinner-party disposition. I was only able to do it because I was pulling the strings on this little show. "Now then, shall I decant the wine while we await our two guests?"

"I'm the host here," Mimi said, reasserting herself. "And don't you forget it."

Andreas von Rauch was the first to arrive, and with Teutonic promptness he knocked on the door at precisely eight o'clock.

"Princess Bonaparte, thank you so much for the invitation," he said, giving her two quick kisses, and then whipped out a bouquet of flowers from behind his back.

"Why thank you, Andreas, these are gorgeous, do come in." She beckoned him inside. "It's just a small affair, you really needn't have bothered."

"Nonsense," he said, turning to shake hands with me. "Detective Lefort, I'm delighted to see you here."

"He's a regular guest, having saved my life as I'm sure you know," Mimi said. "We've been friends ever since. He's quite the storyteller, in fact."

"I had no idea," von Rauch said, throwing me a sideways glance. "I've only seen his professional side, but maybe tonight?"

"Oh, I think tonight is as good as any to see a different side of me," I said. "But first, let me get you a glass of wine. Red, I assume?"

"Wonderful, thank you." He shrugged off his coat and handed it to an obedient Cassie Lau. Thankfully, it was too dark to see the daggers she was sending his way with her eyes, so without even acknowledging her he turned to talk to Mimi. I went into the kitchen, where the decanter sat on the counter.

"Need wineglasses?" Étienne asked, pointing to the sideboard, where half a dozen sat gleaming.

"Just one for now." I nodded my head toward the living room. "You probably heard, Satan arrived and wants his Bordeaux."

"Oh, I heard." Darden grimaced. "And if I'm playing waiter, I had better be the one to take it in to him."

"No, the plan was for you to appear at the end, remember?"

"That will make him suspicious, if I'm only there to clear away dishes or hand out coats."

"If he recognizes you from the hospital we'll have some explaining to do."

"Recognize me?" Darden smiled and shook his head. "There is no chance of that, I promise you."

"How can you be so sure?"

"Because first of all he'd have to see me. An Indian man carrying a tray? No chance at all."

I found a silver tray for Darden to carry the wine on, and followed as he took it out to von Rauch, who swept it up without so much as a glance at the man bringing it to him. That done, Darden gave me a *Told you so* look as he headed back into the safety of the kitchen.

As he did so, there was another knock at the door.

"Who might that be?" von Rauch asked, smiling.

"Your colleague is the only one not here, so I'm assuming him," Mimi said, and went to let him in. I could have been mistaken, but von Rauch's smile tightened just a fraction at the mention of his colleague. And when Denis Berger walked in the smile disappeared altogether, although because he was von Rauch he covered the moment with a sip of his wine.

Tension between the two? I wondered. *Or maybe the German just doesn't like surprises.*

Berger did an even poorer job of disguising his emotions, visibly flinching when he saw Cassie Lau and me standing there next to each other. I positively glowed inside when she handed him a glass of red wine and his hand shook so much he almost spilled it.

"What happened to your face?" Mimi asked, after the introductions were complete. Berger immediately touched his fingertips to the welt on his cheek and mumbled something about a tree branch. I was watching von Rauch at that point because, as much as I reveled in both of them being uncomfortable, I needed to see if he was becoming suspicious. The firm set of his jaw suggested he was, or at least might look for a chance to find a quiet moment with Berger, so I whispered to Mimi that we needed to get things moving. For once, she took my directions without an argument and steered the two guests of honor to the dining table. I walked over with Virginia Hall, and we took our seats, too.

"We don't want to violate curfew too badly, after all," she said lightheartedly, and we all laughed to join in. With a few easy gestures, and just as we'd planned, she installed von Rauch at one end of the table, with Berger to his left, and me beside Berger. To my left, at the other end of the table, Mimi took her seat. Virginia Hall sat next to her and across from me, with Nicola between her and von Rauch. I could tell by the look on her face she was less than enthused to be so close to him, but we all had our parts to play and the seating arrangement mattered. I immediately took out my cigarettes and offered them around, putting my matchbox in front of me in case someone needed a light.

"Henri, put those away, we're about to eat," Mimi chided, and I did so but left the matches on the table.

Our first course was escargots, and it was their garlic that had been enchanting me since I'd walked into her apartment that evening. On a good night I'd put away twelve to kick off a meal, but usually I'd show some restraint and tackle just a half dozen. No one said a word when the special snail plates appeared with just three on them. Cassie put two small baskets of bread on the table, and we happily helped ourselves so we could swab and soak up every drop of garlic butter on our plates. Like every delicacy these days, this was one to be savored and each of us did so, me as much as anyone. We were all quiet in the moment, too, as if talk could dilute or sour the heady flavors of the dish.

Cassie and Étienne Darden cleared the plates away, their eyes down and movements deliberate, as if they'd been born to play waiters. I looked at Virginia. She'd been quiet throughout, but I could understand that. Better to be quiet and process what I'd told her than risk saying something that would mess up the evening's plan. Talking across the table, Mimi and von Rauch were in the middle of a discussion about playwrights.

"Other than Goethe, no Germans really spring to mind," Mimi was saying.

"And I think of him as a novelist," von Rauch said, thoughtful. "Yes, it's strange how we can be so strong in other areas of literature, and in the arts generally, but not when it comes to the theater."

I turned to Berger on my right and spoke quietly to him. "I'm more of a wine man than theater; how about you, Berger?"

He'd been quiet since arriving, unsurprisingly, and now he responded with as few words as possible.

"I like both."

"Well, why don't you follow me into the kitchen to see what we're drinking next? I sprained my wrist earlier, might need help with the cork."

"Use your other hand," he said, not moving.

I mouthed the word "now" and he reluctantly got up and followed me into the kitchen.

"Don't make this more difficult than you have to," I said, my voice low but firm. "I'm looking for an excuse to publish those photos."

"How do I know you won't, no matter what I do?"

"You don't. But your best bet for me to be charitable is to do as I say, and do it right away. Am I clear?"

He glanced at our two makeshift waitstaff, who were watching with interest, and nodded. *"Oui."*

"Good. Do you have details for me?"

"Tuesday, like I said before. The train is coming in from Lyons, that's where he is now, and it arrives at Gare de Lyon at noon."

"His name?"

"Dr. Klaus Scheffler. I met him once."

"Good. What does he look like?"

Berger shrugged. "Like anyone. Average height and weight, nothing to really . . . Wait, when he's outside he always wears a bowler hat."

"A bowler hat?"

"Yes, those stupid hats the British wear."

"What else?"

"That's all." He looked at me. "What are you going to do?"

"Just keep an eye on him, nothing more than that."

"If you try anything, the reprisals will be bad."

"I'm well aware of that," I said, handing him a wine bottle. "Which is why all I want to do is keep an eye on him. Open that, will you?"

I watched as he did so, then took the bottle from him and we went back to the table.

"Have you heard of Bertolt Brecht, Henri?" Mimi asked when we sat.

"You still discussing Germany's lack of theatrical talent?" I poured wine for Virginia Hall, and then myself. "And no, I haven't."

"A damned communist, that one," von Rauch said. "Shame, he has talent; why he'd want to waste it chasing stupidity I will never know."

Cassie and Étienne interrupted the discussion by bringing in a large pot of coq au vin, and two dishes of mixed vegetables.

"This is a bit of a peasant dish, I'm afraid," Mimi said. "But it's the one I could find ingredients for."

"It smells delicious," von Rauch said, and he wasn't wrong. Nicola, who'd also been quiet most of the evening, was staring wide-eyed at the pot and I wondered if she'd just jump straight in.

"Thank you. I'm not a great cook but it is fun to have company again," Mimi said. She ladled out small portions to us, and we helped ourselves to the vegetables. I homed in on some carrots, delighted to see more again so soon. Beside me, Berger seemed to have lost his appetite, taking one spoonful of vegetables, which sat idle in the middle of his plate as he pushed his portion of chicken around with his fork.

We ate in silence for a few minutes, then the conversation started up again and moved from literature to cinema, and then on to the perfidies of the British. Which, as it turned out, was the one subject we all agreed on. We ate as we talked, and a casual observer would never have known there was a war on, let alone mortal enemies sitting at the same table. Of course, it helped that von Rauch, and to a large extent Denis Berger, had no clue what was about to happen. As with the escargot, forks and knives were eventually put down and our plates thoroughly scrubbed clean with scraps of bread.

"That was exquisite," I said truthfully. "I can't wait for the chocolate cake dessert."

"Very amusing, Henri. There aren't enough eggs in Paris to bake a cake, you know that."

"You know, if you do this again," von Rauch piped up. "And if you see fit to invite me back, please take the liberty of providing me with a list of ingredients. I'm sure I can find enough eggs for a cake. Maybe even for a soufflé."

"A soufflé would be something, wouldn't it?" I said to Mimi.

"Yes, specifically because it would be beyond my cooking skills."

"Not mine," Nicola said.

"I can vouch for that," I said, and looked up as the invisible staff came to clear plates. My stomach tightened and I dipped my left hand into my jacket pocket for my cigarettes, and put my right on the matchbox. I watched out of the corner of my eye as Cassie Lau moved to clear Nicola's plate, putting her beside von Rauch at the very moment Nicola nudged an almost-empty wine bottle with her elbow.

In one swift, and rehearsed, motion Cassie Lau stooped

and caught it, her eyes on me as her head paused at von Rauch's chest level, a smile on her face. He instinctively turned to look at her, smiling instinctively at the deftness of her catch, a smile that froze in place when he saw that she'd undone the top two buttons of her blouse. For a moment he was as still as a statue except for his eyes, which opened as wide as I'd ever seen them. For my part, I already had the matchbox in my hand and pressed down on the top of it, just as Virginia Hall had shown me. If I'd aimed it right, the single photo I had time to take would capture Dr. Andreas von Rauch, with his mouth grinning and eyes gaping at one of Paris's most exclusive sex workers, her top undone and, from my angle anyway, a good amount of flesh showing. I hadn't figured out the intricacies of Nazi racism, but I had to think her being half Chinese wouldn't hurt our cause, either.

We just had to hope I'd aimed it right.

CHAPTER TWENTY-NINE

We finished the meal with a poor selection of cheeses, which allowed me to take a second photo of the man at the end of the table. This time, it was with Étienne Darden beside him, delivering a sliver of Camembert. And how right the poor fellow had been—he donned a jacket for his performance, and von Rauch didn't come close to noticing the change in attire, so invisible was Étienne Darden to him.

It made for a good photograph, though, one that, arguably, showed Herr von Rauch dining out with an Indian man, even sharing a portion of cheese with him. Again, assuming I'd pointed the tiny camera in the right direction and hit the button at the right time.

When it was time for them to leave, von Rauch just about

snatched his coat from Cassie Lau, who'd been chastised by Mimi for forgetting to do up her shirt properly.

"In the old days," von Rauch had said gravely as he put it on, "she'd have gotten a good thrashing for that earlier display."

I fought a smile with all my might, eventually having to turn away so I didn't have to make up an explanation for my response to the night's greatest moment of irony. Berger squirmed at the comment, which made it all the more enjoyable for me.

Once they'd gone, though, I had a much less enjoyable task.

"Étienne, we need to talk," I said.

"Are you going to help me?" he asked.

"Let's go upstairs to my apartment." I let the others know we were leaving, and turned to Cassie Lau. "Madame, thank you so much for your help tonight, and this past week."

"It was my pleasure. I wish there was more that I could do."

"If I can think of anything, I will let you know." *One more soldier for the Moulins, perhaps?* I then led Étienne Darden up one more flight to my apartment and poured him a glass of wine.

"This doesn't bode well." He sat on the couch and I in my usual armchair across from him. "You could have just said yes."

"It's going to be up to you."

"I don't understand. You know I will sign in exchange for help disappearing."

"And that can happen. But they want something in return."

"You're getting the statement."

"As far as they are concerned, that's for me." I lit two cigarettes and gave him one. "They want something for themselves."

"What?"

"They want you to kill a man."

He stopped mid-drag on his cigarette and slowly exhaled. "What did you say?"

"They know about Aktion T4 and they want to put a stop to it."

"They want me to kill the new doctor?"

"Exactly."

"Henri, my god." He pointed to the floor. "We just had two of the bastards downstairs. If killing them is what these people want, why didn't we do it then?"

"For a lot of reasons. Mostly because the risk to Mimi, Nicola, all of us would have been astronomical. Even if we'd somehow gotten away with it—and I don't see how you kill two people on the fifth floor and dispose of their bodies without anyone noticing—there would be reprisals. Plus, one of the many things I've learned in my job is that the most successful criminals don't commit their crimes in their own backyards, let alone their own homes."

"I can accept that, but there will be reprisals anyway."

"Maybe not."

"What do you mean?"

"Look, on the one hand you could try and assassinate that bastard on the quiet. Shoot or stab him when no one's around, make his body disappear. Right?"

"I'm not a killer, Henri. I wouldn't know how to do all that, or even if I could do it."

"What did you do in the last war?"

"I went to school. I was a child."

"Ah, so no experience to fall back on. But that's all right because I don't think that's the best way."

"Why not?"

"Because von Rauch is many things, but he's not an idiot. If his new doctor disappears under suspicious circumstances, just like his last one did, then he's going to start pushing for answers. And from what I hear, when these people start doing that, it gets ugly fast."

"Henri, listen to me. I don't think I can kill someone in cold blood, however you think it should be done."

I took a deep breath. "I don't mean to be harsh, but take a look around. People have died, are dying every day, to fight these bastards."

"Do you know why I work at the hospital?"

"Is this where you give me some sentimental horseshit about wanting to help people?"

"It's not horseshit, it's true. I got my hands dirty every day, I'm not afraid of blood, vomit, piss; I cleaned that up daily. But I'm not capable of killing someone in cold blood."

"I didn't say it would be easy, but everyone is capable of it. And it's hardly cold blood, either."

"Of course it is."

"What about the children these people are murdering? How about you lift a finger, a trigger finger, for them?"

"With more killing?"

"You'd be *stopping* more killing. Look, I think I know how this can work, but you're going to have to do it." He started to protest. "Just hear what I have to say. We can talk more about your reservations after."

"They aren't just reservations. I told you, I can't just—"

"Wait and listen first." I'd smoked my cigarette to its natural death and stubbed out the butt in the ashtray on the coffee table. "Have you even shot a gun before?"

"No, why would I have?" he asked.

"*Merde.* Well, it's not difficult, the mechanics of it."

"So you say."

"Never mind the details, for now anyway, but let me lay out the big picture, how I think this can and should work." I lit another smoke and wished I'd had one glass of wine fewer than I had. "There's something the Germans can't stand . . . well, a lot of things, obviously, but von Rauch typifies the need to look good, to look professional and proper. Which means the last thing they want is bad publicity and embarrassment. They will be getting the former, but with our help he might escape a little of the latter."

"Honestly, I don't know what you're talking about."

"I'm talking about how this happens. Our new doctor has to die in a very public place, and in a very public way."

Darden was staring at me as if I were insane. "You want me to kill a German in front of as many witnesses as possible."

"Exactly! See, I knew you'd get it."

"I get that you're utterly mad. Why would I even consider that as a plan?"

"Ah, that's the second part of my plan. Or the first part, I don't think it matters. Anyway, I will have your statement, we will have what I saw in Rennes, and we will have Denis Berger in handcuffs. And trust me, I know how to make that man talk."

"What do you need my statement for then?"

"Because I only have two witnesses and one of them was involved, which doesn't do a lot for his credibility, unless I have corroboration. And you are my corroboration. See how it works?"

"I see that, now, yes, but can't even begin to imagine shooting someone in public. That's a guaranteed death sentence, and you might remember I came to you to avoid that."

"Do you know what Virginia Hall, who you just met, does?" I asked.

"I have no idea, and I don't think I care."

"She's a journalist. An international correspondent for a major newspaper."

"And?"

"It brings me back to what I was saying about the Nazis hating to look bad. And it could be more powerful even than just making them look bad. Virginia is going to write a news story about Aktion T4, what it is and how it works. That story will hit the newsstands, she thinks on the front page, in America the very next day after this shooting, which will be part of the story." I looked over at Darden, but he didn't seem impressed. "Look, the world is going to be furious about this, undoubtedly. More particularly, Americans safe in their cozy lives the other side of the Atlantic will be horrified."

"Oh, of course." I could see it in his face, the penny was dropping. "And the absolute last thing the Germans want is for the Americans to take sides."

"They will hate looking bad, most definitely, but yes, anything that pushes America toward joining the Brits will terrify them."

"You think they will shut the program down after that."

"Not only shut it down, but I don't think there will be any reprisals for killing Dr. Scheffler."

"Why not?"

"Think about it. They've just been exposed for having a program that's based on murdering disabled children, the most vulnerable people in our society. They can't very well start imprisoning or even shooting innocent civilians to make up for the murder of one of the program's doctors, one of the men responsible for selecting victims for the program."

Darden helped himself to a cigarette. "You're actually starting to make a little bit of sense."

"Thank you." I felt a swell of relief he'd seen it my way.

"But why not just run the story without killing him? Wouldn't the public pressure be enough that way?"

"No. Étienne, we have this one chance, one moment in time, to stop this program for good. We need to throw everything we can at it, and a public shooting of the doctor makes sure this hits the front pages. At least, that's how Virginia explained it."

"And you know her well enough to trust her opinion."

"She knows more about newspapers than I do."

"This all assumes I'm willing and able to kill him." Darden's voice was quiet.

"You are definitely able, you just have to pull a trigger. Maybe a couple of times, but that's it."

"That's it?" Darden grimaced. "Maybe for you it's not a hard thing, but I don't see how I can do it."

"You have to. If you don't, the man lives and goes on to kill more children."

"I still think that woman's story would shut the program down by itself, without him having to be killed."

"No, Étienne, I'm afraid not, and for one big reason. If you don't kill him, you don't get your help disappearing. Which means I don't get my signed statement, and *that* means we're left with a story the Germans can deny. She'll have unnamed sources, no one to quote, no eyewitness to what was going on. It's possible they wouldn't even run the story like that, she said. No, I'm sorry but any way we look at this, your participation is vital."

"Your friends drive a hard bargain." Darden shook his head, defeated. "I imagine even if they do run the story with unnamed sources, the Germans will figure out a few names to go after. And without protection, I'll be on that list for certain."

"You were there at the hospital, you know about it."

"And who would care if a dark-skinned Indian man gets shot for passing information?"

"I would, for one. So how about you do this, and then we get you as far away as fast as possible?"

"I still don't know if I can kill a man like that."

"Don't think of it as killing a man. You're putting down a child-killing monster."

"Which happens to be true." He stubbed out his cigarette. "Even if I agreed, how would it work?"

"I'll talk to my contact. Whatever plan they have to make you safe after can be worked into my plan, I'm sure."

"You really think they can protect me in a situation like that?"

"Honestly, I don't know. I'll be there, too, though, if that's any consolation."

He gave me a resigned smile. "Well, you are a cop."

"An armed cop, who might come in handy. Well?"

"It's not as if I have much of a choice, the way you put it."

"I'm afraid that's true, too."

He sat back and looked me in the eye. "Then it looks like I'm doing it. You have a pen and my statement?"

CHAPTER THIRTY

Monday, December 9, 1940

I set off early the next morning, heading down into a cold wind that threatened to pluck the hat from my head and toss it into the Seine. I had one hand clamped on top of my head to save it, and my eyes watered as I was buffeted across Pont Saint-Michel. I was on my way to the Préfecture early because I had no way of contacting Daniel Moulin to give him Étienne Darden's response. I hoped Daniel would think of the same thing, and just show up to work.

At the far side of the bridge a man stepped out in front of me and I was surprised to see Daniel's brother Jean.

"*Bonjour*, Detective," he said. "Do you have an answer for me?"

"I do, and a little more than that. Can we go somewhere and talk just for a moment?"

"I just need to know where he lives so we can go get him."

"And I need a few minutes of your time before you do that."

"Not at the Préfecture." He pointed back the way I'd come. "That café is open, you can buy me a coffee."

Five minutes later we were unwrapping ourselves in the warmth of the café, and settling into creaking wooden chairs. I ordered two coffees and hoped against hope that'd be what we actually got.

"What do we need to talk about?" Jean Moulin asked, once we were settled.

"The plan for taking out this new doctor."

"That's not your concern."

"You're wrong, it's very much my concern."

"What makes you think so?" The café owner slid two cups of coffee in front of us, so I waited to answer.

"The whole point of killing this doctor is to stop Aktion T4, right?"

"Yes."

"So what's your plan to stop them just sending another doctor next week? And what's your plan to avoid reprisals, mass arrests, or whatever else those bastards feel like doing when we kill one of their own?"

"We've done this before, you know, Detective. We'll come up with something."

"You don't even know yet?"

"I only just found out I have a willing triggerman." He sniffed at his coffee the way we all do nowadays, just to get an idea of what we might be tasting.

"I wouldn't say 'willing.' He'll do it, but it took some persuading."

"As long as he does, I don't much care how he feels about it."

I sniffed at my own cup and was surprised to smell proper coffee. I took a sip and while it was weak, it tasted like the real thing.

"It pays to come out early, perhaps," I said, nodding toward my cup.

"It helps more when the owner is a friend," he said.

"Ah. I couldn't tell from your interaction."

"You can imagine the reasons for that." He took a sip himself. "So, here we are. I'm guessing you do have a plan in mind, and you'd like me to hear it."

"I do."

"Then by all means."

"It happens at the Gare de Lyon, as soon as he steps off the train."

He arched an immaculate eyebrow. "Bold. Or reckless."

"*Les deux*," I said. *Both.* "But with good reason."

"Explain."

"I have a journalist friend, an American, who can put a story about Aktion T4 in her newspaper, and the public killing of one of the program's doctors in a Paris train station will move it to the front page."

A smile slowly spread across his face. "The Boche would hate that. In fact, 'hate' isn't a strong enough word for how they'd feel."

"Exactly. The world knowing they are killing kids? Add to that their fear of America joining the British side, this would absolutely help with that."

"And the reprisals angle?" Moulin asked.

"The story helps with that, too. They can't round up a bunch of innocents with those headlines still out there."

"Maybe." We sipped our coffee in unison as I gave him a

moment to think. "But they will want someone's head for this. I can't believe they'd not string someone up."

"I agree, but—"

"Wait, you're not thinking of sacrificing this Darden fellow, are you?" He looked more intrigued than horrified.

"No, not at all. If he does this, it's part of a deal for you to whisk him away to safety."

"Your plan would change that," he said hurriedly. "I'm not saying we wouldn't try, but if he shoots someone in a public place like that, there's no telling whether we can get him safely away."

"I know. And I'm working on a separate plan for that."

"Which is?"

"Which is none of your concern," I said with a smile. "It's more of a plan B. I'll let you know when you need to know. Isn't that how you people operate, anyway?"

"It is." He slugged back the rest of his coffee. "Did you think I'd argue with you about your public assassination idea?"

"Of course. People in charge, in my experience, don't usually like to be told how to do their job."

"True enough. But this is a new job, and I'm new at it, so when someone has a good idea, I'll take it." It was his turn to smile. "I might even take credit for it, if it works."

"Be my guest. Having my name anywhere near all this would be counterproductive to my work as a detective."

"You mean, since you work for the Germans now."

"*With*, not for," I said. "And only when there's a gun to my head, like in this case."

"Daniel told me how they obtained your cooperation, I'm sorry. But hopefully this will take care of that."

"Hopefully." I drained my own coffee. "If not, I might be applying for your services myself."

"Understood. By the way, will you be there?"

"At the Gare de Lyon? Yes, I will."

"I thought so. Do me one favor, though."

"What?"

"Hang back and don't get involved. Whatever you see, whatever you hear, whatever happens, trust that I have things under control and don't intervene. Can you do that?"

"Yes, I can do that."

"*Bien.* Now, if you will give me Monsieur Darden's address, I have an assassin to train, and very little time to do it."

•   •   •

The relief was almost overwhelming, but I had one promise still to fulfill, so when I left the café I headed back to my apartment building and climbed the stairs to Mimi's front door.

"I've transitioned to tea in the mornings," she said. "Like the English have. It's easier to get and I rather like it."

"Just don't start cooking like the English, whatever you do. And no thanks, I managed to find a half-decent coffee."

"Lucky you." She was stirring a half spoonful of sugar into her tea as we talked, and my blood pressure spiked at the *chink-chink-chink* of her spoon against the sides of the cup.

"I think the sugar is stirred in, Mimi, you can stop that."

"Misophonia strikes again," she said, laying the spoon on the saucer. "You really can't help yourself; it's just fascinating the way a polite, mild-mannered man becomes instantly rude. Aggressive almost."

I held up a hand in apology. "I can't help myself, you're right, but I am sorry."

"Oh, I'm not offended in the slightest. Does it build up inside you or is it instant? Like with me stirring, describe how you felt."

"I've told you before, all about it."

"Tell me again, now."

"It's annoying, not angering, right away. But I try to control it and hope the noise stops. When it doesn't stop, I just . . . explode a little inside, and some of that leaks out. Usually in the form of an angry request to the person making the noise."

"Yes, the disproportionate thing intrigues me. Most people have noises they don't like, that's normal. But for you, the anger is . . . yes, disproportionate."

"Fascinating, I'm sure. But speaking of getting angry, I promised I'd tell you what your friend Andreas has been up to."

"'Friend' is a little strong, Henri. He's a German soldier after all."

"A Nazi, you meant to say."

"I don't know if he is, though. We've not talked about it, but I think he's an old-fashioned type, and I can't imagine he approves of Hitler and his minions. He can't very well say so out loud, though, so it's a difficult position to be in."

"He's really got you fooled, hasn't he?"

"Try to see things with a little more nuance, Henri. People aren't all good or all bad, for heaven's sake. He's not automatically a bad man because he's a German. He's not even automatically a Nazi because he wears a German uniform sometimes."

"Mimi, I'm afraid I'm about to break your heart."

"Meaning what exactly?"

"You know your missing children and that hard-to-pinpoint munitions factory in Rennes?"

"What about them? Just because we haven't found it, doesn't mean it doesn't exist. They work very hard to keep—"

"There's no such factory, Mimi. And Andreas von Rauch is the senior doctor in a program called Aktion T4, which takes children with deformities, or mental handicaps, and murders them. I went to the hospital in Rennes where they're kept, observed for a while, and then killed."

"No, that can't be true. It's not possible."

"It is true. Your other guest, the quiet Dr. Denis Berger, confirmed all of this, and like I said I saw some of those kids in the hospital myself."

"And Andreas is . . ."

"He's one of three doctors who approve the selection and murder, yes. The senior doctor. He's in charge."

Mimi's face had paled and there were tears in her eyes. "You're one hundred percent sure of all this?"

"I am. I'm sorry."

"Why send them to Rennes?"

"It makes them harder to find when people like you start looking. I imagine they started their own rumor about a munitions factory just to give people like you a wild goose to chase after."

"But why? Why would they do such an awful thing?"

"They are obsessed with human perfection. That's why they hate anyone who doesn't look like them. Jews, Black people, cripples, people born with disabilities. They see them all as deficient, defective, and they want to eliminate them. These kids, they ship their bodies back here to Paris, where von Rauch and his colleagues examine them, looking for reasons they are the way they are. They'd call it research, I'm sure."

"And you had me invite those monsters into my home?"

"As part of a plan to stop all this. I've already talked to Virginia, she's going to expose the program in her newspaper, cause as much outrage as possible. Once the world reads about this, I think there will be universal condemnation."

"Do you think that will stop them?"

"Not by itself, but other things are planned."

"Like what?"

"*Non.*" I wagged a finger. "Much better, much safer, that you don't know."

"Does it involve more killing?" she asked.

"Yes, and I know how you feel about killing."

"Good." She had regained some color in her cheeks, but still looked shell-shocked. "Also know that in this case, I can get over my feelings. Children, for God's sake, how could they?"

"I know. I'm sorry."

"Well, you were right about one thing."

"What's that?"

"If you told me all this before dinner last night, I'd have . . . Well, I don't know what I would have done, but it wouldn't be serve escargot and coq au vin."

I smiled. "That's what I thought."

"Do you mind telling me why I had two servers?"

"I think, if you don't mind, that's something else I'd like to keep up my sleeve for now."

"Ever the mysterious Henri Lefort. Well then, should we talk about that hearing test?"

"Absolutely, good idea." I rose to my feet and picked up my hat. "Just not today."

CHAPTER THIRTY-ONE

Tuesday, December 10, 1940

On Tuesday, I didn't go into the Préfecture, just like I hadn't the previous day, which I spent alternating between fretting and relaxing. Two glasses of wine at lunch had helped nicely with both of those, but today I was more purposeful in making sure I was rested and fed before the noontime fireworks began. Earlier in the day I'd tried to find Daniel Moulin to find Jean Moulin to find out what the plan was, how it was going to happen, but I couldn't locate the first to fetch the second, so I was going into this blind.

I did not like that one bit. *Every* major police operation starts with a plan, with those involved understanding their roles, their positions, their responsibilities. But on this one, I was going to waltz into a firefight, with no idea which direction it was coming from. I knew Étienne Darden would be the triggerman, which I did not like one bit, but exactly where and when I had no clue. And I couldn't very well spot him and follow him about like a puppy dog without making myself look suspicious, and possibly giving him away.

Still, I made sure I got to the train station an hour before Klaus Scheffler was due in, although the breakfast I'd so carefully scrounged up almost made a reappearance when I saw the black-and-red swastika flag the Boche had draped over part of the station's clock tower. The fact that I'd been able to see it from about a half mile away should have given me time to get used to it, but I just felt sicker with every closing step. It was a relief to step past it and enter the cavernous station, where the sonorous voice of the announcer and the *clickity-clack* of the giant timetable were familiar and reassuring.

I bought myself a newspaper and tried to ignore Virginia Hall, who I spotted ensconced at a café inside the station, sipping at something hot. She'd insisted on witnessing the mayhem firsthand so she could describe everything in lurid detail, and I'd only put up a fight because I thought I should. It was, therefore, not much of a fight. Frankly, anything that got people's attention I was in favor of.

Paper in hand, I settled on a bench against the wall, one where I could see the timetable and therefore know as soon as anyone which platform the new doctor would be arriving at. There seemed to be an awful lot of gray uniforms milling around, which was far from ideal, of course, but there also wasn't a damn thing I could do about it.

A man roughly my age, but in considerably worse condition, shuffled toward me from the direction of the lavatories. He wore a long, tattered black overcoat, gray trousers that might once have been another color, and from under a grubby beret his hair was long and greasy. His face and hands were grimy, too, and if he'd just been to use the facilities clearly his mother hadn't taught him to wash up afterward. He plopped down on the bench beside me and stared at me.

"This is mine," he said.

"The bench?"

"Go sit somewhere else, I lie down here."

"No thanks. You can lie down when I get up, which will be when I decide to get up, not when you tell me to."

"You're a Boche. You have an accent like a Boche."

"No, I'm not. I'm a policeman and if you don't shut up I'll find somewhere you can lie down and it's a lot less comfortable than this bench."

"You'd arrest me? For talking?" He spat on the ground. "See, you're a Boche. Our police don't do that."

I glanced over at him and realized I'd been wrong about him not washing his hands. I meant hand. His left arm was missing, and I expect that made hygiene a little more challenging when you live rough.

"You lose that in the last war?"

"I didn't lose it. I always kept it in the same place so I could find it, but then you bastards starting throwing ordinance at my trench and there it was, all of a sudden, just gone."

"I told you, I'm not one of them." I reached into my jacket and pulled out my credentials. I held them up. "You like playing with words, can you read what this says?"

"I lost my arm, not my eyes or my ability to read. So where's that accent from? As slight as it is, it's there all right."

"The Pyrénées," I lied. "I grew up there and never learned to speak like a Parisian."

"Good for you," he said earnestly. "You in the last war? Or too young?"

"Both," I said. "The recruiters weren't good with numbers, and fifteen looked as good as sixteen to them, so they let me in."

"The only numbers they cared about were how many of us they could send to the front."

"And I was too dumb to know the best place to be was at the back," I said.

"You got a smoke, soldier?"

"Call me Henri." I pulled out a half-empty packet and box of matches. "Here, keep them. My sister's trying to get me to quit anyway."

"*Merci.* But have one more with me. I can't smoke your cigarettes by myself." I took one and he deftly opened the matchbox, took out a match, and struck it alight with one hand. He lit both cigarettes and inhaled deeply. "Real tobacco. You must be high-ranking."

"You just have to arrest the right people, the ones with good smokes."

"I suppose you could arrest me and get them back, if you wanted."

"Yeah, about that. My apologies, I'm a little irritable these days."

"No problem." He held up the cigarette and admired it. "You more than made up for it." Then he squinted and looked at me. "You meeting someone?"

"I am, sort of."

"Either a pretty girl to woo, or a criminal to arrest. I don't see you holding flowers or chocolates, so I'm guessing a criminal."

"You have no idea."

"So tell me." He tapped his wrist. "I don't have a watch, but have plenty of time."

"The less you know, the better." I looked up as the large timetable clacked and announced the platform for Dr. Scheffler's train. "But do me, and more importantly yourself, a favor and steer clear of platform three when the noon train from Lyons comes in."

"There's going to be some shooting? Can't say I miss being around flying bullets."

"Shooting and some very angry Boche."

"Now that I do enjoy. I'll sit and watch from here, though, don't worry."

We sat quietly, him resting his head back against the wall with his eyes closed, and me reading my newspaper. I glanced up every thirty seconds or so, peering over the top of the pages to see if I could spot Étienne Darden or either of the Moulin brothers. I also studied every male who looked to be between the ages of eighteen and sixty, wondering if they were part of the resistance movement and here to help. But none of the men I saw gave me any clues, so wondering was all I could manage.

With twenty minutes still to go, I couldn't bear to sit any longer. I folded up the newspaper and dropped it gently onto my new friend's lap, then stood. That's when I locked eyes with Andreas von Rauch, who stood about forty feet away under the timetable, and his surprise was as readable as the train times. He looked around and I could see his head stop moving when he came to face where Virginia Hall was sitting.

I cursed silently at myself for not telling her to be more discreet, and cursed myself for parading about the place and being spotted so easily. And spotted by a man who I should have guessed would be here. It made perfect sense that, as important as this Scheffler character was to the program, its head doctor would come to the station to meet the man himself. No doubt with a gleaming Mercedes parked outside.

Von Rauch wasn't a man easily fooled, and I didn't much like the grim expression on his face as he strode toward me, clearly determined to get some answers. He stopped in front of me and his eyes narrowed just enough for me to notice.

"Detective Lefort. What a surprise."

"A pleasant one, I trust."

"Unless you are here to arrest me, of course."

"Have you done something arrestable?" I asked lightly.

"I am here merely to meet a new colleague. Quite innocent, I assure you."

"Well, I'm glad to hear that."

"And you?" he still had me fixed with his suspicious gaze.

"Also meeting someone." My stomach dropped when I looked over his shoulder toward the station's entrance and saw Étienne Darden ambling in the direction of the large timetable. In other words, ambling toward us.

"Did you notice that Ms. Hall is here, too?" von Rauch asked, suspicion dripping from his words.

"I saw her on the way in, but she looked busy so I didn't want to interrupt."

"How strange that all three of us should be here at this very moment. Don't you think?"

I think the plan has changed, is what I think. I also wondered if anyone from Moulin's group was watching us. *Surely they'd put eyes on von Rauch, too?*

"You have a suspicious mind, monsieur. That's supposed to be my role."

"Do you know who I'm here to meet?" he asked, his eyes narrowing further.

Merde. Now or never

In the last war, maybe once a week there was a moment where things went sideways, or completely and utterly backward, and you had to do something to avoid being left in the mud with your head blown off or your guts hanging out. We called those "act or die" moments and, standing there in front of von Rauch, I felt like I was in one. I wasn't going to be able to feed him any horseshit likely to make him happy and continue on his way. He was too smart for that.

Act or die.

"Let me show you something," I said, and put a hand on his arm to steer him away from the approaching Étienne Darden, and toward Virginia Hall.

"Show me what?" Von Rauch seemed more surprised than offended, so I kept him moving until we were close to Hall's table. She was reading a newspaper and had a large shoulder bag hanging from the back of her chair. She looked up, surprised, and I thought I saw a flash of fear for a split second, but then she saw my face and, I hoped at the time, realized she needed to play along.

"Here we are. Virginia, so nice to see you again. Mind if we sit with you for a moment?"

I sat von Rauch with his back to where Étienne Darden was now looking up at the timetable. He had a long, brown wool coat on, and if a machine gun was concealed beneath it, I couldn't tell. He was a porter not a soldier, or even a *flic*, so I would be surprised if they expected him to kill with a handgun.

"I only have two minutes," von Rauch was saying. "The train I'm meeting will be in soon."

"Mind if I borrow this?" I said politely to Virginia Hall, as I picked up her newspaper. I leaned forward and discreetly drew my gun, hiding it on my lap with the paper.

"Not at all." She smiled and waited for me to take the lead.

"*Merci beaucoup.*" I turned to von Rauch. "Now then, you murdering prick, please be aware that I have a gun trained on your groin and in about three minutes you will understand precisely why I will have no hesitation pulling the trigger and why, if I do so, not only will your compatriots not arrest me, they will probably give me a goddamn medal."

Von Rauch sat frozen, his eyes wide and his mouth wider, and as the blood drained from his face in fear and outrage, I knew I'd never see a finer sight.

CHAPTER THIRTY-TWO

Étienne Darden had moved away from the timetable and slowly toward platform three. I was relieved to be able to watch him from my spot at the table, but I tried to be subtle about it because I didn't want to spook von Rauch before I'd laid out the situation to him. By now, he'd gained back some composure.

"If you do indeed have a gun pointed at me, you are in very serious trouble," he said.

"Shut up, Nazi. Now's the time for you to listen and keep your mouth shut."

"I'm not a Nazi—"

"Here's what's happening, and what's going to happen. Your friend Scheffler is not going to be joining your horrific little experiment, Aktion T4."

"What? How do you know about that?" he sputtered.

"Because in France you can't go around killing children without someone spilling their guts about it."

"Research. It's just a research project."

"Is that so? And how exactly do you get your research subjects?"

"From a hospital in Rennes. They are already deceased when they come to me, so I don't see—"

"It's too late for that," I interrupted again. "We know how it works and, more importantly, why those children are dead by the time they come to you."

"So, you *are* here to arrest me."

"No. I'm here to kill you if you so much as move a muscle."

"Then what? What are you doing here?"

"It takes three of you to sign off on each . . . subject. Right?"

He nodded and I watched as understanding dawned on his face. "If you're not arresting me, then you're not arresting Scheffler, either."

"Arresting in a different sense, shall we say?"

"You're going to . . . you're going to kill him?" He seemed horrified by the idea, which made me angrier.

"You don't like the idea of murder, all of a sudden."

Von Rauch's face hardened. "They were cripples from birth, all of them. Or mentally defective. That man is a respected German doctor, a high-ranking—"

"Nazi. I told you to shut up and listen."

He didn't. "I don't know how you think you're going to get away with this, Lefort. You're in for a very unpleasant ending."

"Like Jean Grabbin, perhaps?"

The switch in direction threw him off for a moment, and I

THE DARK EDGE OF NIGHT

could see Virginia beside us looking at us in turn, almost like she was watching a tennis match.

"What are you saying?"

"That was you in the hospital truck, wasn't it? That night I went in and found Grabbin dead. You'd already killed him and were there to remove his body. The driver ducked down, it was you trying to hide your face from me."

"I don't know what—"

"No one knew Grabbin was dead, so it wasn't sent by the hospital morgue. And if it had been there for some other reason, its driver would have made himself known, but you left the moment you saw me. You knew what I'd find." I glared at him. "You weren't even there for Grabbin's body, were you? You were there to take the children back. My god you disgust me."

Von Rauch's demeanor seemed to shift a little, and when he spoke he was defiant. "I didn't care about Grabbin alive, why should I care about him dead?"

"So you admit you killed him."

"In front of a policeman and a journalist?" he scoffed. "Hardly."

"Yet you did. You killed him after the funeral. You had your obedient Frenchman Berger following me to make sure I didn't take Grabbin in for questioning or otherwise impede his trip home. Where you were waiting for him. Did he just let you in, or did you have to use force?"

"That man murdered a German doctor, a member of the Reich! And he stole bodies from the hospital for some reason I can scarcely imagine."

"For a reason you would never understand, that's true. You killed him, didn't you?"

"I executed an enemy, one guilty of murder." Von Rauch sneered. "Just try arresting me for that and see what happens to you."

"I told you already, I'm not arresting you," I said. "But please do not forget that my gun is pointed right at your twig and berries."

"I haven't forgotten, and you will pay for it with your life."

"Unlikely." I wished I felt as confident as I sounded, but at least von Rauch didn't move.

"How the hell do you expect to get away with this?" he demanded. "Look around, you fool, there are soldiers everywhere. You can't assassinate him and survive."

"Oh, I'm not the one doing it. My role is to make sure there are no arrests and no reprisals."

"That would be some trick." Back came the sneer, and I barely resisted the urge to wipe it off his face with my fist.

Instead, I gave him one of my own, and said, "Some trick it will be. And I do apologize, I forgot to mention that you're going to help me."

"Me?" That really surprised him, which I enjoyed greatly.

"Yes, you." I turned to Virginia. "Do you have them?"

"I most certainly do," she said, reaching into her shoulder bag. "And I must say, you did a good job; they turned out well."

"Why, thank you." I took the large envelope that she'd offered and, rather awkwardly with just one hand, I looked inside to see three photographs, and to my delight the top one at least seemed to be of exceptional quality.

"What is that?" von Rauch asked.

"We'll get to the envelope in a minute," I said. "But I need you to understand what's going on. Virginia here is a journalist, as you quite rightly pointed out. She will be writing a story about Aktion T4 that will make for fascinating reading back in America. Added to that, the imminent and public demise of your colleague will ensure that her story is on the front page with a large headline no one will miss. First of all in her newspaper and then many more, I'm sure." I suddenly remembered Eric Sevareid, the journalist I'd met at a café. I'd be contacting him for sure. "Am I right about that, Virginia?"

"Most definitely. And in fact I gave my editor a summary of the story and he was so excited he almost fainted."

"Look at that, Andreas, we're halfway to making your name famous all over the world."

Von Rauch had visibly paled as the implications dawned on him. And I'd figured that being the man he was, the German doctor would be very high on the list of those desperate to maintain the image of the noble, decent invader, the myth that we were about to explode. And his name would be front and center.

"I'll have you sh—" he began, but the fight had left his voice, and I hoped the rest of him, so I quickly interrupted.

"You'll do no such thing," I said, opening the envelope and sliding the photographs onto the table between us. "We have copies of these, yes?" I asked Virginia.

"Many," she said, her eyes sparkling with delight. "The doctor is welcome to keep them."

"Somehow I doubt he will want to." I gave her a wink and turned back to von Rauch. "The top one is from a series I took using your colleague Dr. Berger as a model. He was very accommodating." I showed von Rauch the picture of Berger naked and shackled to the cross, with Mistress Lau looking serious beside him. "You may recognize her, too, yes?"

"I've never seen her before in my life," he protested. "This is an outrage, it's disgusting, it's . . . it's. . . ."

"It's the man you hired, is what it is. And if you look at this photograph . . ." I showed him the next one, which was taken by the matchbox camera at dinner. It showed Cassie Lau's face and, more importantly, her cleavage very close to a smiling von Rauch. "Perhaps you recognize her now?"

"Good god, how did—?"

"It doesn't really matter how, though, does it? Nor what the truth behind the picture is. It's all about how it looks, I would suggest." When he said nothing, I went on. "And from here it looks quite bad. For you. And about to get worse."

He looked at me, and for the first time I saw real fear in his eyes. I marveled that this man, anyone really, could be more in fear of a bad name than a gun pointed at his privates, but von Rauch was that man.

"Take a look at our third and final picture, would you?"

He picked it up and his hand was trembling. "That's the boy from the other night."

"He's a man, not a boy." I leaned in, my voice low but angry. "Apart from killing children, I think the thing I detest about you is how you look down on people because of the color of their skin or their race, and you're not worthy to lick the boots of a single one of them."

"Why are you showing me this picture?" His voice was almost a whisper.

"Because it shows you not only living it up with a dark gentleman from the subcontinent, which your superiors will detest, but he's the man who's about to ensure there will be no more children selected for murder by you."

"He's . . . here?"

I nodded slowly. "So just think what happens if that photo-graph of you falls into certain hands. You at a dinner party with the dark-skinned man who killed Dr. Scheffler. Not a great look for you, especially since you were at that dinner party with him barely twenty-four hours before the assassination."

I let him think about that for a second, and when he did he reached the conclusion I intended him to reach. He just tried not to.

"They wouldn't suspect me of being a part of this!"

"Well, I don't know if that's true or not. Considering the 'they' you're referring to will undoubtedly be the Gestapo, I'd say you're wrong. And let's not forget, they do have a reputation for ask-ing very pointed questions for a day or two before reaching their conclusions, so even if they end up believing you . . ." I spread my hands in mock sympathy. "I think we can all agree that it will be a very uncomfortable couple of days, yes?"

Behind him, Étienne Darden was still inching his way toward the platform, and my stomach tightened with the anticipation, and some fear for the man himself. Past him, I could see the front of the train rumbling toward us all, belching out steam and smoke from the coal that powered it.

Von Rauch turned to watch too.

"Stay seated, please," I said, giving him a glimpse of my gun so he knew that was an order, not a request.

We watched as the train slowed, and I was surprised to see a young boy—he looked to be no more than ten—walk up to Éti-enne Darden and hand him a note. They both then stood there for a moment watching, like us, as the train shuddered and clanked to a final halt. As it let out a last hiss of steam the air in the station seemed to quiver, and a split second later three explosions, one immediately after the other, had us diving for the ground.

I looked up and saw that the windows in one carriage had been blown out. Smoke poured from the gaping holes into the station, and orange flames rose up inside the carriage to lick at the air, to suck in more to feed itself and grow. I put a hand on von Rauch's leg to keep him in place but everyone else was running and screaming, the civilians away from the train and the German soldiers toward it.

Meanwhile, Étienne Darden hadn't moved, and like Virginia Hall, von Rauch, and me, he just stared at a burning railway carriage. After a moment, the boy said something and Darden scrunched up the piece of paper, dropped it on the platform, and together they walked away.

CHAPTER THIRTY-THREE

Wednesday, December 11, 1940

"Do you want me to arrest him?" I asked Becker. He'd made me wait by the phone for an hour before he called back, but I didn't have much else to do so I didn't mind too much. "Seemed wise to get your opinion on that before actually doing it."

"Very wise," Becker said. "From what you've told me, your evidence isn't strong."

"It was helped considerably by his admission to me."

"Which he will no doubt deny."

"I'm sure he will. But you fellows specialize in getting the truth out of people, don't you? I mean, especially when you've decided what the truth is going to be."

"I dare say we could persuade him to repeat his confession," Becker said stiffly. "Whether we would want to is another matter."

"So are you telling me not to arrest him?"

He was quiet for a moment. "In light of Tuesday's events and today's news in America, I think the arrest of von Rauch would best be done by us."

"As long as you do; that bastard shouldn't get away with murder."

"And if I don't?" The tone was almost mocking, and he didn't need to say the *There's not a damn thing you can do about it* part.

"What will happen to him?" I asked, a little more politely.

"Not your concern anymore. But if you must know, I expect he will remain in his position for a day or two to shut things down, then quietly disappear back to Berlin."

"And Aktion T4?"

"Not *my* concern. I hardly see how it can continue now, though, given what the president of the United States said." He made a clucking sound of disapproval. "Children, even crippled children."

"A little too much even for you?" I couldn't help myself, and instantly regretted provoking him, but fortunately it seemed he was used to ignoring insolents like me.

"You arrested Monsieur Berger, I gather."

"And with the greatest of pleasure. He's singing like one of von Rauch's opera stars in the hope of saving his own neck from Madame Guillotine."

"That's a matter for you people." His voice dripped with indifference. "Well, I suppose you did as instructed. You can close your case."

"I'd be happy—" I began, but he'd already hung up.

• • •

I stopped at Mimi's door on my way home, and was delighted to find Virginia Hall there.

"I have some champagne," Mimi said. "We should celebrate."

"Maybe later," I said. I wanted to enjoy this moment without the aid of alcohol, at least until the sun went down. I'd seen a lot of my comrades from the last war descend into a bottle and not be able to climb back out. It was a quick and easy slide, from what I'd seen, and so I tended to steer clear of the two substances that seemed to affect me most: champagne and brandy. "Are we seeing you both for dinner?" I asked.

"Most certainly," Mimi said, and Virginia nodded at me with a smile on her face. One that was infectious, as it turned out. She was dressed casually, in slacks and a dark blue wool sweater, and a matching beret sat on the table beside us.

I had an urge to ask her to put it on, but my urges with women tended to land me in trouble so I just grinned back at her and said, "Great. Excellent."

"Thanks for the wonderful news story, Henri," she said.

"You're very welcome, although I wouldn't mind staying out of the headlines for a little while."

"Yes, you did a fine job," Mimi said. "I still can't believe Andr— that von Rauch character was such a callous monster."

I let the tiniest of smiles play on my lips, and said, "Somewhere in the back of my head, I feel like maybe someone warned you he might not be so wonderful. Does that ring a bell with you at all?"

"Now you listen to me, Henri." Mimi put her hands on her

hips and gave me a stern look. "All I ever said about him was that—"

"That he was a gentleman from a good family," I interrupted, "and on the important moral issues he'd be on the same page as me, a poor and humble workingman."

"All right, Henri, you don't have to—"

But I was enjoying myself and, to her left, Virginia was trying and failing to suppress a smile.

"Oh, but I do, Mimi, you know I do." I wagged my finger, mimicking her sternness. "I do hope you learned an important lesson here."

"And what might that be?"

"That murderous people come from all walks of life, and so-called good families aren't exempt."

"That may be so," Mimi said, "but I still think it's true that there are good and noble families who—"

"I'm not done." Interrupting Mimi, without being scolded for it, was turning out to be as much fun as being right about something. "One more suggestion for you."

"And what might that be?"

"Next time you're psychoanalyzing someone, feel free to reach out for help." I gave her my biggest grin. "Or I'll put that another way: I told you so."

And then, having gotten the last word with her for the first (and likely last) time, I turned on my heel and showed myself out.

Upstairs, Nicola welcomed me with a kiss on each cheek and an unusually long hug.

"Congratulations, you genius," she said. "And what a relief."

"Genius, thank you. Any chance I can get that in writing?"

"None whatsoever."

"Well, fair enough." I shrugged off my coat and hung it by the door. "Honestly, it was good work all around. Including you, so thank you for your help."

"Mimi did more than I did. And talking of her, I need to go find some food."

"Best leave her alone for an hour. Or maybe better to interrupt her in case she's plotting revenge."

"What on earth are you talking about?"

I laughed and told her about the exchange we'd just had.

Nicola shook her head when I finished, but she was smiling. "You know, it's all right to be noble in victory. Even when it comes to Mimi."

"I wouldn't know, I never win with her. Maybe next time."

"If there is a next time," she said. "Anyway, we'll see her for dinner and in the meantime I happen to know that someone's selling *brebis*, so I'm going to run out and get some."

"My favorite cheese," I said, rubbing my hands together at the prospect of a piece of real *brebis*.

"Well, it's from the Pyrénées where you're from." She laughed for a moment, then stood up to leave.

"You know, on that subject," I said. "I think I will tell him."

"Tell who what?"

"Daniel. About me. That is, if you don't mind."

"I think it's a wonderful idea. He knows I'm your sister and hasn't told anyone. I really do think you can trust him to keep your secret."

"Our secret," I corrected. "If I can't trust him after all that's happened this past week, I can't trust anyone."

"Very true." There was a knock at the door and she smiled again. "Now's your chance."

"That's him?"

"Or Mimi coming for revenge, but I suspect it's Daniel."

"You sure he won't want to go cheese shopping with you?"

"Very sure." She opened the door and swapped kisses with Moulin, who presented her with a small bouquet of flowers that, in normal times, most women would have taken as an insult. *"Merci, cheri."*

I gave him a wave from the couch as Nicola pulled on her coat.

"Are you going somewhere?" Moulin asked her.

"I need to pick up some cheese. Won't be long."

"You want some company? I could use the exercise."

"Well, well, full of surprises, aren't you?" Nicola laughed. "Actually, no. Henri has something he wants to talk to you about."

"Sounds intriguing," Moulin said, glancing at me.

"Oh, you have no idea. Come sit."

Nicola let herself out, and Moulin wandered over to me, where we shook hands before he took over her spot on the couch.

"First of all," I said. "Did Étienne Darden get somewhere safe?"

A grin spread over his face and he said, "I'm sorry, I have absolutely no idea who you are talking about."

"Ah, yes, excellent. I am curious about one thing, though, if you can explain it."

"Ask, and if I can I will."

"The change in plan at the train station. The way it was done, or rather who did it."

"Let me answer that with a question. Apart from him and us, who knew what was going to happen?"

I thought for a moment. "Just me, I suppose."

"Correct." He sat there and just stared at me, waiting for me to get it. Which I eventually did.

"It was a test. And of me, not him."

Moulin clapped his hands with delight. "You really are a good detective. I was worried you might figure it out before everything happened."

"If the Boche swooped in and arrested him, you'd know I was the leak. This was about testing me."

"In large part, yes. We knew we had to take out Scheffler, of course, and we weren't about to let a complete amateur take that on. He was terrible in training, by the way. I don't think he was even capable of doing it."

"He told me that, but he agreed anyway."

"That's also what it was about. If we're going to help people, we not only need to trust them like we now trust you. We need them to be willing to do things, even if it turns out they can't. It's resolve as much as action that will win the day for us."

"You're optimistic."

"Not in the short term, but eventually, yes, I believe we will have France back."

"I'm glad to hear that. Shall we move on?"

"To?"

"I have another secret I'd like you to keep."

"I'm good at that."

"I'm telling you because I know that, and because if you're going to be around Nicola a lot, you should know the truth."

"About?"

"Me."

"You've already told me you're her brother. There's more? Or is that not really true?"

"I'm her brother, all right. But . . ." I took a deep breath and dove in headfirst. "I'm her brother Michel."

"I don't understand."

"I'll tell you the short version for now, then you can ask questions if you like." He nodded, so I went on. "As a baby I was left with my abusive father in New York City, while my twin brother Henri came back to France with our mother. I was eventually taken from my father and placed in various foster homes, each worse than the last. When I was fifteen, my foster father was attacking his wife, the only decent adult I'd been around. Anyway, I hit him, just once to stop him beating her, and then I just left. That same day I joined the US Army and soon after I was shipped over here."

"And you were Michel Lefort."

"Correct. Near the end of the war, I found out that I had a brother and volunteered for a specific mission, a joint American-French thing, when I heard he was going on it. Everyone on the mission was killed, including him, except me."

"But why did you take his name?"

"Remember how I said I hit my foster father?" He nodded again. "I hit him with an ashtray, and apparently split his skull. I didn't even realize." Moulin's eyes widened with surprise. "And that's not the worst of it. He'd been strangling his wife and it turns out he killed her. Problem was, when their bodies were found the authorities assumed I'd done it, killed them both and fled."

"Oh no. That's awful."

"*Oui.* Right before I went on that mission, my commanding officer told me there were arrest warrants for me. For murder. My brother was the last one in that group to die, and when he did I had a split second to make a decision—to survive that mission and face being hung for murder . . ."

"Or become Henri," Moulin said. "That's insane."

"Fortunately, I didn't realize how insane it was until after I'd committed to it. By then . . ." I shrugged. "Well, Nicola helped, of course, and now it's who I am."

"If anyone found out," Moulin began. "There's no statute of limitations on murder, is there?"

"Right. You can see why I don't tell people freely."

"You could still be arrested, tried, and . . . Well, in theory."

"A theory I'd rather not see tested, as you might imagine."

"Well, you have my word. Your secret is safe with me."

"*Merci.*"

"Your accent!" he said suddenly, smiling. "That's why you tell people you're from the Pyrénées. Oh my God, how did you come up with that?"

"Nicola, if I remember rightly."

"She's a smart one," Moulin said. "I'm glad you had her to help you; that must have been quite the transition."

"I couldn't have done it without her."

"Who else knows?"

"Just you and Mimi," I said. "Which means we can laugh about it over dinner."

"It's a laughing matter?"

"It is now. Wasn't then."

"I can imagine. But truly, Henri, thank you for trusting me with that secret. I will never tell a soul."

"We've shared a few this week," I said. "You know, I often wonder, if someone did find out, would people even believe it?"

"Like you said, best not to test some theories. And I do have a question for you, since we were speaking of trust and willingness earlier."

He was staring at me intently, and I thought that maybe he was more interested in my reaction to whatever he was about to ask, more so than in whatever answer I gave him.

"I'm listening," I said.

"If there were future events that we needed assistance with. Perhaps another Étienne Darden in need. Would you be available?"

"Risk my neck to give the Germans a bloody nose?"

"Again."

"Again. I suppose I did, yes." I thought of my very explicit threats to von Rauch, and the lengths I'd gone to for blackmail material. "I wouldn't be opposed to you approaching me about it. Discretion assured, even if it wasn't something I wanted to get involved with."

"Understood. Although you should know your name is already on a list of friendlies, so I'm glad you're on board for a slightly more active role."

"I said you could approach me," I reminded him.

"I've not known you long, Henri. But I think long enough to know what will happen if, or when, I do."

"You're probably right." I stood. "Sometimes I just can't help myself. On that note, I should open some wine; it's not too early."

"Yes, and Nicola said we're celebrating your solving the case. Or closing it out, at least."

"Hopefully the Germans will deal with von Rauch in their usual unforgiving manner. So that means we're celebrating two things."

He cocked his head. "What's the other one?"

"Well now," I said with a wry smile. "Didn't I just join the Resistance?"

AUTHOR'S NOTE

While most of my characters are fictional, I do enjoy dropping in a few real people from time to time. Of course, everything I have them do and say is entirely a product of my imagination but, even so, I thought you might like to hear a little about the real them.

Princess Marie Bonaparte (1882–1962), known to Henri and Nicola as Mimi, heads the list, of course. Born in the town of Saint-Cloud, France, she was an only child and the great-grand-niece of Emperor Napoleon. As in my books, she was fascinated by psychology and sexuality, and even consulted Freud in 1925 to address what was described at the time as her "frigidity." At the start of World War II she arranged for Freud and his family to leave Vienna to escape the Nazis (this story was made into a 2004 movie called *Princess Marie*). She died of leukemia in

Saint-Tropez in France in 1962, and her ashes were interred in the tomb of her husband, Prince George of Greece, in Athens.

Virginia Hall (1906–1982) was an American who worked with the English and American spy services during World War II. She did indeed lose her foot in a hunting accident, as I write in the book, and she even had a nickname for her prosthetic foot: Cuthbert. Originally from Baltimore, Maryland, she always had a hankering for travel and adventure, and ended up as a spy because her (multiple) applications to the State Department to become a diplomat were either ignored or rejected. To escape the Nazis' clutches she once crossed the Pyrénées on foot, covering up to fifty miles a day as she was guided over a 7,500 foot pass—in November! Her code names were Diane and Marie (coincidentally) but the Germans named her Artemis and the Limping Lady, and tried everything they could to get their hands on her, never succeeding. She was awarded the Distinguished Service Cross by the Americans, the Croix de Guerre by the French, and the Most Excellent Order of the British Empire by the English. She died in July 1982 and is buried in Pikesville, Maryland. Her exploits are detailed in the most excellent book *A Woman of No Importance* by Sonia Purnell.

Eric Sevareid (1912–1992) was an American writer and journalist, who worked for CBS from 1939 to 1977. He was one of several elite journalists hired by the news icon Edward R. Murrow, and Sevareid was the first to report on the fall of Paris in 1940.

The One-Two-Two was a brothel opened in 1924 by **Marcel Jamet** and his first wife Fernande, who called herself Doriane (she later left him and he remarried). The brothel was named after its address: 122 rue de Provence and, in its heyday, had twenty-two decorated rooms where forty to sixty-five prostitutes worked for up to three hundred clients per day. It didn't open until 4:00 P.M. and stayed open until 4:00 A.M., during which time the girls working there had to have four sex sessions a day, at twenty francs each (excluding tips), and two sessions on Sundays. There was also a bar, a refectory for the girls, and even a doctor's office.

Jean Moulin (1899–1943) was a civil servant who became one of the best-known leaders of the Resistance. He did have a brother, Joseph, but he died in 1907. (He also had a sister, but there was no Daniel Moulin.) Jean studied law and got his law degree in July 1921, and in 1939 was appointed prefect of the Eure-et-Loir department, based in Chartres. A resister from the first, Moulin met Charles de Gaulle, the voice of the Free French, in London, after which he parachuted back into France to begin his Resistance work. On June 21, 1943, he was betrayed and arrested at a meeting of fellow Resistance leaders. He was tortured daily by the infamous Klaus Barbie, the Butcher of Lyons, enduring indescribable agonies but never giving information to his captors. The precise details of his demise are not clear, but there's no doubt the Nazis tortured him to death.

Aktion T4 was, sadly, also very real. The term itself wasn't used until postwar trials for some of those involved in the program, which was a horrific campaign of mass murder. The doctors involved identified those they believed were genetically or otherwise physically or mentally inferior, targeting them on this basis for "involuntary euthanasia," which we would just call murder. Not really operational in France, the program ran mostly in Germany, Austria, Poland, and what is now the Czech Republic, and it's believed it resulted in the deaths of approximately 300,000 people. Many of those were children, and while hard numbers are difficult to come by, author Christopher Browning, who wrote *The Origins of the Final Solution: The Evolution of Nazi Jewish Policy, September 1939–March 1942*, said that just by the end of 1941 over five thousand children had been killed. It's reported that the last child to be killed under Aktion T4 was Richard Jenne on May 29, 1945, in the children's ward of a state hospital in Bavaria, Germany—more than three weeks after US Army troops had occupied the town.

ACKNOWLEDGMENTS

My first thank-you goes to you, the reader. Thank you for giving your valuable time to my book, for daring to share Henri's world, for cheering him along (I hope) and making all the work, the love, the sweat that goes into creating a finished novel worthwhile.

My second thank-you goes to a champion, someone who took a chance with a never-published writer, someone who hangs up her agenting cloak after shepherding me through thirteen published novels. Ann Collette, you have been my advisor, mentor, friend, and (as mentioned!) champion. And thank you for putting me in good hands going forward, how typical of such a kind and professional agent. Time now to read for pleasure, enjoy the river-walk and the people watching. Thank you for everything, you will always be my friend.

Thanks always to my family, Sarah, Blake, and the real Henry and Nicola. All of you inspire me, all of the time.

To Leslie Gelbman, Grace Gay, Lisa Bonvissuto, Kayla Janas, Steve Erickson, Martin Quinn, and all the good folks at St. Martin's, a million thanks for making the dream of this book, this series, a reality.

My thanks to Professor Eric Smoodin for his assistance on French cinema, and to Andre Glasburg and Marcella Sampic for their advice and informational help with pretty much all things French.

And I want to thank, too, some people who have supported me from the beginning, and continue to do so: Mike Luna, a good friend and my own personal book dealer; and Allison Finch, whose great taste in literature is only outdone by her great kindness to me and the world. Gratitude, too, to my new friends at Cofer & Connelly, among whom I have found a home—especially Rick Cofer, Liz Duggan, Megan Rue, Natalia Tsokos, Skye Allen, Justin Newsom, Sarah Wolf, Heather Hellums, Esmeralda Quintana, Camila Montoya, Sarah Dugan, and the amazing Merissa Johnson.

"A satisfying puzzle in a carefully crafted setting."
—KIRKUS REVIEWS

WINTER 1940: With soldiers parading down the Avenue des Champs-Élysées, Nazi flags dangling from the Arc de Triomphe, and the Eiffel Tower defaced with German propaganda, Parisians have little to celebrate as Christmas approaches. Police Inspector Henri Lefort's wishes for a quiet holiday season are dashed when the Gestapo orders him to investigate the disappearance of Dr. Viktor Brandt, a neurologist involved in a secret project at one of Paris's hospitals.

Being forced onto a missing persons case for the enemy doesn't deter Henri from conducting his real job. A Frenchman has been beaten to death in what appears to be a botched burglary, and catching a killer is more important than locating a wayward scientist. But when Henri learns that the victim's brother is a doctor who worked at the same hospital as the missing German, his investigation takes a disturbing turn.

Uncovering a relationship between the two men—one that would not be tolerated by the Third Reich—Henri must tread carefully. And when he discovers that Dr. Brandt's experimental work is connected to groups of children being taken from orphanages, Henri risks bringing the wrath of both the SS and the Gestapo upon himself and everyone he loves.

MARK PRYOR is a former newspaper reporter and felony prosecutor, originally from England but now working as a criminal defense attorney in Austin, Texas. He is the author of the Hugo Marston mystery series, set in Paris, London, and Barcelona. Mark is also the author of the psychological thriller *Hollow Man* and its sequel, *Dominic*. As a prosecutor, he appeared on CBS News's *48 Hours* and Discovery Channel's *Investigation Discovery: Cold Blood.*

Cover design by Rowen Davis and David Baldeosingh Rotstein

Cover art: Paris © Stephen Mulcahey/Arcangel; man © Donald Jean/Arcangel; planes © Sergey Kamshylin/Shutterstock

Author photo: Nick Berard

MINOTAUR BOOKS
ST. MARTIN'S PUBLISHING GROUP
120 BROADWAY, NEW YORK, NY 10271
PRINTED IN THE UNITED STATES OF AMERICA
www.minotaurbooks.com

US $19.00 / CAN $25.00
ISBN 978-1-250-33867-9

51900 >

9 781250 338679